Wife in Name Only

Charlotte M. Braeme

Wife in Name Only

By

Charlotte M. Braeme

(Bertha M. Clay)

By The Same Author In Uniform Style

Dora Thorne
From Gloom to Sunlight
Her Martyrdom
Golden Heart
Her Only Sin
Lady Damer's Secret
The Squire's Darling
Her Mother's Sin
Wife in Name Only
Wedded and Parted
Shadow of a Sin

Chapter I.

It was the close Of an autumn day, and Dr. Stephen Letsom had been standing for some time at his window watching the sun go down. It faded slowly out of the western sky. There had been a golden flush with the sunset which changed into crimson, then into purple, and finally into dull gray tints that were forerunners of the shades of night. Dr. Stephen Letsom had watched it with sad, watchful eyes. The leaves on the trees had seemed to be dyed first in red, then in purple. The chrysanthemums changed color with every phase of the sunset; there was a wail in the autumn wind as though the trees and flowers were mourning over their coming fate. There was something of sadness in the whole aspect of nature.

The doctor evidently shared it. The face looking from the window was anything but a cheerful one. Perhaps it was not the most judicious manner in which the doctor could have spent his time—above all, if he wished to give people an impression that he had a large practice. But Dr. Letsom had ceased to be particular in the matter of appearances. He was to all intents and purposes a disappointed man. Years before, when his eyes were bright with the fires of youth, and hope was strong in his heart, he had invested such money as he possessed in the purchase of a practice at Castledene, and it had proved to be a failure—why, no one exactly knew.

Castledene was one of the prettiest little towns in Kent. It had a town-hall, a market-place, a weekly market, and the remains of a fine old castle; but it was principally distinguished for its races, a yearly event which brought a great influx of visitors to the town. It was half buried in foliage, surrounded by dense woods and green hills, with a clear, swift river running by. The inhabitants were divided into three distinct classes—the poor, who gained a scanty livelihood by working in the fields, the shop-keepers, and the gentry, the latter class consisting principally of old maids and widows, ladies of unblemished gentility and limited means. Among the latter Dr. Letsom was not popular. He had an unpleasant fashion of calling

1

everything by its right name. If a lady would take a little more stimulant than was good for her he could not be persuaded to call her complaint "nervousness;" when idleness and ennui preyed upon a languid frame, he had a startling habit of rousing the patient by a mental cautery. The poor idolized him, but the ladies pronounced him coarse, abrupt; and when ladies decide against a doctor, fate frowns upon him.

How was he to get on in the world? Twenty years before he had thought less of getting on than of the interests of science or of doing good; now those ideas were gradually leaving him—life had become a stern hand-to-hand fight with hard necessity. The poor seemed to be growing poorer—the difficulty of getting a fee became greater— the ladies seemed more and more determined to show their dislike and aversion.

Matters were growing desperate, thought Dr. Letsom on this autumn night, as he stood watching the chrysanthemums and the fading light in the western sky. Money was becoming a rare commodity with him. His housekeeper, Mrs. Galbraith had long been evincing signs of great discontent. She had not enough for her requirements— she wanted money for a hundred different things, and the doctor had none to give her. The curtains were worn and shabby, the carpets full of holes, the furniture, though clean and well preserved, was totally insufficient. In vain the doctor assured her he had not the means; after the fashion of weak-minded women, she grumbled incessantly. On this night he felt overwhelmed with cares. The rent due the preceding June had not been paid; the gas and coal accounts were still unsettled; the butcher had sent in his "little bill;" the baker had looked anything but pleased at the non-payment of his. The doctor sadly wanted a new hat—and he had hardly money in hand for the week's expenses. What was to be done?

Mrs. Galbraith retired to rest in a very aggrieved state of mind, and the doctor stood watching the stars, as they came out in the darkening sky. He was tired of the struggle; life had not been a success with him; he had worked hard, yet nothing had prospered. In youth he had loved a bright, pretty girl, who had looked forward to becoming his wife; but he had never married, because he had not had the means, and the pretty girl died a disappointed woman. Now, as he watched the stars, he fancied them shining on her grave; fancied the grass waving above her head; studded with large white daisies; and he wished that he were lying by her side, free from care, and at rest. Strong man as he was his eyes grew dim with tears, and his lips trembled with a deep-drawn, bitter sob.

He was turning away, with a feeling of contempt for his own weakness, when he was startled by the sound of a vehicle driven furiously down Castle street. What vehicle could it be at that hour of the night—nearly eleven? Stephen Letsom stood still and watched. He saw a traveling carriage, with two horses, driven rapidly up to the door of the principal hotel—the Castle Arms—and there stand for some few minutes. It was too dark for him to see if any one alighted from it, or what took place; but, after a time the horses' heads were turned, and then, like a roll of thunder, came the noise of the carriage-wheels.

The vehicle drew up before his door, and the doctor stood for a few moments as though paralyzed. Then came a violent peal of the doorbell; and he knowing that Mrs. Galbraith had retired for the evening, went to answer it. There indeed, in the starlight, were the handsome traveling carriage, the pair of gray horses, and the postilion. Stephen Letsom looked about him like one in a dream. He had been twenty years in the place, yet no carriage had ever stopped at his door.

He heard a quick, impatient voice, saying:

"Are you the doctor—Dr. Letsom?"

Looking in the direction of the sound, the doctor saw a tall, distinguished-looking man, wrapped in a traveling cloak—a man whose face and manner indicated at once that he belonged to the upper ranks of society. Dr. Stephen Letsom was quick to recognize that fact.

"I am the doctor," he replied, quietly.

"Then for Heaven's sake, help me! I am almost mad. My wife has been suddenly taken ill, and I have been to the hotel, where they tell me they have not a room in which they can lodge her. The thing is incredible. You must help me."

"I will do what I can," returned the doctor.

Had fortune indeed knocked at his door at last?

He went to the carriage-door, and, looking inside, saw a lady, young and beautiful, who stretched out her hands to him, as though appealing for help.

"I am very ill," she moaned, feebly.

Dr. Letsom guessed so much from her pallid face and shadowed eyes.

"What is the matter with your wife?" he asked of the strange gentleman, who bent down and whispered something that made Dr. Letsom himself look anxious.

"Now doctor," said the traveler, "it is useless to raise objections You see how the matter stands; my wife must stop here. The hotel is full of visitors—people who are here for the races. There is nowhere else for her to go—she must stay here."

"At my house?" interrogated the doctor. "It is impossible."

"Why?" asked the stranger, quickly.

"Because I am not married—I have no wife, no sister."

"But you have women-servants, surely?" was the hasty rejoinder.

"Only one, and she is not over-clever."

4

"You can get more. My wife must have help. Send all over the place—get the best nurses, the best help possible. Do not study expense. I will make you a rich man for life if you will only help me now."

"I will help you," said Dr. Letsom.

For a moment his thoughts flew to the green grave under the stars. Riches would come too late, after all; they could not bring back life to the dead.

"Wait one moment," said the doctor; and he hastened to rouse his housekeeper, who, curious and interested, exerted herself so as to satisfy even the stranger.

Then the strange lady, all white and trembling, was helped down from the parlor into the doctor's shabby little parlor.

"Am I going to die?" she asked, raising her large blue eyes to the doctor's face.

"Certainly not," he replied, promptly; "you must not think of dying."

"But I am very ill; and last night I dreamed that I was dead."

"Have you any brandy in the house?" asked the traveler. "See how my wife trembles."

Alas for the poor doctor! There was neither brandy nor wine. With an impatient murmur, the stranger called the postilion and sent him to the Castle arms with such an order as made Mrs. Galbraith open her eyes in wonder. Than, without seeming to notice the doctor or his servant, he flung himself on his knees by the lady's side, and kissed the beautiful white face and colorless lips.

"My darling," he cried, "this is my fault. I ought not to have asked you to undertake such a journey. Can you ever forgive me?"

She kissed him.

"You did all for the best, Hubert," she said, then adding, in a whisper: "Do you think I shall die?"

Then the doctor thought it right to interpose.

"There is no question of death," he said; "but you must be quiet. You must have no agitation—that would injure you."

Then he and Mrs. Galbraith led the beautiful, trembling girl to the room which the latter had hastily prepared for her, and, when she was installed therein, the doctor returned to the stranger, who was pacing, with quick, impatient steps, up and down the little parlor.

"How is she?" he cried, eagerly.

The doctor shook his head.

"She is young and very nervous," he replied. "I had better tell you at once that she will not be able to leave Castledene for a time—all thought of continuing the journey must be abandoned."

"But she is in no danger?" cried the traveler, and Stephen Letsom saw an agony of suspense in his face.

"No, she is not in danger; but she requires and must have both rest and care."

"She shall have anything, if Heaven will only spare her. Doctor, my best and safest plan will be to make a friend of you, to confide in you, and then we can arrange together what had better be done. Can you spare me five minutes?"

Stephen Letsom nodded assent, and sat down to listen to as strange a story as he bad ever heard.

"I should imagine," said the strange gentleman, "that no man likes to plead guilty to a folly. I must do so. Let me first of all introduce myself to you as Lord Charlewood. I am the only son of the Earl of Mountdean, and my father lies dying in Italy. I came of age only last year, and at the same time I fell in love. Now I am not in any way dependent on my father—the title and estate are entailed—but I love him. In these degenerate days it seems perhaps strange to hear a son say that he loves his father. I have obeyed him all my life from this motive. I would give my life for him. But in one respect I have done that which will cause him great annoyance and anger. I have married without his knowledge."

The doctor looked up with greater interest; perhaps his thoughts reverted to the grave in the starlight. Lord Charlewood moved uneasily in his chair.

"I cannot say that I am sorry," he continued, "for I love my wife very dearly; but I do wish now that I had been less hurried, less precipitate. My wife's great loveliness must be my excuse. She is the daughter of a poor curate, the Reverend Charles Trevor, who came two years ago to supply temporarily the place of the Rector of Lynton. He brought his daughter with him; and the first moment I saw her I fell in love with her. My heart seemed to go out from me and cleave to her. I loved her with what I can see now was the selfish ardor of a young man. I had but one thought—to win her. I wrote to my father, who was in Italy, and asked his consent. He refused it in the most decided manner, and told me to think no more of what after all was but a boy's fancy. He was then staying near the Lake of Como—staying for the benefit of his health—and I went over to see him. I pleaded, prayed, urged my great love—all in vain. The earl, my father, only laughed at me, and said all young men suffered from the fever called love. I came back to England, and found that Mr. Trevor was dead. Madaline, his daughter, was left alone in the world. She raised her beautiful face to mine, poor child, and tried to smile while she talked of going out into the world and of working hard for her daily bread; and, as I listened, my love seemed to grow stronger and deeper. I caught her in my arms, and swore that nothing should part us—that, come what would, she must be my wife. She was very unwilling—not that she did not love me, but because she was afraid of making my father angry; that was her great objection. She knew my love for him and his affection for me. She would not come between us. It was in vain that I prayed her to do as I wished. After a time she consented to a compromise—to marry me without my father's knowledge. It was a folly, I own; now I see clearly its imprudence—then I imagined it the safest and surest way. I persuaded her, as I had persuaded myself, that, when my father once knew that we were married, he would forgive us, and all would go well. We were married eleven mouths since, and I have been so happy since then that it has seemed to me but a single day. My beautiful young wife was frightened at the bold step we had taken, but I soothed her. I did not take her home to Wood Lynton, but, laying aside all the trappings of wealth and title, we have traveled from place to place as Mr. and Mrs. Charlewood, enjoying our long honeymoon. If we liked any one particular spot we remained in it. But a letter from Italy came like a thunderbolt—my father had grown rapidly worse and wanted to see me at once. If I had been content to go at once, all would have been well. I could not endure that he should die without seeing, loving, and blessing my wife Madaline. I told her my desire, and she consented most cheerfully to accompany me. I ought to have known that—in her state of health—traveling was most injurious; but I was neglectful of the fact—I listened only to my heart's desire, that my father should see my wife before he died. We started on our fatal journey—only this morning. At first my wife seemed to enjoy it; and then I saw all the color fading from her sweet face. I saw her lips grow white and tremble, and I became alarmed. It was not until we reached Castledene that she gave in and told me she could go no further. Still you say there is no danger, and that you do not think she will die?"

"Danger? No, I see none. Life and death lie in the hands of One above us; but, humanely speaking, I see no danger."

"Of course we cannot get on now," observed Lord Charlewood "at least Lady Charlewood cannot. How long do you think my suspense will last?"

"Not much longer," was the calm reply. "By noon to-morrow all will be safe and well, I hope."

"I must wait until then," said Lord Charlewood. "I could not leave my wife while even the faintest shadow of danger lies over her. If all be well, I can start the day after to-morrow; and, please Heaven, I shall be in time to see my father. You think I shall have good news for him?"

"I have every hope that you will be able to tell him that the heir of the Mountdeans is thriving and well."

Lord Charlewood smiled.

"Such news as that will more than reconcile him to our marriage," he said. After a pause he continued: "It is a most unfortunate matter; yet I am just as well pleased that my son and heir should be born in England. Doctor, there is another thing I wish to say. I know perfectly well what these little country towns are—everything is a source of gossip and sensation. If it were known that such an incident as this had happened to me, the papers would be filled with it; and it might fall out that my father, the earl, would come to know of it before I myself could tell him. We had better take all proper precautions against such a thing. I should prefer that we be known here only as Mr. and Mrs. Charlewood. No one will think of connecting the surname with the title."

"You are quite right," agreed the doctor.

"Another thing I wish to add is that I want you to spare no expense—send for the best nurse, the best help it is possible to get. Remember that I am a rich man, and that I would give my whole fortune, my life itself a thousand times over, to save or to serve my wife."

Then came a summons for the doctor from the room above, and Lord Charlewood was once more left alone. He was a young man, and was certainly both a good and honorable one. He had never deliberately done anything wicked—on the contrary he had tried always to do what was best; yet, as he stood there, a strange sense of something wanting came over him. The young wife he loved with such passionate worship was in the hour of need, and he could render no assistance.

Later on a strange hush had fallen over the doctor's house. It was past 1 in the morning; the sky was overcast; the wind was moaning fitfully, as though a storm was brewing in the autumn air. The dew lay thick and heavy on the ground. Inside the house was the strange hush that dangerous sickness always brings with it. The doctor had in haste summoned the best nurse in Castledene, Hannah Furney, who shook her head gravely when she saw the beautiful pale face. An hour passed, and again Dr. Letsom sought his distinguished guest.

"I am sorry not to bring better news," he said. "Lady—Mrs Charlewood—is not so well as I had hoped she would be. Dr. Evans is considered very clever. I should like further advice. Shall I send for him?"

The sudden flash of agony that came into Lord Charlewood's face was a revelation to Dr. Letsom; he laid his hand with a gentle touch on the stranger's arm.

"Do not fear the worst," he said. "She is in the hands of Heaven. I am taking only ordinary precautions. I do not say she is in danger—I merely say that she is not so well as I should like to see her."

Another hour passed, the church clock at Castledene was striking two, and Dr. Evans had joined the grave-faced group around the sick woman's bed. He, too, had looked with compassion on the beautiful young face—he, too, had bent forward to listen to the whisper that parted the white lips.

"Am I going to die?" she asked.

He tried to smile and say something about hope; but Nurse Furney knew, and she turned away lest the sick woman's questioning eyes should read what her face betrayed.

Three o'clock struck. A sweet voice, abrupt and clear, broke the silence of the solemn scene.

"Hubert. Where is Hubert? I must see him."

"Tell him to come," said Dr. Evans to Dr. Letsom, "but do not tell him there is any danger."

A few minutes later Lord Charlewood stood by the side of his young wife.

"Hubert," she said to him, with outstretched hands, "Hubert, my husband, I am so frightened. They do not tell me the truth. Am I going to die?"

He bent down to kiss her.

"Die, my darling? No, certainly not. You are going to live, to be what you always have been, the dearest, sweetest wife in the world." And he believed implicitly what he said.

Then came a strange sleep, half waking, half dreaming. Lady Charlewood fancied that she was with her husband on the seashore, and that the waves were coming in so fast that they threatened to drown her, they were advancing in such great sheets of foam. Once more she clung to him, crying:

"Help me, Hubert; I shall be drowned—see how the tide is coming in!"

Then the doctor bade him leave her—he must go down to the shabby, lowly little room, where the gas was burning, and the early dawn of the morning was coming in. The agony of unrest was on him. He thought how useless was money, after all; here he was with thousands at his command, yet he could not purchase help or safety for her whom his soul loved best. He was helpless, he could do nothing to assist her; he could trust only to Heaven.

He went from the window to the door; he trembled at the solemn silence, the terrible hush; he longed for the full light of day. Suddenly he heard a sound that stirred the very depths of his heart—that brought a crimson flush to his face and tears to his eyes. It was the faint cry of a little child. Presently he heard the footsteps of Dr. Letsom; and the next minute the doctor was standing before him, with a grave look on his face.

"You have a little daughter," he said—"a beautiful little girl—but your wife is in danger; you had better come and see her."

Even he—the doctor—accustomed to scenes of sorrow and desolation was startled by the cry of pain that came from the young man's lips.

Chapter II.

Five o'clock! The chimes had played the hour, the church clock had struck; the laborers were going to the fields, the dairy-maids were beginning their work; the sky had grown clear and blue, the long night of agony was over. The Angel of Death had spread his wings over the doctor's house, and awaited only the moment when his sword should fall.

Inside, the scene had hardly changed. The light of the lamp seemed to have grown so ghostly that the nurse had turned it out, and, drawing the blinds, let the faint morning light come in. It fell on the beautiful face that had grown even whiter in the presence of death. Lady Charlewood was dying; yet the feeble arms held the little child tightly. She looked up as her husband entered the room. He had combated by a strong effort all outward manifestations of despair.

"Hubert," whispered the sweet, faint voice, "see, this is our little daughter."

He bent down, but he could not see the child for the tears that filled his eyes.

"Our little daughter," she repeated; "and they say, Hubert, that I have given my life for hers. Is it true?"

He looked at the two doctors; he looked at the white face bearing the solemn, serene impress of death. It would be cruel to deceive her now, when the hands that caressed the little child were already growing colder.

"Is it true, Hubert?" she repeated, a clear light shining in her dying eyes.

"Yes, my darling, it is true," he said, in a low voice.

"I am dying—really dying—when I have my baby and you?" she questioned. "Oh, Hubert, is it really true?"

Nothing but his sobs answered her; dying as she was, all sweet, womanly compassion awoke in her heart.

"Hubert," she whispered—"oh, my darling, if you could come with me!—I want to see you kiss the baby while it lies here in my arms."

He bent down and kissed the tiny face, she watching him all the time.

"You will be very kind to her, darling, for my sake, because you have loved me so much, and call her by my name—Madaline. Tell her about me when she grows up—how young I was to die, how dearly I loved you, and how I held her in my arms. You will not forget?"

"No," he said, gently; "I shall not forget."

The hapless young mother kissed the tiny rosebud face, all the passion and anguish of her love shining in her dying eyes; and then the nurse carried the babe away.

"Hubert," said Lady Charlewood, in a low, soft, whisper, "may I die in your arms, darling?"

She laid her head on his breast, and looked at him with the sweet content of a little child.

"I am so young," she said, gently, "to die—to leave you Hubert. I have been so happy with you—I love you so much."

"Oh, my wife, my wife!" he groaned, "how am I to bear it?"

The white hands softly clasped his own.

"You will bear it in time," she said. "I know how you will miss me; but you have the baby and your father—you will find enough to fill your life. But you will always love me best—I know that, Hubert. My heart feels so strange; it seems to stop, and then to beat slowly. Lay your face on mine, darling."

He did just as she requested, whispering sweet, solemn words of comfort; and then, beneath his own he felt her lips grow cold and still. Presently he heard one long, deep-drawn sigh. Some one raised the sweet head from his breast, and laid it back upon the pillow. He knew she was dead.

He tried to bear it; he said to himself that he must be a man, that he had to live for his child's sake. He tried to rise, but the strength of his manhood failed him. With a cry never forgotten by those who heard it, Lord Charlewood fell with his face on the ground.

Seven o'clock. The full light of day was shining in the solemn chamber; the faint golden sunbeams touched the beautiful white face, so still and solemn in death; the white hands were folded, and lay motionless on the quiet heart. Kindly hands had brushed back the golden-brown hair; some one had gathered purple chrysanthemums and laid them round the dead woman, so that she looked like a marble bride on a bed of flowers. Death wore no stern aspect there; the agony and the torture, the dread and fear, were all forgotten; there was nothing but the sweet smile of one at perfect rest.

They had not darkened the room, after the usual ghostly fashion—Stephen Letsom would not have it so—but they had let in the fresh air and the sunshine, and had placed autumn flowers in the vases. The baby had been carried away—the kind-hearted nurse had charge of it. Dr. Evans had gone home, haunted by the memory of the beautiful dead face. The birds were singing in the morning sun; and Lord Charlewood, still crushed by his great grief, lay on the couch in the little sitting-room where he had spent so weary a night.

"I cannot believe it," he said, "or, believing, cannot realize it. Do you mean to tell me, doctor, that she who only yesterday sat smiling by my side, life of my life, soul of my soul, dearer to me than all the world, has gone from me, and that I shall see her no more? I cannot, I will not believe it! I shall hear her crying for me directly, or she will come smiling into the room. Oh, Madaline, my wife, my wife!"

Stephen Letsom was too clever a man and too wise a doctor to make any endeavor to stem such a torrent of grief. He knew that it must have its way. He sat patiently listening, speaking when he thought a word would be useful; and Lord Charlewood never knew how much he owed to his kind, unwearied patience.

Presently he went up to look at his wife, and, kneeling by her side, nature's great comforter came to him. He wept as though his heart would break—tears that eased the burning brain, and lightened the heavy heart. Dr. Letsom was a skillful, kindly man; he let the tears flow, and made no effort to stop them. Then, after a time, disguised in a glass of wine, he administered a sleeping potion, which soon took effect. He looked with infinite pity on the tired face. What a storm, a tempest of grief had this man passed through!

"It will be kinder and better to let him sleep the day and night through, if he can," said Stephen to himself. "He would be too ill to attend to any business even if he were awake."

So through the silent hours of the day Lord Charlewood slept, and the story spread from house to house, until the little town rang with it—the story of the travelers, the young husband and wife, who, finding no room at the hotel, had gone to the doctors, where the poor lady had died. Deep sympathy and pity were felt and expressed; kind-hearted mothers wept over the babe; some few were allowed to enter the solemn death chamber; and these went away haunted, as Dr. Evans was, by the memory of the lovely dead face. Through it all Lord Charlewood slept the heavy sleep of exhaustion and fatigue, and it was the greatest mercy that could have befallen him.

The hour of wakening was to come—Stephen Letsom never forgot it. The bereaved man was frantic in his grief, mad with the sense of his loss. Then the doctor, knowing how one great sorrow counteracts another, spoke of his father, reminding him that if he wished to see him alive he must take some little care of himself.

"I shall not leave her!" cried Lord Charlewood. "Living or dead, she is dearer than all the world to me—I shall not leave her!"

"Nor do I wish you to do so," said the doctor. "I know you are a strong man—I believe you to be a brave one; in grief of this kind the first great thing is to regain self-control. Try to regain yours, and then you will see for yourself what had better be done."

Lord Charlewood discerned the truth.

"Have patience with me," he said, "a little longer; the blow is so sudden, so terrible, I cannot yet realize what the world is without Madaline."

A few hours passed, and the self-control he had struggled for was his. He sent for Dr. Letsom.

"I have been thinking over what is best," he said, "and have decided on all my plans. Have you leisure to discuss them with me?"

The question seemed almost ironical to the doctor, who had so much more time to spare than he cared to have. He sat down by Lord Charlewood's side, and they held together the conversation that led to such strange results.

"I should not like a cold, stone grave for my beautiful wife," said Lord Charlewood. "She was so fair, so *spirituelle*, she loved all nature so dearly; she loved the flowers, trees, and the free fresh air of heaven. Let her be where she can have them all now."

The doctor looked up with mild reproach in his eyes.

"She has something far better than the flowers of this world," he said. "If ever a dead face told of rest and peace, hers does; I have never seen such a smile on any other."

"I should like to find her a grave where the sun shines and the dew falls," observed Lord Charlewood—"where grass and flowers grow and birds sing in the trees overhead. She would not seem so far away from me then."

"You can find many such graves in the pretty church-yard here in Castledene," said the doctor.

"In time to come," continued Lord Charlewood, "she shall have the grandest marble monument that can be raised, but now a plain white cross will be sufficient, with her name, Madaline Charlewood; and, doctor, while I am away you will have the grave attended to—kept bright with flowers—tended as for some one that you loved."

Then they went out together to the green church-yard at the foot of the hill, so quiet, so peaceful, so calm, and serene, that death seemed robbed of half its terrors; white daisies and golden buttercups studded it, the dense foliage of tall lime-trees rippled above it. The graves were covered with richly-hued autumn flowers; all was sweet, calm, restful. There was none of earth's fever here. The tall gray spire of the church rose toward, the clear blue sky.

Lord Charlewood stood looking around him in silence.

"I have seen such a scene in pictures," he said. "I have read of such in poems, but it is the first I have really beheld. If my darling could have chosen for herself, she would have preferred to rest here."

On the western slope, where the warmest and brightest sun beams lay, under the shade of the rippling lime-trees, they laid Lady Charlewood to rest. For long years afterward the young husband was to carry with him the memory of that green grassy grave. A plain white cross bore for the present her name; it said simply:

In Loving Memory of
MADALINE CHARLEWOOD,
who died in her 20th year.
ERECTED BY HER SORROWING HUSBAND.

"When I give her the monument she deserves," he said. "I can add no more."

They speak of that funeral to this day in Castledene—of the sad, tragic story, the fair young mother's death, the husband's wild despair. They tell how the beautiful stranger was buried when the sun shone and the birds sang—how solemnly the church-bell tolled, each knell seeming to cleave the clear sunlit air—how the sorrowing young husband, so suddenly and so terribly bereft, walked first, the chief mourner in the sad procession; they tell how white his face was, and how at each toll of the solemn bell he winced as though some one had struck him a terrible blow—how he tried hard to control himself, but how at the grave, when she was hidden forever from his sight, he stretched out his hands, crying, "Madaline, Madaline!" and how for the remainder of that day he shut himself up alone, refusing to hear the sound of a voice, to look at a human face—refusing food, comfort, grieving like one who has no hope for the love he had lost. All Castledene grieved with him; it seemed as though death and sorrow had entered every house.

Then came the morrow, when he had to look his life in the face again—life that he found so bitter without Madaline. He began to remember his father, who, lying sick unto death, craved for his presence. He could do no more for Madaline; all his grief, his tears, his bitter sorrow, were useless; he could not bring her back; he was powerless where she was concerned. But with regard to his father matters were different—to him he could take comfort, healing, and consolation. So it was decided that he should at once continue his broken journey.

What of little Madaline, the child who had her dead mother's large blue eyes and golden hair? Again Lord Charlewood and the doctor sat in solemn conclave; this time the fate of the little one hung in the balance.

Lord Charlewood said that if he found his father still weak and ill, he should keep the secret of his marriage. Of course, if Madaline had lived, all would have been different—he would have proudly owned it then. But she was dead. The child was so young and so feeble, it seemed doubtful whether it would live. What need then to grieve the old earl by the story of his folly and his disobedience? Let the secret remain. Stephen Letsom quite agreed with him in this; no one knew better than himself how dangerous was the telling of bad or disagreeable news to a sick man. And then Lord Charlewood added:

"You have indeed been a friend in need to me, Dr. Letsom. Money can no more repay such help as yours than can thanks; all my life I shall be grateful to you. I am going now to Italy, and most probably shall remain there until the earl, my father, grows better, or the end comes. When I return to England, my first care shall be to forward your views and prospects in life; until then I want you to take charge of my child."

Stephen Letsom looked up, with something like a smile.

"I shall be a rough nurse," he observed.

"You understand me," said Lord Charlewood. "You have lived here so long that you know the place and every one in it, I have been thinking so much of my little one. It would be absurd for me to take her to Italy; and as, for my father's sake, I intend to keep my marriage a secret for some time longer, I cannot send her to any of my own relatives or friends. I think the best plan will be for you to find some healthy, sensible woman, who would be nurse and foster-mother to her."

"That can easily be managed," remarked Stephen Letsom.

"Then you will have both child and nurse entirely under your own control. You can superintend all arrangements made for the little one's benefit. I have thought of offering to send you five hundred per annum, from which you can pay what you think proper for the child. You can purchase what is needful for her, and you will have an income for yourself. That I beg you accept in return for the services you have rendered me."

Dr. Letsom expressed his gratitude. He thanked Lord Charlewood and began at once to look around for some one who would be a fitting person to take care of little Madaline. Lord Charlewood had expressed a desire to see all settled before leaving for Italy.

Among the doctor's patients was one who had interested him very much—Margaret Dornham. She had been a lady's-maid. She was a pretty, graceful woman, gentle and intelligent—worthy of a far better lot than had fallen to her share. She ought to have married a well-to-do tradesman, for whom she would have made a most suitable wife; but she had given her love to a handsome ne'er do well, with whom she had never had one moment of peace or happiness. Henry Dornham had never borne a good character; he had a dark, handsome face—a certain kind of rich, gypsy-like beauty—but no other qualifications. He was neither industrious, nor honest, nor sober. His handsome face, his dark eyes, and rich curling hair had won the heart of the pretty, graceful, gentle lady's-maid, and she had married him—only to rue the day and hour in which she had first seen him.

They lived in a picturesque little cottage called Ashwood, and there Margaret Dornham passed through the greatest joy and greatest sorrow of her life. Her little child, the one gleam of sunshine that her darkened life had ever known, was born in the little cottage, and there it had died.

Dr. Letsom, who was too abrupt for the ladies of Castledene, had watched with the greatest and most untiring care over the fragile life of that little child. He had exerted his utmost skill in order to save it. But all was in vain; and on the very day that Lord Charlewood arrived at Castledene the child died.

When a tender nurse and foster-mother was needed for little Madaline, the doctor thought of Margaret Dornham. He felt that all difficulty was at an end. He sent for her. Even Lord Charlewood looked with interest at the graceful, timid woman, whose fair young face was so deeply marked with lines of care.

"Will I take charge of a little child?" she replied to the doctor's question. "Indeed I will, and thank Heaven for sending me something to keep my heart from breaking."

"You feel the loss of your own little one very keenly?" said Lord Charlewood.

"Feel it, sir? All the heart I have lies in my baby's grave."

"You must give a little of it to mine, since Heaven has taken its own mother," he said, gently. "I am not going to try flu bribe you with money—money does not buy the love and care of good women like you—but I ask you, for the love you bore to your own child, to be kind to mine. Try to think, if you can, that it is your own child brought back to you."

"I will," she promised, and she kept her word.

"You will spare neither expense nor trouble," he continued, "and when I return you shall be most richly recompensed. If all goes well, and the little one prospers with you, I shall leave her with you for two or three years at least. You have been a lady's-maid, the doctor tells me. In what families have you lived?"

"Principally with Lady L'Estrange, of Verdun Royal, sir," she replied. "I left because Miss L'Estrange was growing up, and my lady wished to have a French maid."

In after years he thought how strange it was that he should have asked the question.

"I want you," said Lord Charlewood, "to devote yourself entirely to the little one; you will be so liberally paid as not to need work of any other kind. I am going abroad, but I leave Dr. Letsom as the guardian of the child; apply to him for everything you want, as you will not be able to communicate with me."

He watched her as she took the child in her arms. He was satisfied when he saw the light that came into her face: he knew that little Madaline would be well cared for. He placed a bank note for fifty pounds in the woman's hands.

"Buy all that is needful for the little one," he said.

In all things Margaret Dornham promised obedience. One would have thought she had found a great treasure. To her kindly, womanly heart, the fact that she once more held a little child in her arms was a source of the purest happiness The only drawback was when she reached home, and her husband laughed coarsely at the sad little story.

"You have done a good day's work, Maggie," he said; "now I shall expect you to keep me, and I shall take it easy."

He kept his word, and from that day made no further effort to earn any money.

"Maggie had enough for both," he said—"for both of them and that bit of a child."

Faithful, patient Margaret never complained, and not even Dr. Letsom knew how the suffering of her daily life had increased even though she was comforted by the love of the little child.

Chapter III.

Madaline slept in her grave—her child was safe and happy with the kindly, tender woman who was to supply its mother's place. Then Lord Charlewood prepared to leave the place where he had suffered so bitterly. The secret of his title had been well kept. No one dreamed that the stranger whose visit to the little town had been such a sad one was the son of one of England's earls. Charlewood did not strike any one as being a very uncommon name. There was not the least suspicion as to his real identity. People thought he must be rich; but that he was noble also no one ever imagined.

Mary Galbraith, the doctor's housekeeper, thought a golden shower had fallen over the house. Where there had been absolute poverty there was now abundance. There were no more shabby curtains and threadbare carpets—everything was new and comfortable. The doctor seemed to have grown younger—relieved as he was from a killing weight of anxiety and care.

The day came when Lord Charlewood was to say good-by to his little daughter, and the friends who had been friends indeed. Margaret Dornham was sent for. When she arrived the two gentlemen were in the parlor, and she was shown in to them. Every detail of that interview was impressed on Margaret's mind. The table was strewn with papers, and Lord Charlewood taking some in his hand, said:

"You should have a safe place for those doctor. Strange events happen in life. They might possibly be required some day as evidences of identification."

"Not much fear of that," returned the doctor, with a smile. "Still, as you say, it is best to be cautious."

"Here is the first—you may as well keep it with the rest," said Lord Charlewood; "it is a copy of my marriage certificate. Then you have here the certificates of my little daughter's birth and of my poor wife's death. Now we will add to these a signed agreement between you and myself for the sum I have spoken about."

Rapidly enough Lord Charlewood filled up another paper, which was signed by the doctor and himself; then Stephen Letsom gathered them all together. Margaret Dornham saw him take from the sideboard a plain oaken box bound in brass, and lock the papers in it.

"There will be no difficulty about the little lady's identification while this lasts," he said, "and the papers remain undestroyed."

She could not account for the impulse that led her to watch him so closely, while she wondered what the papers could be worth.

Then both gentlemen turned their attention from the box to the child. Lord Charlewood would be leaving directly, and it would be the last time that he, at least, could see the little one. There was all a woman's love in his heart and in his face, as he bent down to kiss it and say farewell.

"In three years' time, when I come back again," he said, "she will be three years old—she will walk and talk. You must teach her to say my name, Mrs. Dornham, and teach her to love me."

Then he bade farewell to the doctor who had been so kind a friend to him, leaving something in his hand which made his heart light for many a long day afterward.

"I am a bad correspondent, Dr. Letsom," he said; "I never write many letters—but you may rely upon hearing from me every six months. I shall send you half-yearly checks—and you may expect me in three years from this at latest; then my little Madaline will be of a manageable age, and I can take her to Wood Lynton."

So they parted, the two who had been so strangely brought together—parted with a sense of liking and trust common among

Englishmen who feel more than they express. Lord Charlewood looked round him as he left the town.

"How little I thought," he said, "that I should leave my dead wife and living child here! It was a town so strange to me that I hardly even knew its name."

On arriving at his destination, to his great joy, and somewhat to his surprise, Lord Charlewood found that his father was better; he had been afraid of finding him dead. The old man's joy on seeing his son again was almost pitiful in its excess—he held his hands in his.

"My son—my only son! why did you not come sooner?" he asked. "I have longed so for you. You have brought life and healing with you; I shall live years longer now that I have you again."

And in the first excitement of such happiness Lord Charlewood did not dare to tell his father the mournful story of his marriage and of his young wife's untimely death. Then the doctors told him that the old earl might live for some few years longer, but that he would require the greatest care; he had certainly heart-disease, and any sudden excitement, any great anxiety, any cause of trouble might kill him at once. Knowing this Lord Charlewood did not dare to tell his secret; it would have been plunging his father into danger uselessly; besides which the telling of it was useless now—his beautiful wife was dead, and the child too young to be recognized or made of consequence. So he devoted himself to the earl, having decided in his own mind what steps to take. If the earl lived until little Madaline reached her third year, then he would tell him his secret; the child would be pretty and graceful—she would, in all probability, win his love. He could not let it go on longer than that. Madaline could not remain unknown and uncared for in that little county town; it was not to be thought of. Therefore, if his father lived, and all went well, he would tell his story then; if, on the contrary, his health failed, then he would keep his secret altogether, and his father would never know that he had disobeyed him.

There was a wonderful affection between this father and son. The earl was the first to notice the change that had come over his bright, handsome boy; the music had all gone from his voice, the ring from his laughter, the light from his face. Presently he observed the deep mourning dress.

"Hubert," he asked, suddenly, "for whom are you in mourning?"

Lord Charlewood's face flushed. For one moment he felt tempted to answer—

"For my beloved wife whom Heaven has taken from me."

But he remembered the probable consequence of such a shock to his father, and replied, quietly:

"For one of my friends, father—one whom you did not know." And Lord Mountdean did not suspect.

Another time the old earl placed his arm round his son's neck.

"How I wish, Hubert," he said, "that your mother had lived to see you a grown man! I think—do not laugh at me, my son—I think yours is perfect manhood; you please me infinitely."

Lord Charlewood smiled at the simple, loving praise.

"I have a woman's pride in your handsome face and tall, stately figure. How glad I am, my son, that no cloud has ever come between us! You have been the best of sons to me. When I die you can say to yourself that you have never once in all your life given me one moment's pain. How pleased I am that you gave up that foolish marriage for my sake! You would not have been happy. Heaven never blesses such marriages."

He little knew that each word was as a dagger to his son's heart.

"After you had left me and had gone back to England," he continued, "I used to wonder if I had done wisely or well in refusing you your heart's desire; now I know that I did well, for unequal marriages never prosper. She, the girl you loved, may have been very beautiful, but you would never have been happy with her."

"Hush, father!" said Lord Charlewood, gently. "We will not speak of this again."

"Does it still pain you? tell me, my son," cried the earl.

"Not in the way you think," he replied.

"I would not pain you for the world—you know that, Hubert. But you must not let that one unfortunate love affair prejudice you against marriage. I should like to see you married, my son. I should like you to love some noble, gentle lady whom I could call daughter; I should like to hold your children in my arms, to hear the music of children's voices before I go."

"Should you love my children so much, father?" he asked.

"Yes, more than I can tell you. You must marry, Hubert, and then, as far as you are concerned, I shall not have a wish left unfulfilled."

There was hope then for his little Madaline—hope that in time she would win the old earl's heart, and prevent his grieving over the unfortunate marriage. For two years and a half the Earl of Mountdean lingered; the fair Italian clime, the warmth, the sunshine, the flowers, all seemed to join in giving him new life. For two years and a half he improved, so that his son had begun to hope that he might return to England, and once more see the home he loved so dearly—Wood Lynton; and, though during this time his secret preyed upon him through every hour of every day, causing him to long to tell his father, yet he controlled the longing, because he would do nothing that might in the least degree retard his recovery. Then, when the two years and a half had passed, and he began to take counsel with himself how he could best break the intelligence, the earl's health suddenly failed him, and he could not accomplish his purpose.

During this time he had every six months sent regular remittances to England, and had received in return most encouraging letters about little Madaline. She was growing strong and beautiful; she was healthy, fair, and happy. She could say his name; she could sing little baby-songs. Once, the doctor cut a long golden-brown curl from her little head and sent it to him; but when he received it the earl lay dying, and the son could not show his father his little child's hair. He died as he had lived, loving and trusting his son, clasping his hand to the last, and murmuring sweet and tender words to him. Lord Charlewood's heart smote him as he listened, he had not merited such implicit faith and trust.

"Father," he said, "listen for one moment! Can you hear me? I did marry Madaline—I loved her so dearly, I could not help it—I married her; and she died one year afterward. But she left me a little daughter. Can you hear me, father?"

No gleam of light came into the dying eyes, no consciousness into the quiet face; the earl did not hear. When, at last, his son had made up his mind to reveal his secret, it was too late for his father to hear—and he died without knowing it. He died, and was brought back to England, and buried with great pomp and magnificence; and then his son reigned in his stead, and became Earl of Mountdean. The first thing that he did after his father's funeral was to go down to Castledene; he had made all arrangements for bringing his daughter and heiress home. He was longing most impatiently to see her; but when he reached the little town a shock of surprise awaited him that almost cost him his life.

Chapter IV.

Dr. Letsom had prospered; one gleam of good fortune had brought with it a sudden outburst of sunshine. The doctor had left his little house in Castle street, and had taken a pretty villa just outside Castledene. He had furnished it nicely—white lace curtains were no longer an unattainable luxury; no house in the town looked so clean, so bright, or so pretty as the doctor's People began to look up to him; it was rumored that he had had money left to him—a fortune that rendered him independent of his practice. No sooner was that quite understood than people began to find out that after all he was a very clever man. No sooner did they feel quite convinced that he was indifferent about his practice than they at once appreciated his services; what had been called abruptness now became truth and sincerity He was declared to be like Dr. Abernethy—wonderfully clever, though slightly brusque in manner. Patients began to admire him; one or two instances of wonderful cures were noted in his favor; the world, true to itself, true to its own maxims, began to respect him when it was believed that he had good fortune for his friend. In one year's time he had the best practice in the town, the ladies found his manner so much improved.

He bore his good-fortune as he had borne his ill-fortune, with great equanimity; it had come too late. If but a tithe of it had fallen to his share twelve years earlier, he might have made the woman he loved so dearly his wife. She might have been living—- loving happy, by his side. Nothing could bring her back—the good-fortune had come all too late; still he was grateful for it. It was pleasant to be able to pay his bills when they became due, to be able to help his poorer neighbors, to be able to afford for himself little luxuries such as he had long been without. The greatest happiness he had now in life was his love for little Madeline. The hold she had taken of him was marvelous from the first moment she held out her baby-hands until the last in which he saw her she was his one dream of delight. At first he had visited Ashwood as a matter of duty; but, as time passed on those visits became his dearest pleasures. The child began to know him, her lovely little face to brighten for him; she had no fear of him, but would sit on his knee and lisp her pretty stories and sing her pretty songs until he was fairly enchanted.

Madaline was a lovely child. She had a beautiful head and face, and a figure exquisitely molded. Her smiles were like sunshine; her hair had in it threads of gold; her eyes were of the deep blue that one sees in summer. It was not only her great loveliness, but there was about her a wonderful charm, a fascination, that no one could resist.

Dr. Letsom loved the child. She sat on his knee and talked to him, until the whole face of the earth seemed changed to him. Besides his great love for the little Madaline, he became interested in the story of Margaret Dornham's life—in her love for the handsome, reckless ne'er-do-well who had given up work as a failure—in her wonderful patience, for she never complained—in her sublime heroism, for she bore all as a martyr. He heard how Henry Dornham was often seen intoxicated—heard that he was abusive, violent. He went afterward to the cottage, and saw bruises on his wife's delicate arms and hands—dark cruel marks on her face; but by neither word nor look did she ever betray her husband. Watching that silent, heroic life, he became interested in her. More than once he tried to speak to her about her husband—to see if anything could be done to reclaim him. She knew that all efforts were in vain—there was no good in him; still more she knew now that there never had been such good as she had hoped and believed. Another thing pleased and interested the doctor—it was Margaret Dornham's passionate love for her foster child. All the love that she would have lavished on her husband, all the love that she would have given to her own child, all the repressed affection and buried tenderness of heart were given to this little one. It was touching pitiful, sad, to see how she worshiped her.

"What shall I do when the three years are over, and her father comes to claim her?" she would say to the doctor. "I shall never be able to part with her. Sometimes I think I shall run away with her and hide her."

How little she dreamed that there was a prophecy in the words!

"Her father has the first claim," said Dr. Letsom. "It may be hard for us to lose her, but she belongs to him."

"He will never love her as I do," observed Margaret Dornham.

Of the real rank and position of that father she had not the faintest suspicion. He had money, she knew; but that was all she knew—and money to a woman whose heart hungers for love seems very little.

"There is something almost terrible in the love of that woman for that child," thought the doctor. "She is good, earnest, tender, true, by nature; but she is capable of anything for the little one's sake."

So the two years and a half passed, and the child, with her delicate, marvelous grace, had become the very light of those two lonely lives. In another six months they would have to lose her. Dr. Letsom knew very well that if the earl were still living at the end of the three years his son would tell him of his marriage.

On a bright, sunshiny day in June the doctor walked over to Ashwood. He had a little packet of fruit and cakes with him, and a wonderful doll, dressed most royally.

"Madaline!" he cried, as he entered the cottage, and she came running to him, "should you like a drive with me to-morrow?" he asked. "I am going to Corfell, and I will promise to take you if you will be a good girl."

She promised—for a drive with the doctor was her greatest earthly delight.

"Bring her to my house about three to-morrow afternoon, Mrs. Dornham," said Dr. Letsom, "and she shall have her drive."

Margaret promised. When the time came she took the little one, dressed in her pretty white frock; and as they sat in the drawing-room, the doctor was brought home to his house—dead.

It was such a simple yet terrible accident that had killed him. A poor man had been injured by a kick from a horse. For want of better accommodation, he had been carried up into a loft over a stable, where the doctor attended him. In the loft was an open trap-door, through which trusses of hay and straw were raised and lowered. No one warned Dr. Letsom about it. The aperture was covered with straw, and he, walking quickly across, fell through. There was but one comfort—he did not suffer long. His death was instantaneous; and on the bright June afternoon when he was to have taken little Madaline for a drive, he was carried home, through the sunlit streets, dead.

Margaret Dornham and the little child sat waiting for him when the sad procession stopped at the door.

"The doctor is dead!" was the cry from one to another.

A terrible pain shot through Margaret's head. Dead! The kindly man, who had been her only friend, dead! Then perhaps the child would be taken from her, and she should see it no more!

An impulse, for which she could hardly account, and for which she was hardly responsible, seized her. She must have the box that contained the papers, lest, finding the papers, people should rob her of the child. Quick as thought, she seized the box—which always stood on a bracket in the drawing-room—and hid it under her shawl. To the end of her life she was puzzled as to why she had done this. It would not be missed, she knew, in the confusion that was likely to ensue. She felt sure, also, that no one, save herself and the child's father, knew of its contents.

She did not wait long in that scene of confusion and sorrow. Clasping the child in her arms, lest she should see the dead face, Margaret Dornham hurried back to the cottage, bearing with her the proofs of the child's identity.

The doctor was buried, and with him all trace of the child seemed lost. Careful search was made in his house for any letters that might concern her, that might give her father's address; but Stephen Letsom had been faithful to his promise—he had kept the secret. There was nothing that could give the least clew. There were no letters, no memoranda; and, after a time, people came to the conclusion that it would be better to let the child remain where she was, for her father would be sure in time to hear of the doctor's death and to claim her.

So September came, with its glory of autumn leaves. Just three years had elapsed since Lady Charlewood had died; and then the great trouble of her life came to Margaret Dornham.

Chapter V.

On the day after Dr. Letsom's death, Margaret Dornham's husband was apprehended on a charge of poaching and aiding in a dangerous assault on Lord Turton's gamekeepers. Bail was refused for him, but at the trial he was acquitted for want of evidence. Every one knew he was guilty. He made no great effort to conceal it. But he defied the whole legal power of England to prove him guilty. He employed clever counsel, and the result was his acquittal. He was free; but the prison brand was on him, and his wife felt that she could not endure the disgrace.

"I shall go from bad to worse now, Maggie," he said to her. "I do not find prison so bad, nor yet difficult to bear; if ever I Bee by any lucky hit I can make myself a rich man, I shall not mind a few years in jail as the price. A forgery, or something of that kind, or the robbery of a well-stocked bank, will be henceforward my highest aim in life."

She placed her hand on his lips and prayed him for Heaven's sake to be silent. He only laughed.

"Nature never intended me to work—she did not indeed, Maggie. My fellow-men must keep me; they keep others far less deserving."

From that moment she knew no peace or rest. He would keep his word; he would look upon crime as a source of profit; he would watch his opportunity of wrong-doing, and seize it When it came.

In the anguish of her heart she cried aloud that it must not be at Ash wood; anywhere else, in any other spot, but not there, where she had been known in the pride of her fair young life—not there, where people had warned her not to marry the handsome reckless, ne'er-do-well, and had prophesied such terrible evil for her if she did marry him—not there, where earth was so fair, where all nature told of innocence and purity. If he must sin, let it be far away in large cities where the ways of men were evil.

She decided on leaving Ashwood. Another and perhaps even stronger motive that influenced her was her passionate love for the child; that was her one hope in life, her one sheet-anchor, the one thing that preserved her from the utter madness of desolation.

The three years had almost elapsed; the doctor was dead, and had left nothing behind him that could give any clew to Madaline's identity, and in a short time—she trembled to think how short—the father would come to claim his child, and she would lose her. When she thought of that, Margaret Dornham clung to the little one in a passion of despair. She would go away and take Madaline with her—keep her where she could love her—where she could bring her up as her own child, and lavish all the warmth and devotion of her nature upon her. She never once thought that in acting thus she was doing a selfish, a cruel deed—that she was taking the child from her father, who of all people living had the greatest claim upon her.

"He may have more money than I have," thought poor, mistaken Margaret, "but he cannot love her so much; and after all love is better than money."

It was easy to manage her husband. She had said but little to him at the time she undertook the charge of little Madaline, and he had been too indifferent to make inquiries. She told him now, what was in some measure quite true, that with the doctor's death her income had ceased, and that she herself not only was perfectly ignorant of the child's real name, but did not even know to whom to write. It was true, but she knew at the same time that, if she would only open the box of papers, she would not be ignorant of any one point; for those papers she had firmly resolved never to touch, so that in saying she knew nothing of the child's identity she would be speaking the bare truth.

At first Henry Dornham was indignant. The child should not be left a burden and drag on his hands, he declared—it must go to the work-house.

But patient Margaret clasped her arms round his neck, and whispered to him that the child was so clever, so pretty, she would be a gold-mine to them in the future—only let them get away from Ashwood, and go to London, where she could be well trained and taught. He laughed a sneering laugh, for which, had he been any other than her husband, she would have hated him.

"Not a bad plan, Maggie," he said; "then she can work to keep us. I, myself, do not care where we go or what we do, so that no one asks me to work."

He was easily persuaded to say nothing about their removal, to go to London without saying anything to his old friends and neighbors of their intentions. Margaret knew well that so many were interested in the child that she would not be allowed to take her away if her wish became known.

How long the little cottage at Ashwood had been empty no one knows. It stood so entirely alone that for weeks together nothing was seen or known of its inhabitants. Henry Dornham was missed from his haunts. His friends and comrades wondered for a few days, and then forgot him; they thought that in all probability he was engaged in some not very reputable pursuit.

The rector of Castledene—the Rev. John Darnley—was the first really to miss them. He had always been interested in little Madaline. When he heard from the shop keepers that Margaret had not been seen in the town lately, he feared she was ill, and resolved to go and see her. His astonishment was great when he found the cottage closed and the Dornhams gone—the place had evidently been empty for some weeks. On inquiry he found that the time of their departure and the place of their destination was equally unknown. No one knew whither they had gone or anything about them. Mr. Darnley was puzzled; it seemed to him very strange that, after having lived in the place so long, Margaret Dornham should have left without saying one word to any human being.

"There is a mystery in it," thought the rector. He never dreamed that the cause of the mystery was the woman's passionate love for the child.

All Castledene wondered with him—indeed, for some days the little town was all excitement. Margaret Dornham had disappeared with the child who had been left in their midst. Every one seemed to be more or less responsible for her; but neither wonder nor anything else gave them the least clew as to whither or why she had gone. After a few day's earnest discussion and inquiry the excitement died away, when a wonderful event revived it. It was no other than the arrival of the new Earl of Mountdean in search of his little girl.

This time the visitor did not take any pains to conceal his title. He drove to the "Castle Arms," and from there went at once to the doctor's house. He found it closed and empty. The first person he asked told him that the doctor had been for some weeks dead and buried.

The young earl was terribly shocked. Dead and buried—the kindly man who had befriended him in the hour of need! It seemed almost incredible. And why had no one written to him? Still he remembered the address of his child's foster-mother. It was Ashwood Cottage; and he went thither at once. When he found that too closed and deserted, it seemed to him that fortune was playing him a trick.

He was disconcerted; and then, believing that this at least was but a case of removal, he decided upon going to the rector of the parish, whom he well remembered. He surely would be able to give him all information.

Mr. Darnley looked up in wonder at the announcement of his visitor's name—the Earl of Mountdean. What could the earl possibly want of him?

His wonder deepened as he recognized in the earl the stranger at the burial of whose fair young wife he had assisted three years before. The earl held out his hand.

"You are surprised to see me, Dr. Darnley? You recognize me, I perceive."

The rector contrived to say something about his surprise, but Lord Mountdean interrupted him hastily:

"Yes, I understand. I was traveling as Mr. Charlewood when my terrible misfortune overtook me here. I have returned from Italy, where I have been spending the last three years. My father has just died, and I am here in search of my child. My child," continued the earl, seeing the rector's blank face—"where is she? I find my poor friend the doctor is dead, and the house where my little one's foster-mother lived is empty. Can you tell me what it means?"

He tried to speak calmly, but his handsome face had grown quite white, his lips were dry and hot, his voice, even to himself, had a strange, harsh sound.

"Where is she?" he repeated. "The little one—my Madaline's child? I have a strange feeling that all is not well. Where is my child?"

He saw the shadow deepen on the rector's face, and he clasped his arm.

"Where is she?" he cried. "You cannot mean that she is dead? Not dead, surely? I have not seen her since I left her, a little, feeble baby; but she has lived in my heart through all these weary years of exile. My whole soul has hungered and thirsted for her. By night and by day I have dreamed of her, always with Madaline's face. She has spoken sweet words to me in my dreams, always in Madaline's voice. I must see her. I cannot bear this suspense. You do not answer me. Can it be that she too is dead?"

"No, she is not dead," replied the rector. "I saw her two months since, and she was then living—well, beautiful, and happy. No, the little one is not dead."

"Then tell me, for pity's sake, where she is!" cried the earl, in an agony of impatience.

"I cannot. Two months since I was at Ashwood Cottage Margaret Dornham's worthless husband was in some great trouble. I went to console his wife; and then I saw the little one. I held her in my arms, and thought, as I looked at her, that I had never seen such a lovely face. Then I saw no more of her; and my wonder was aroused on hearing some of the tradespeople say that Mrs. Dornham had not been in town for some weeks. I believed she was ill, and went to see. My wonder was as great as your own at finding the house closed. Husband, wife, and child had disappeared as though by magic from the place, leaving no clew or trace behind them."

The rector was almost alarmed at the effect of his words. The young earl fell back in his chair, looking as though the shadow of death had fallen over him.

Chapter VI.

It was but a child, the rector thought to himself, whom its father had seen but a few times. He did not understand that to Lord Mountdean this child—his dying wife's legacy—was the one object in life, that she was all that remained to him of a love that had been dearer than life itself. Commonplace words of comfort rose to his lips, but the earl did not even hear them. He looked up suddenly, with a ghastly pallor still on his face.

"How foolish I am to alarm myself so greatly!" he said. "Some one or other will be sure to know whither the woman has gone. She may have had some monetary trouble, and so have desired to keep her whereabouts a secret; but some one or other will know. If she is in the world I will find her. How foolish I am to be so terribly frightened! If the child is living what have I to fear?"

But, though his words were brave and courageous, his hands trembled, and the rector saw signs of great agitation. He rang for wine, but Lord Mountdean could not take it—he could do nothing until he had found his child.

In few words he told the rector the story of his marriage.

"I thought," he said, "that I could not do better for the little one than leave her here in the doctor's care."

"You were right," returned the rector; "the poor doctor's love for the child was talked about everywhere. As for Margaret Dornham, I do not think, if she had been her own, she could have loved her better. Whatever else may have gone wrong, take my word for it, there was no lack of love for the child; she could not have been better cared for—of that I am quite sure."

"I am glad to hear you say so; that is some comfort. But why did no one write to me when the doctor died?"

"I do not think he left one shred of paper containing any allusion to your lordship. All his effects were claimed by some distant cousin, who now lives in his house. I was asked to look over his papers, but there was not a private memorandum among them—not one; there was nothing in fact but receipted bills."

Lord Mountdean looked up.

"There must be some mistake," he observed. "I myself placed in his charge all the papers necessary for the identification of my little daughter."

"May I ask of what they consisted?" said the rector.

"Certainly—the certificate of my marriage, of my beloved wife's death, of my little daughter's birth, and an agreement between the doctor and myself as to the sum that was to be paid to him yearly while he had charge of my child."

"Then the doctor knew your name, title, and address?"

"Yes; I had no motive in keeping them secret, save that I did not wish my marriage to be known to my father until I myself could tell him—and I know how fast such news travels. I remember distinctly where he placed the papers. I watched him."

"Where was it?" asked Mr. Darnley. "For I certainly have seen nothing of them."

"In a small oaken box with brass clasps, which stood on a sideboard. I remember it as though it were yesterday."

"I have seen no such box," said the rector. "Our wisest plan will be to go at once to the house where his cousin, Mr. Grey, resides, and see if the article is in his possession. I am quite sure, though, that he would have mentioned it if he had seen it."

Without a minute's delay they drove at once to the house, and found Mr. Grey at home. He was surprised when he heard the name and rank of his visitor, and above all when he understood his errand.

"A small oaken box with brass clasps?" he said. "No; I have nothing of the kind in my possession; but, if your lordship will wait, I will have a search made at once."

Every drawer, desk, and recess were examined in vain. There was no trace of either the box or the papers.

"I have an inventory of everything the doctor's house contained—it was taken the day after his death," said Mr. Grey; "we can look through that."

Item after item was most carefully perused. The list contained no mention of a small oaken box. It was quite plain that box and papers had both disappeared.

"Could the doctor have given them into Mrs. Dornham's charge?" asked the earl.

"No," replied the rector—"I should say certainly not. I am quite sure that Mrs. Dornham did not even know the child's surname. I remember once asking her about it; she said it was a long name, and that she could never remember it. If she had had the papers, she would have read them. I cannot think she holds them."

Then they went to visit Mrs. Galbraith, the doctor's housekeeper. She had a distinct recollection of the box—it used to stand on the sideboard, and a large-sized family Bible generally lay on the top of it. How long it had been out of sight when the doctor died she did not know, but she had never seen it since. Then they drove to the bank, thinking that, perhaps, for greater security, he might have deposited it there. No such thing had been heard of. Plainly enough, the papers had disappeared; both the earl and the rector were puzzled.

"They can be of no possible use to any one but myself," said Lord Mountdean. "Now that my poor father is dead and cannot be distressed about it, I shall tell the whole world—if it cares to listen—the story of my marriage. If I had wanted to keep that or the birth of my child a secret, I could have understood the papers being stolen by one wishing to trade with them. As it is, I cannot see that they are of the least use to any one except myself."

They gave up the search at last, and then Lord Mountdean devoted himself to the object—the finding of his child.

In a few days the story of his marriage was told by every newspaper in the land; also the history of the strange disappearance of his child. Large rewards were offered to any one who could bring the least information. Not content with employing the best detective skill in England, he conducted the search himself. He worked unwearyingly.

"A man, woman, and child could not possibly disappear from the face of the earth without leaving some trace behind," he would say.

One little gleam of light came, which filled him with hope—they found that Margaret Dornham had sold all her furniture to a broker living at a town called Wrentford. She had sent for him herself, and had asked him to purchase it, saying that she, with her husband, was going to live at a distance, and that they did not care about taking it with them. He remembered having asked her where she was going, but she evaded any reply. He could tell no more. He showed what he had left of the furniture and tears filled Lord Mountdean's eyes as he saw among it a child's crib. He liberally rewarded the man, and then set to work with renewed vigor to endeavor to find out Margaret Dornham's destination.

He went to the railway stations; and, though the only clew he succeeded in obtaining was a very faint one, he had some reason for believing that Margaret Dornham had gone to London.

In that vast city he continued the search, until it really seemed that every inch of ground had been examined. It was all without result—Margaret Dornham and her little foster-child seemed to have vanished.

"What can be the woman's motive?" the earl would cry, in despair. "Why has she taken the child? What does she intend to do with it?"

It never occurred to him that her great, passionate love for the little one was the sole motive for the deed she had done.

The papers were filled with appeals to Margaret Dornham to return to Castledene, or to give some intelligence of her foster-child. The events of the story were talked about everywhere; but, in spite of all that was done and said, Lord Mountdean's heiress remained undiscovered. Months grew into years, and the same mystery prevailed. The earl was desperate at first—his anguish and sorrow were pitiful to witness; but after a time he grew passive in his despair. He never relaxed in his efforts. Every six months the advertisements with the offers of reward were renewed; every six months the story was retold in the papers. It had become one of the common topics of the day. People talked of the Earl of Mountdean's daughter, of her strange disappearance, of the mysterious silence that had fallen over her. Then, as the years passed on, it was agreed that she would never be found, that she must be dead. The earl's truest friends advised him to marry again. After years of bitter disappointment, of anguish and suspense, of unutterable sorrow and despair, he resigned himself to the entire loss of Madaline's child.

Nature had made Philippa L'Estrange beautiful, circumstances had helped to make her proud. Her father, Lord L'Estrange, died when she was quite a child, leaving her an enormous fortune that was quite under her own control. Her mother, Lady L'Estrange, had but one idea in life, and that was indulging her beautiful daughter in her every caprice. Proud, beautiful, and wealthy, when she most needed her mother's care that mother died, leaving her sole mistress of herself. She was but seventeen then, and was known as one of the wealthiest heiresses and loveliest girls of the day. Her first step was, in the opinion of the world, a wise one; she sent for a widowed cousin, Lady Peters, to live with her as chaperon. For the first year after her mother's death she remained at Verdun Royal, the family estate. After one year given to retirement, Philippa L'Estrange thought she had mourned for her mother after the most exemplary fashion She was just nineteen when she took her place again in the great world, one of its brightest ornaments.

An afternoon in London in May. The air was clear and fresh; there was in it a faint breath of the budding chestnuts, the hawthorn and lilac; the sun shone clear and bright, yet not too warmly.

On this afternoon Miss L'Estrange sat in the drawing-room of the magnificent family mansion in Hyde Park. The whole world could not have produced a more marvelous picture. The room itself was large, lofty, well proportioned, and superbly furnished; the hangings were of pale-rose silk and white lace the pictures and statues were gems of art, a superb copy of the Venus of Milo gleaming white and shapely from between the folds of rose silk, also a marble Flora, whose basket was filled with purple heliotropes, and a Psyche that was in itself a dream of beauty; the vases were filled with fairest and most fragrant flowers. Nothing that art, taste, or luxury could suggest was wanting—the eye reveled in beauty. Miss L'Estrange had refurnished the room in accordance with her own ideas of the beautiful and artistic.

The long windows were opened, and through them one saw the rippling of the rich green foliage in the park; the large iron balconies were filled with flowers, fragrant mignonette, lemon-scented verbenas, purple heliotropes, all growing in rich profusion. The spray of the little scented fountain sparkled in the sun. Every one agreed that there was no other room in London like the grand drawing-room at Verdun House.

There was something on that bright May afternoon more beautiful even than the flowers, the fountains, the bright-plumaged birds in their handsome cages, the white statues, or the pictures; that was the mistress and queen of all this magnificence, Philippa L'Estrange. She was reclining on a couch that had been sent from Paris—a couch made of finest ebony, and covered with pale, rose-colored velvet. If Titian or Velasquez had seen her as she lay there, the world would have been the richer by an immortal work of art; Titian alone could have reproduced those rich, marvelous colors; that perfect, queenly beauty. He would have painted the picture, and the world would have raved about its beauty. The dark masses of waving hair; the lovely face with its warm Southern tints; the dark eyes lighted with fire and passion; the perfect mouth with its proud, sweet, imperial, yet tender lips; the white, dimpled chin; the head and face unrivaled in their glorious contour; the straight, dark brows that could frown and yet soften as few other brows could; the white neck, half hidden, half revealed by the coquettish dress; the white rounded arms and beautiful hands—all would have struck the master. Her dress fell round her in folds that would have charmed an artist. It was of some rich, transparent material, the pale amber hue of which enhanced her dark loveliness. The white arms were half shown, half covered by rich lace—in the waves of her dark hair lay a yellow rose. She looked like a woman whose smile could be fatal and dangerous as that of a siren, who could be madly loved or madly hated, yet to whom no man living could be indifferent.

She played for some few minutes with the rings on her fingers, smiling to herself a soft, dreamy smile, as though her thoughts were very pleasant ones; then she took up a volume of poems, read a few lines, and then laid the book down again. The dark eyes, with a gleam of impatience in them, wandered to the clock.

"How slowly those hands move!" she said.

"You are restless," observed a calm, low voice; "watching a clock always makes time seem long."

"Ah, Lady Peters," said the rich, musical tones, "when I cease to be young, I shall cease to be impatient."

Lady Peters, the chosen confidante and chaperon of the brilliant heiress, was an elderly lady whose most striking characteristic appeared to be calmness and repose. She was richly dressed in a robe of black *moire*, and she wore a cap of point lace; her snowy hair was braided back from a broad white brow; her face was kindly, patient, cheerful; her manner, though somewhat stately, the same. She evidently deeply loved the beautiful girl whose bright face was turned to hers.

"He said three in his note, did he not, Lady Peters?"

"Yes, my dear, but it is impossible for any one to be always strictly punctual; a hundred different things may have detained him."

"But if he were really anxious to see me, he would not let anything detain him," she said.

"Your anxiety about him would be very flattering to him if he knew it," remarked the elder lady.

"Why should I not be anxious? I have always loved him better than the whole world. I have had reason to be anxious."

"Philippa, my dear Philippa, I would not say such things if I were you, unless I had heard something really definite from himself."

The beautiful young heiress laughed a bright, triumphant laugh.

"Something definite from himself! Why, you do not think it likely that he will long remain indifferent to me, even if he be so now — which I do not believe."

"I have had so many disappointments in life that I am afraid of being sanguine," said Lady Peters; and again the young beauty laughed.

"It will seem so strange to see him again. I remember his going away so well. I was very young then—I am young now, but I feel years older. He came down to Verdun Royal to bid us good-by, and I was

48

in the grounds. He had but half an hour to stay, and mamma sent him out to me,"

The color deepened in her face as she spoke, and the light shone in her splendid eyes—there was a kind of wild, restless passion in her words.

"I remember it all so well! There had been a heavy shower of rain in the early morning, that had cleared away, leaving the skies blue, the sunshine golden, while the rain-drops still glistened on the trees and the grass. I love the sweet smell of the green leaves and the moist earth after rain. I was there enjoying it when he came to say good-by to me—mamma came with him. 'Philippa,' she said, 'Norman is going; he wants to say good-by to his little wife.' He always calls me his little wife. I saw him look very grave. She went away and left us together. 'You are growing too tall to be called my little wife, Philippa,' she said, and I laughed at his gravity. We were standing underneath a great flowering lilac-tree—the green leaves and the sweet flowers were still wet with the rain. I remember it so well! I drew one of the tall fragrant sprays down, and shaking the rain-drops from it, kissed it. I can smell the rich, moist odor now. I never see a lilac-spray or smell its sweet moisture after rain but that the whole scene rises before me again—I see the proud, handsome face that I love so dearly, the clear skies and the green trees. 'How long shall you be away, Norman?' asked him. 'Not more than two years,' he replied. 'You will be quite a brilliant lady of fashion when I return, Philippa; you will have made conquests innumerable.' 'I shall always be the same to you,' I replied; but he made no answer. He took the spray of lilac from my hands. 'My ideas of you will always be associated with lilacs,' he said; and that is why, Lady Peters, I ordered the vases to be filled with lilacs to-day. He bent down and kissed my face. 'Good-by, Philippa,' he said, 'may I find you as good and as beautiful as I leave you.' And then he went away. That is just two years ago; no wonder that I am pleased at his return."

Lady Peters looked anxiously at her.

"There was no regular engagement between you and Lord Arleigh, was there, Philippa?"

"What do you call a regular engagement?" said the young heiress. "He never made love to me, if that is what you mean—he never asked me to be his wife; but it was understood—always understood."

"By whom?" asked Lady Peters.

"My mother and his. When Lady Arleigh lived, she spent a great deal of time at Verdun Royal with my mother; they were first cousins, and the dearest of friends. Hundreds of times I have seen them sitting on the lawn, while Norman and I played together. Then they were always talking about the time we should be married. 'Philippa will make a beautiful Lady Arleigh,' his mother used to say. 'Norman, go and play with your little wife,' she would add; and with all the gravity of a grown courtier, he would bow before me and call me his little wife."

"But you were children then, and it was perhaps all childish folly."

"It was nothing of the kind," said the heiress, angrily. "I remember well that, when I was presented, my mother said to me, 'Philippa, you are sure to be very much admired; but remember, I consider you engaged to Norman. Your lot in life is settled; you are to be Lady Arleigh of Beechgrove.'"

"But," interposed Lady Peters, "it seems to me, Philippa, that this was all your mother's fancy. Because you played together as children—because, when you were a child he called you his little wife—because your mother and his were dear friends, and liked the arrangement—it does not follow that he would like it, or that he would choose the playmate of his childhood as the love of his manhood. In all that you have said to me, I see no evidence that he loves you, or that he considers himself in any way bound to you."

"That is because you do not understand. He has been in England only two days, yet, you see, he comes to visit me."

"That may be for old friendship's sake," said Lady Peters. "Oh, my darling, be careful! Do not give the love of your heart and soul for nothing."

"It is given already," confessed the girl, "and can never be recalled, no matter what I get in return. Why, it is twenty minutes past three; do you think he will come?"

Philippa L'Estrange rose from the couch and went to the long open window.

"I have never seen the sun shine so brightly before," she said; and Lady Peters sighed as she listened. "The world has never looked so beautiful as it does to-day. Oh, Norman, make, haste! I am longing to see you."

She had a quaint, pretty fashion of calling Lady Peters by the French appellation *maman*. She turned to her now, with a charming smile. She shook out the perfumed folds of her dress—she smoothed the fine white lace.

"You have not told me, *maman*," she said, "whether I am looking my best to-day. I want Norman to be a little surprised when he sees me. If you saw me for the first time to-day, would you think me nice?"

"I should think you the very queen of beauty," was the truthful answer.

A pleased smile curved the lovely, scarlet lips.

"So will Norman. You will see, *maman*, there is no cause for anxiety, none for fear. You will soon be wondering why you looked so grave over my pretty love story."

"It seems to me," observed Lady Peters, "that it is a one sided story. You love him—you consider yourself betrothed to him. What will you say or do, Philippa, if you find that, during his travels, he has learned to love some one else? He has visited half the courts of Europe since he left here; he must have seen some of the loveliest women in the world. Suppose he has learned to love one—what then?"

The beautiful face darkened.

"What then, *maman*? I know what I should do, even in that case. He belonged to me before he belonged to any one else, and I should try to win him back again."

"But if his word were pledged?"

"He must break his pledge. It would be war to the knife; and I have an idea that in the end I should win."

"But," persisted Lady Peters, "if you lost—what then?"

"Ah, then I could not tell what would happen! Love turns to burning hate at times. If I failed I should seek revenge. But we will not talk of failure. Oh, *maman*, there he is."

How she loved him! At the sound of his footsteps a crimson glow shone in her face, a light shone in the depth of her splendid dark eyes; the scarlet lips trembled. She clenched her fingers lest a sound that might betray her should escape her.

"Lord Arleigh," announced a servant at the door.

Tall, stately, self-possessed, she went forward to greet him. She held out her hand; but words failed her, as she looked once more into the face she loved so well.

"Philippa!" cried the visitor, in tones of wonder. "I expected to find you changed, but I should not have known you."

"Am I so greatly altered?" she asked.

"Altered?" he repeated, "I left you a pretty school-girl—I find you a queen." He bowed low over the white hand.

"The queen bids you welcome," she said, and then after introducing Lady Peters, she added: "Should you not really have known me, Norman?"

He had recovered from his first surprise, and Lady Peters, who watched him closely, fancied that she detected some little embarrassment in his manner. Of one thing she was quite sure— there was admiration and affection in his manner, but there was nothing resembling love.

He greeted her, and then took a seat, not by Philippa's side, but in one of the pretty lounging chairs by the open window.

"How pleasant it is to be home again!" he said. "How pleasant, Philippa, to see you!" And then he began to talk of Lady L'Estrange. "It seems strange," he went on, "that your mother and mine, after being such true friends in life, should die within a few days of each other. I would give the whole world to see my mother again. I shall find Beechgrove so lonely without her."

"I always recognize a good man," put in Lady Peters, "by the great love he bears his mother."

Lord Arleigh smiled.

"Then you think I am a good man?" he interrogated. "I hope, Lady Peters, that I shall never forfeit your good opinion."

"I do not think it likely," said her ladyship.

Philippa grew impatient on finding his attention turned, even for a few moments, from herself.

"Talk to me, Norman," she said; "tell me of your travels—of what you have seen and done—of the new friends you have made."

"I have made no new friends, Philippa," he said; "I love the old ones best."

He did not understand the triumphant expression of the dark eyes as they glanced at Lady Peters. He told her briefly of the chief places that he had visited, and then he said:

"What a quantity of flowers you have, Philippa! You still retain your old love."

She took a spray of lilac from one of the vases and held it before him. Again Lady Peters noted confusion on his face.

"Do you remember the lilac, and what you said about it?" she asked.

"Yes," he replied, "I was in Florence last year when they were in flower, and I never looked at the beautiful blooming trees without fancying that I saw my cousin's face among the blossoms."

"Why do you call me 'cousin?'" she asked, impatiently.

He looked up in surprise.

"You are my cousin, are you not, Philippa?"

"I am only your second cousin," she said; "and you have never called me so before."

"I have always called you 'cousin' in my thoughts," he declared. "How remiss I am!" he exclaimed, suddenly. "You will think that I have forgotten what little manners I had. I never congratulated you on your success."

"What success?" she asked, half impatiently.

"I have not been twenty-four hours in London, yet I have heard on all sides of your charms and conquests. I hear that you are the belle of the season—that you have slain dukes, earls, marquises, and baronets indiscriminately. I hear that no one has ever been more popular or more admired that Philippa L'Estrange. Is it all true?"

"You must find out for yourself," she said, laughingly, half disappointed that he had laid the spray of lilac down without any further remark, half disappointed that he should speak in that light, unconcerned fashion about her conquests; he ought to be jealous, but evidently he was not.

Then, to her delight, came a summons for Mrs. Peters; she was wanted in the housekeeper's room.

"Now we are alone," thought Philippa, "he will tell me that he is pleased to see me. He will remember that he called me his little wife."

But, as Lady Peters closed the door, he took a book from the table, and asked her what she had been reading lately—which was the book of that season. She replied to his questions, and to the remarks that followed; but they were not what she wanted to hear.

"Do not talk to me about books, Norman," she cried at last. "Tell me more about yourself; I want to hear more about you."

She did not notice the slight flush that spread over his face.

"If we are to talk about ourselves," he said, "I should prefer you to be the subject. You have grown very beautiful, Philippa."

His eyes took in every detail of the rich amber costume—the waving mass of dark hair—the splendid face, with its scarlet lips and glorious eyes—the white hands that moved so incessantly. He owned to himself that in all his travels he had seen nothing like the imperial loveliness of this dark-eyed girl.

"Does it please you to find me what you call beautiful?" she asked, shyly.

"Of course it does. I am very proud of you—proud to be known as the cousin of Philippa L'Estrange."

Nothing more! Had he nothing more than this to be proud of? Was he so blind that he could not see love in the girl's face—so deaf that he could not hear it in the modulations of her musical voice? She bent her beautiful face nearer him.

"We were always good friends, Norman," she said, simply, "you and I?"

"Yes, we were like brother and sister," he responded, "How we quarreled and made friends! Do you remember?"

"Yes—but we were not like brother and sister, Norman. We did not call each other by such names in those days, did we?"

"I never could find names pretty enough for you," he replied laughingly.

She raised her eyes suddenly to his.

"You cared for me a great deal in those days, Norman," she said, gently. "Tell me the truth—in your travels have you ever met any one for whom you care more?"

He was perfectly calm and unembarrassed.

"No, cousin, I have not. As I told you before, I have really made no friends abroad for whom I care much—a few pleasant acquaintances, nothing more."

"Then I am content," she said.

But he was deaf to the passionate music of her voice. Then the distance between them seemed to grow less. They talked of her home, Verdun Royal; they talked of Beechgrove, and his plans for living there. Their conversation was the intimate exchange of thought of old friends; but there was nothing of love. If she had expected that he would avail himself of Lady Peters' absence to speak of it, she was mistaken. He talked of old times, of friendship, of childhood's days, of great hopes and plans for the future—of anything but love. It seemed to be and perhaps was the farthest from his thoughts.

"I am going to Beechgrove in a week," he said; "you will give me permission to call and see you every day, Philippa?"

"I shall be pleased to see you—my time is yours," she answered but he did not understand the full meaning of the words.

Then Lady Peters came in and asked if he would join them at dinner.

"Philippa likes gayety," she said; "we have never had one quiet evening since the season began; she has a ball for to-night."

"Yes," laughed the heiress; "the world is very sweet to me just now, Norman; but I will give up my ball and stay at home purposely to sing to you, if you will dine with us."

"That is a temptation I cannot resist," he returned. "I will come. All your disappointed partners will, however, vent their wrath on me, Philippa."

"I can bear it," she said, "and so can you. Now I can let you go more willingly, seeing that I shall soon see you again."

And then he went away. After he had gone she spoke but little; once she clasped her arms round Lady Peters' neck and kissed the kindly face.

"Do not speak to me," she said, "lest I should lose the echo of his voice;" and Lady Peters watched her anxiously, as she stood with a rapt smile on her face, as of one who has heard celestial music in a dream.

The Arleighs of Beechgrove had for many generations been one of the wealthiest as well as one of the noblest families in England. To Norman, Lord Arleigh, who had succeeded his father at the early age of twenty, all this good gift of fame, fortune, and wealth had now fallen. He had inherited also the far-famed Arleigh beauty. He had clear-cut features, a fair skin, a fine manly frame, a broad chest, and erect, military bearing; he had dark hair and eyes, with straight, clear brows, and a fine, handsome mouth, shaded by a dark mustache Looking at him it was easy to understand his character. There was pride in the dark eyes, in the handsome face, in the high-bred manner and bearing, but not of a common kind.

In accordance with his late father's wish, he had gone through the usual course of studies. He had been to Eton and to Oxford; he had made the usual continental tour; and now he had returned to live as the Arleighs had done before him—a king on his own estate. There was just one thing in his life that had not pleased him. His mother, Lady Arleigh, had always evinced the greatest affection for her cousin, the gentle Lady L'Estrange. She had paid long visits to Verdun Royal, always taking her son with her; and his earliest recollection was of his mother and Lady L'Estrange sitting side by side planning the marriage of their two children, Philippa and Norman. He could remember many of his mother's pet phrases—"So suitable," "A perfect marriage," "The desire of my heart." All his mother's thoughts and ideas seemed to begin and end there. He had been taught, half seriously, half in jest, to call Philippa his little wife, to pay her every attention, to present her with jewels and with flowers, to make her his chief study. While be was still a boy he had only laughed at it.

Philippa was a beautiful, high-sprited girl. Her vivacity and animation amused him. He had spoken the truth in saying that he had met no one he liked better than his old friend. He had seen beautiful girls, lovely women, but he had not fallen in love. Indeed, love with the Arleighs was a serious matter. They did not look lightly upon it. Norman. Lord Arleigh, had not fallen; in love, but he had begun to think very seriously about Philippa L'Estrange. He had been fond of her as a child, with the kind of affection that often exists between children. He had called her his "little wife" in jest, not in earnest. He had listened to the discussions between the two ladies as he would have listened had they been talking about adding a new wing to the house. It was not until he came to the years of manhood that he began to see how serious the whole matter was. Then he remembered with infinite satisfaction that there had been nothing binding, that he had never even mentioned the word "love" to Philippa L'Estrange, that he had never made love to her, that the whole matter was merely a something that had arisen in the imagination of two ladies.

He was not in the least degree in love with Philippa. She was a brunette—he preferred a blonde; brunette beauty had no charm for him. He liked gentle, fair-haired women, tender of heart and soul— brilliancy did not charm him. Even when, previously to going abroad, he had gone down to Verdun Royal to say good-by, there was not the least approach to love in his heart. He had thought Philippa very charming and very picturesque as she stood under the lilac-trees; he had said truly that he should never see a lilac without thinking of her as she stood there. But that had not meant that he loved her.

He had bent down, as he considered himself in courtesy bound, to kiss her face when he bade her adieu; but it was no lover's kiss that fell so lightly on her lips. He realized to himself most fully the fact that, although he liked her, cared a great deal for her, and felt that she stood in the place of a sister to him, he did not love her.

But about Philippa herself? He was not vain; the proud, stately Lord Arleigh knew nothing of vanity. He could not think that the childish folly had taken deep root in her heart-he would not believe it. She had been a child like himself; perhaps even she had forgotten the nonsense more completely than he himself had. On his return to England, the first thing he heard when he reached London was that his old friend and playfellow—the girl he had called his little wife— was the belle of the season, with half London at her feet.

Chapter VII.

Lord Arleigh had been so accustomed to think of Philippa as a child that he could with difficulty imagine the fact that she was now a lovely girl, and one of the wealthiest heiresses in London. He felt some curiosity about her. How would she greet him? How would she receive him? He wrote to her at once, asking permission to visit her, and he came away from that visit with his eyes a little dazzled, his brain somewhat dazed, but his heart untouched. His fancy was somewhat disturbed by the haunting memory of dark, splendid eyes, lighted with fire and passion, and a bright, radiant face and scarlet lips—by a *mélange* of amber, lace, and perfume—but his heart was untouched. She was beautiful beyond his fairest dreams of woman—he owned that to himself—but it was not the kind of beauty that he admired it was too vivid, too highly colored, too brilliant. He preferred the sweet, pure lily to the queenly rose. Still he said to himself that he had never seen a face or figure like Miss L'Estrange's. No wonder that she had half London at her feet.

He was pleased with her kind reception of him, although he had not read her welcome aright; he was too true a gentleman even to think that it was love which shone in her eyes and trembled on her lips— love which made her voice falter and die away—love which caused her to exert every art and grace of which she was mistress to fascinate him. He was delighted with her—his heart grew warm under the charm of her words, but he never dreamed of love.

He had said to himself that there must be no renewal of his childish nonsense of early days—that he must be careful not to allude to it; to do so would be in bad taste—not that he was vain enough to think she would attach any importance to it, even if he did so; but he was one of nature's gentlemen, and he would have scorned to exaggerate or to say one word more than he meant. Her welcome had been most graceful, most kind—the beautiful face had softened and changed completely for him. She had devoted herself entirely to him; nothing in all the wide world had seemed to her of the least interest except himself and his affairs—books, music, pictures, even herself, her own triumphs, were as nothing when compared with him. He would have been less than mortal not to have been both pleased and flattered.

Pressed so earnestly to return to dinner, he had promised to do so; and evening, the sweet-scented May evening, found him once more at Hyde Park. If anything, Philippa looked more lovely. She wore her favorite colors—amber and white—a dress of rich amber brocade, trimmed with white lace; the queenly head was circled with diamonds; jewels like fire gleamed on the white breast; there was a cluster of choice flowers in her bodice. He had seen her hitherto as a girl; now he was to see her as the high-bred hostess, the mistress of a large and magnificent mansion.

He owned to himself that she was simply perfect. He had seen nothing in better taste, although he had been on intimate terms with the great ones of the earth. As he watched her, he thought to himself that, high and brilliant as was her station, it was not yet high enough for her. She flung a charm so magical around her that he was insensibly attracted by it, yet he was not the least in love—nothing was further from his thoughts. He could not help seeing that, after a fashion, she treated him differently from her other guests. He could not have told why or how; he felt only a certain subtle difference; her voice seemed to take another tone in addressing him, her face another expression as though she regarded him as one quite apart from all others.

The dinner-party was a success, as was every kind of entertainment with which Philippa L'Estrange was concerned. When the visitors rose to take their leave, Norman rose also. She was standing near him.

"Do not go yet, Norman," she said; "it is quite early. Stay, and I will sing to you."

She spoke in so low a tone of voice that no one else heard her. He was quite willing. Where could he feel more at home than in this charming drawing-room, with this beautiful girl, his old friend and playmate?

She bade adieu to her visitors, and then turned to him with such a smile as might have lost or won Troy.

"I thought they would never go," she said; "and it seems to me that I have barely exchanged one word with you yet, Norman."

"We have talked many hours," he returned, laughing.

"Ah, you count time by the old fashion, hours and minutes. I forget it when I am talking to one I—to an old friend like you."

"You are enthusiastic," said Lord Arleigh, wondering at the light on the splendid face.

"Nay, I am constant," she rejoined.

And for a few minutes after that silence reigned between them. Philippa was the first to break it.

"Do you remember," she asked, "that you used to praise my voice, and prophesy that I should sing well?"

"Yes, I remember," he replied.

"I have worked hard at my music," she continued, "in the hope of pleasing you."

"In the hope of pleasing me?" he interrogated. "It was kind to think so much of me."

"Of whom should I think, if not of you?" she inquired.

There were both love and reproach in her voice—he heard neither. Had he been as vain as he was proud, he would have been quicker to detect her love for himself.

The windows had been opened because the evening air was so clear and sweet; it came in now, and seemed to give the flowers a sweeter fragrance. Lord Arleigh drew his chair to the piano.

"I want you only to listen," she said. "You will have no turning over to do for me; the songs I love best I know by heart. Shut your eyes, Norman, and dream."

"I shall dream more vividly if I keep them open and look at you," he returned.

Then in a few minutes he began to think he must be in dream-land — the rich, sweet voice, so clear, so soft, so low, was filling the room with sweetest music. It was like no human voice that he remembered; seductive, full of passion and tenderness — a voice that told its own story, that told of its owner's power and charm — a voice that carried away the hearts of the listeners irresistibly as the strong current carries the leaflet.

She sang of love, mighty, irresistible love, the king before whom all bow down; and as she sang he looked at her. The soft, pearly light of the lamps fell on her glorious face, and seemed to render it more beautiful. He wondered what spell was fast falling over him, for he saw nothing but Philippa's face, heard nothing but the music that seemed to steep his senses as in a dream.

How fatally, wondrously lovely she was, this siren who sang to him of love, until every sense was full of silent ecstasy, until his face flushed, and his heart beat fast. Suddenly his eyes met hers; the scarlet lips trembled, the white fingers grew unsteady; her eyelids drooped, and the sweet music stopped.

She tried to hide her confusion by smiling.

"You should not look at me, Norman," she said, "when I sing; it embarrasses me."

"You should contrive to look a little less beautiful then, Philippa," he rejoined. "What was that last song?"

"It is a new one," she replied, "called 'My Queen.'"

"I should like to read the words," said Lord Arleigh.

In a few minutes she had found it for him, and they bent over the printed page together; her dark hair touched his cheek, the perfume from the white lilies she wore seemed to entrance him; he could not understand the spell that lay over him.

"Is it not beautiful?" she said.

"Yes, beautiful, but ideal; few women, I think, would equal this poet's queen."

"You do not know—you cannot tell, Norman. I think any woman who loves, and loves truly, becomes a queen."

He looked at her, wondering at the passion in her voice—wondering at the expression on her beautiful face.

"You are incredulous," she said; "but it is true. Love is woman's dominion; let her but once enter it, and she becomes a queen; her heart and soul grow grander, the light of love crowns her. It is the real diadem of womanhood, Norman; she knows no other."

He drew back startled; her words seemed to rouse him into sudden consciousness. She was quick enough to see it, and, with the *distrait* manner of a true woman of the world, quickly changed the subject. She asked some trifling question about Beechgrove, and then said, suddenly:

"I should like to see that fine old place of yours, Norman. I was only ten when mamma took me there the last time; that was rather too young to appreciate its treasures. I should like to see it again."

"I hope you will see it, Philippa; I have many curiosities to show you. I have sent home treasures from every great city I have visited."

She looked at him half wonderingly, half wistfully, but he said no more. Could it be that he had no thought of ever asking her to be mistress and queen of this house of his?

"You must have a party in the autumn," she said. "Lady Peters and I must be among your guests."

"That will be an honor. I shall keep you to your word, Philippa." And then he rose to go.

The dark, wistful eyes followed him. She drew a little nearer to him as he held out his hand to say good-night.

"You are quite sure, Norman, that you are pleased to see me again?" she interrogated, gently.

"Pleased! Why, Philippa, of course I am. What a strange question!"

"Because," she said, "there seems to be a cloud—a shadow— between us that I do not remember to have existed before."

"We are both older," he explained, "and the familiarity of childhood cannot exist when childhood ceases to be."

"I would rather be a child forever than that you should change to me," she said, quickly.

"I think," he returned, gravely, "that the only change in me is that I admire you more than I have ever done"

And these words filled her with the keenest sense of rapture yet they were but commonplace enough, if she had only realized it.

Chapter VIII.

Lord Arleigh raised his hat from his brow and stood for a few minutes bareheaded in the starlight. He felt like a man who had been in the stifling atmosphere of a conservatory; warmth and perfume had dazed him. How beautiful Philippa was—how bewildering! What a nameless wondrous charm there was about her! No wonder that half London was at her feet, and that her smiles were eagerly sought. He was not the least in love with her; admiration, homage, liking, but not love—anything but that—filled him; yet he dreamed of her, thought of her, compared her face with others that he had seen—all simply because her beauty had dazed him.

"I can believe now in the sirens of old," he said to himself; "they must have had just such dark, glowing eyes, such rich, sweet voices and beautiful faces. I should pity the man who hopelessly loved Philippa L'Estrange. And, if she ever loves any one, it will be easy for her to win; who could resist her?"

How little he dreamed that the whole passionate love of her heart was given to himself—that to win from him one word of love, a single token of affection, she would have given all that she had in the world.

On the day following he received a note; it said simply:

"Dear Norman: Can you join me in a ride? I have a new horse which they tell me is too spirited. I shall not be afraid to try it if you are with me.

"Yours, Philippa."

He could not refuse—indeed, he never thought of refusing—why should he? The beautiful girl who asked this kindness from him was his old friend and playfellow. He hastened to Verdun House and found Philippa waiting for him.

"I knew you would come," she said. "Lady Peters said you would be engaged. I thought differently."

"You did well to trust me," he returned, laughingly; "it would require a very pressing engagement to keep me from the pleasure of attending you."

He had thought her perfect on the previous evening, in the glitter of jewels and the gorgeous costume of amber and while; yet, if possible, she looked even better on this evening. Her riding-habit was neat and plain, fitting close to the perfect figure, showing every gracious line and curve.

Philippa L'Estrange possessed that rare accomplishment among women, a graceful "seat" on horseback. Lord Arleigh could not help noticing the admiring glances cast on her as they entered the park together. He saw how completely she was queen of society. Unusual homage followed her. She was the observed of all observers; all the men seemed to pause and look at her. Lord Arleigh heard repeatedly, as they rode along, the question, "Who is that beautiful girl?" Every one of note or distinction contrived to speak to her. The Prince of Auboine, at that time the most *fêted* guest in England, could hardly leave her. Yet, in the midst of all, Lord Arleigh saw that she turned to him as the sunflower to the sun. No matter with whom she was conversing, she never for one moment forgot him, never seemed inattentive, listened to him, smiled her brightest on him, while the May sun shone, and the white hawthorn flowers fell on the grass— while the birds chirped merrily, and crowds of bright, happy people passed to and fro.

"How true she is to her old friends!" thought Lord Arleigh, when he saw that even a prince could not take her attention from him.

So they rode on through the sunlit air—he fancy free, she loving him every moment with deeper, truer, warmer love.

"I should be so glad, Norman," she said to him, "if you would give me a few riding-lessons. I am sure I need them."

He looked at the graceful figure, at the little hands that held the reins so deftly.

"I do not see what there is to teach you," he observed; "I have never seen any one ride better."

"Still I should be glad of some little instruction from you," she said. "I always liked riding with you, Norman."

"I shall be only too pleased to ride with you every day when I am in town," he told her; and, though he spoke kindly, with smiling lips, there was no warmth of love in his tone.

The day was very warm—the sun had in it all the heat of June. When they reached Verdun House, Philippa said:

"You will come in for a short time, Norman? You look warm and tired. Williams—the butler—is famous for his claret-cup."

He murmured something about being not fatigued, but disinclined for conversation.

"You will not see any one," she said; "you shall come to my own particular little room, where no one dares enter, and we will have a quiet conversation there."

It seemed quite useless to resist her. She had a true siren power of fascination. The next minute saw him seated in the cool, shady *boudoir*, where the mellow light came in, rose-filtered through the silken blinds, and the perfumed air was sweet. Lady Peters, full of solicitude, was there, with the iced claret cup, thinking he was tired and-warm. It was so like home that he could not help feeling happy.

Presently Lady Peters retired for a few minutes, and in came Philippa. She had changed her riding-costume for a white silk *négligé* that fell round her in loose, graceful folds. She wore no flowers, jewels, or ribbons, but the dark masses of her hair were unfastened, and hung round the white neck; there was a warm, bright flush on her face, with the least touch of languor in her manner. She threw herself back in her lounging chair, saying, with a dreamy smile:

"You see that I make no stranger of you, Norman."

From beneath the white silken folds peeped a tiny embroidered slipper; a jeweled fan lay near her, and with it she gently stirred the perfumed air. He watched her with admiring eyes.

"You look like a picture that I have seen, Philippa," he said.

"What picture?" she asked, with a smile.

"I cannot tell you, but I am quite sure I have seen one like you. What picture would you care to resemble?"

A sudden gleam of light came into her dark eyes.

"The one underneath which you would write 'My Queen,'" she said, hurriedly.

He did not understand.

"I think every one with an eye to beauty would call you 'queen,'" he observed, lightly. The graver meaning of her speech had quite escaped him.

Then Lady Peters returned, and the conversation changed.

"We are going to hear an *opéra-bouffe* to-night," said Philippa, when Lord Arleigh was leaving. "Will you come and be our escort?"

"You will have a box filled with noisy chatterers the whole night," he remarked, laughingly.

"They shall all make room for you, Norman, if you will come," she said. "It is 'La Grande Duchesse,' with the far-famed Madame Schneider as her Grace of Gérolstein."

"I have not heard it yet," returned Lord Arleigh. "I cannot say that I have any great admiration for that school of music, but, if you wish it, I will go, Philippa.

"It will increase my enjoyment a hundredfold," she said, gently, "if you go."

"How can I refuse when you say that? I will be here punctually," he promised; and again the thought crossed his mind how true she was to her old friends—how indifferent to new ones!

On that evening Philippa changed her customery style of dress—it was no longer the favorite amber, so rich in hue and in texture, but white, gleaming silk, relieved by dashes of crimson. A more artistic or beautiful dress could not have been designed. She wore crimson roses in her dark hair, and a cluster of crimson roses on her white breast. Her bouquet was of the same odorous flowers. In the theater Lord Arleigh noticed that Philippa attracted more attention than any one else, even though the house was crowded; he saw opera-glasses turned constantly toward her beautiful face.

Miss L'Estrange kept her word, saying but little to those who would fain have engrossed her whole attention—that was given, to Lord Arleigh. She watched his face keenly throughout the performance. He did not evince any great interest in it.

"You do not care for 'La Grande Duchesse?'" she said.

"No—frankly, I do not," he replied.

"Tell me why," said Philippa.

"Can you ask me to do so, Philippa?" he returned, surprised; and then he added, "I will tell you. First of all, despite the taking music, it is a performance to which I should not care to bring my wife and sister."

"Tell me why?" she said, again.

"It lowers my idea of womanhood. I could not forgive the woman, let her be duchess or peasant, who could show any man such great love, who could lay herself out so deliberately to win a man."

She looked at him gravely. He continued:

"Beauty is very charming, I grant—as are grace and talent; but the chief charm to me of a woman is her modesty. Do you not agree with me, Philippa?"

"Yes," she replied, "most certainly I do; but, Norman, you are hard upon us. Suppose that, woman loves a man ever so truly—she must not make any sign?"

"Any sign she might make would most certainly, in my opinion, lessen her greatest charm," he said.

"But," she persisted, "do you not think that is rather hard? Why must a woman never evince a preference for the man she loves?"

"Woman should be wooed—never be wooer," said Lord Arleigh.

"Again I say you are hard, Norman. According to you, a woman is to break her heart in silence and sorrow for a man, rather than give him the least idea that she cares for him."

"I should say there is a happy medium between the Duchess of Gérolstein and a broken heart. Neither men nor women can help their peculiar disposition, but in my opinion a man never more esteems a woman than when he sees she wants to win his love."

He spoke with such perfect freedom from all consciousness that she knew the words could not be intended for her; nevertheless she had learned a lesson from them.

"I am like yourself, Norman," she said; "I do not care for the play at all; we will go home," and they left the house before the Grand Duchess had played her part.

Chapter IX.

Philippa L'Estrange thought long and earnestly over her last conversation with Lord Arleigh. She had always loved him; but the chances are that, if he had been devoted to her on his return, if he had wooed her as others did, she would have been less *empressée*. As it was, he was the only man she had not conquered, the only one who resisted her, on whom her fascinations fell without producing a magical effect. She could not say she had conquered her world while he was unsubdued. Yet how was it? She asked herself that question a hundred times each day. She was no coquette, no flirt, yet she knew she had but to smile on a man to bring him at once to her feet; she had but to make the most trifling advance, and she could do what she would. The Duke of Mornton had twice repeated his offer of marriage—she had refused him. The Marquis of Langland, the great match of the day, had made her an offer, which she had declined. The Italian Prince Cetti would have given his possessions to take her back with him to his own sunny land, but she had refused to go. No woman in England had had better offers of marriage; but she had refused them all. How was it that, when others sighed so deeply and vainly at her feet, Lord Arleigh alone stood aloof?

Of what use were her beauty, wit, grace, wealth, and talent, if she could not win him? For the first time she became solicitous about her beauty, comparing it with that of other women, always being compelled, in the end, to own that she excelled. If Lord Arleigh talked, or danced, or showed attention to any lady, she would critically examine her claim to interest, whether she was beautiful, mentally gifted, graceful. But Philippa detected another thing—if Lord Arleigh did not love her, it was at least certain that he loved no one else.

The whole world was spoiled for her because she had not this man's love. She desired it. Her beauty, her wealth, her talents, her grace, were all as nothing, because with them she could not win him. Then, again, she asked herself, could it be that she could not win him? What had men told her? That her beauty was irresistible. It might be that he did care for her, that he intended to carry out his mother's favorite scheme, but that he was in no hurry, that he wanted her and himself to see plenty of life first. It was easier, after all, to believe that than to think that she had completely failed to win him. She would be quite satisfied if it were so, although it was certainly not flattering to her that he should be willing to wait so long; but, if he would only speak—if he would only say the few words that would set her mind quite at ease—she would be content.

Why did he not love her? She was fair, young, endowed with great gifts; she had wealth, position; she had the claim upon him that his mother and hers had wished the alliance. Why did she fail? why did he not love her? It seemed to her that she was the one person in all the world to whom he would naturally turn—that, above all others, he would select her for his wife; yet he did not evince the least idea of so doing. Why was it?

Twice that night when he had so frankly told her his ideas about women, she had been most careful, most reserved.

"If he likes reserve and indifference," she said to herself, "he shall have plenty of it." Yet it was at the same time so mixed with kindness, with thoughtful consideration for him, that the wonder was he did not succumb. "I must find out," she said to herself, "whether he does really care for me." How to do so she did not quite know—but woman's wits are proverbially keen.

The more she saw of him the better she liked him—his single-mindedness, his chivalry, his faith in women and his respect for them, were greater than she had seen in any other, and she loved him for these qualities. The more she contrasted him with others, the greater, deeper, and wider grew her love. It must be that in time he should care for her.

The Duchess of Aytoun gave a grand ball, to which, as belle of the season, Philippa was invited.

"Shall you go?" she asked of Lord Arleigh.

"I have hardly decided," he replied.

"Do go, Norman; I like waltzing, but I do not care to waltz with every one. Do go, that I may dance with you."

"You do not mind waltzing with me, then?" he said.

The glance she gave him was answer sufficient. He could not kelp feeling flattered.

"I shall be there, Philippa," he said; and then she promised herself on that evening she would try to discover what his sentiments were with regard to her.

She took great pains with her toilet; she did not wish to startle, but to attract—and the two things were very different. Her dress looked brilliant, being of a silvery texture; the trimming was composed of small fern-leaves; a *parure* of fine diamonds crowned her head.

The effect of the dress was striking, and Philippa herself had never looked more lovely. There was a flush of rose-color on her face, a light in her eyes. If ever woman's face told a story, hers did—if ever love softened, made more tender and pure any face on earth, it was hers.

After her toilet was complete, she stood for a few minutes looking in her mirror. The tall, stately figure in the glorious dress was perfect; the face, framed in shining masses of dark hair, was perfect too.

"If I can but win one word from him!" she thought. "If I can but remind him of those childish days when he used to call me his little wife!"

She no sooner made her appearance than, as was usual, she was surrounded by a little court of admirers—the Duke of Mornton first among them. They little guessed that they owed her complacent reception of their compliments to the fact that she was not even attending to them, but with her whole soul in her eyes was watching for Lord Arleigh's arrival. The duke even flattered himself that he was making some progress, because at some chance word from him the beautiful face flushed a deep crimson. How was he to know that Lord Arleigh had at that moment entered the room?

The latter could not help feeling pleased and flattered at the way in which Philippa received him. He was but mortal, and he could not help seeing the dark eyes shine, the scarlet lips tremble, the whole face soften. Presently she placed her hand on his arm, and walked away with him.

"I was growing impatient, Norman," she said; and then, remembering his criticisms on the wooing of women, she hastened to add—"impatient at the want of novelty; it seems to me that in London ball-rooms all the men talk in the same fashion."

Lord Arleigh laughed.

"What are they to do, Philippa?" he asked. "They have each one the same duties to perform—to please their partners and amuse themselves. You would not have a 'hapless lordling' talk about science or metaphysics while he danced, would you?"

"No; but they might find some intelligent remarks to make. You talk well, Norman, and listening to you makes me impatient with others."

"You are very kind," he said, and he took the pretty tablets from her hand.

"You have saved every waltz for me, Philippa. I shall expect to have a dozen duels on my hands before morning."

"'This is my favorite," she said, as the music of the irresistible "Blue Danube" filled the room.

Then it seemed to her that they floated away into another sphere. His arm was round her, his eyes smiling down into hers. With youth, music, beauty, love, there was nothing wanting to complete the charm.

When it was over, he asked her if she would rest.

"No," said Philippa; "I heard the playing of a fountain in the fernery. I should like to go there."

They went through the magnificent suite of rooms, and then through the conservatory into the dim, beautiful fernery, where the lamps glowed like stars, and the cool rippling water fell with a musical rhythm into the deep basin below. They could hear the distant sound of music from the ball-room. It was a time when love, if it lay in a man's heart, would spring, into sweet, sudden life.

"If he loves me," she said to herself, "he will tell me so now."

"I like this better than the ball-room," she said. "By the way, you have not told me if you like my dress?" she added, anxious to bring him to the one subject she had at heart. "Do you remember that when we were children, Norman, you used to criticise my dress?"

"Did I? It was very rude of me. I should not venture to criticise anything so marvelous now. It is a wonderful dress, Philippa; in the light it looks like moonbeams, in the shade like snow. Do you suppose I should ever have the courage to criticise anything so beautiful?"

"Do you really like it, Norman—without flattery?"

"I never flatter, Philippa, not even in jest; you should know that."

"I never heard you flatter," she acknowledged. "I took pains with my toilet, Norman, to please you; if it does so I am well content."

"There is another waltz," said Lord Arleigh; "we will go back to the ball-room."

"Make him love me!" she said to herself, in bitter disdain. "I might as well wish for one of the stars as for his love—it seems just as far off."

Chapter X.

Lord Arleigh did not go to Beechgrove as he had intended. He found so many old friends and so many engagements in London that he was not inclined to leave it. Then, too, he began to notice many little things which made him feel uncomfortable. He began to perceive that people considered him in some kind of way as belonging to Miss L'Estrange; no matter how many surrounded her, when he entered a room they were seen one by one to disappear until he was left alone by her side. At first he believed this to be accidental; after a time he knew that it must be purposely done.

Miss L'Estrange, too, appeared to see and hear him only. If any one wanted to win a smile from her lovely lips, he had but to make way for Lord Arleigh; if any man wanted a kind word, or a kind glance from the beautiful eyes, he had but to praise Lord Arleigh. People soon perceived all this. The last to discover it was Lord Arleigh himself. It dawned but slowly upon him. He began to perceive also that Philippa, after a fashion of her own, appropriated him. She looked upon it as a settled arrangement that he should ride with her every day—that every day he must either lunch or dine with them—that he must be her escort to theater and ball. If he at times pleaded other engagements she would look at him with an air of childish wonder and say:

"They cannot have so great a claim upon you as I have, Norman?"

Then he was disconcerted, and knew not what to answer; it was true that there was no one with so great a claim—it seemed to have been handed down from his mother to him.

His eyes were still further opened one day when a large and fashionable crowd had gathered at Lady Dalton's garden-party. Philippa was, as heretofore, the belle, looking more than usually lovely in a light gossamer dress of white and pink. She was surrounded by admirers. Lord Arleigh stood with a group of gentlemen under a great spreading beech-tree.

"How beautiful she is, that Miss L'Estrange!" said one—Sir Alfred Martindale. "I can believe in the siege of Troy when I look at her; and I think it just as well for mankind that such women are rare."

"If ever there was a human moth," observed another, "it is that unfortunate Duke of Mornton. I have seen some desperate cases in my time, but none so desperate as his."

Lord Arleigh laughed. They were all intimate friends.

"The Duke of Mornton is a great friend of mine," he said. "I can only hope that he may be saved from the ultimate fate of a moth, and that Miss L'Estrange will take pity on him."

He could not help seeing that the three gentleman looked up with an expression of utter wonder.

"Do you mean," asked Sir Alfred, "that you hope Miss L'Estrange will marry the duke?"

"I do not think she could do better," replied Lord Arleigh.

"You are the last man in London I should have expected to hear say so," said Sir Alfred, quietly.

"Am I? Pray may I ask why?"

"Yes, if you acquit me of all intention of rudeness in my reply. I repeat that you are the last man in London whom I should have expected to hear make such a remark, for the simple reason that every one believes you are going to marry Miss L'Estrange yourself."

Lord Arleigh's face flushed hotly.

"Then 'every one,' as you put it, Sir Alfred, takes a great liberty—an unauthorized liberty—with the name of a very charming lady. Miss L'Estrange and myself were much together when children—our mothers were distantly related—and at the present time we are—excellent friends."

"I am sorry," returned Sir Alfred, "if I have said anything to annoy you. I thought the fact was as evident as the sun at noon-day; every one in London believes it."

"Then people take an unwarrantable liberty with the lady's name," said Lord Arleigh.

Some one else remarked, with a slightly impertinent drawl, that he did not believe Miss L'Estrange would consider it a liberty. A flash from Lord Arleigh's dark eyes silenced him.

A few minutes afterward Lord Arleigh found the Duchess of Aytoun and Philippa seated underneath a large acacia-tree. Captain Gresham, a great favorite in the London world, was by Philippa's side. The duchess, with a charming gesture of invitation made room for Lord Arleigh by her side. The gallant captain did not often find an opportunity of making love to the belle of the season. Now that he had found it, he was determined not to lose it—not for fifty Lord Arleighs. So, while the duchess talked to the new-comer, he relentlessly pursued his conversation with Miss L'Estrange.

There was but one music in the world for her, and that was the music of Lord Arleigh's voice. Nothing could ever drown that for her. The band was playing, the captain talking, the duchess conversing, in her gay, animated fashion; but above all, clearly and distinctly, Philippa heard every word that fell from Lord Arleigh's lips, although he did not know it. He believed that she was, as she seemed to be, listening to the captain.

"I have pleasing news concerning you, Lord Arleigh," said the duchess. "I wonder if I may congratulate you?"

"What is it? I do not know of anything very interesting concerning myself," he remarked—"nothing, I am sure, that calls for congratulation."

"You are modest," said the duchess; "but I have certainly heard, and on good authority, too, that you are about to be married."

"I can only say I was not in the least aware of it," he rejoined.

The duchess raised her parasol and looked keenly at him.

"Pray pardon me," she continued; "do not think that it is from mere curiosity that I ask the question. Is there really no truth in the report?"

"None whatever," he replied. "I have no more idea of being married than I have of sailing this moment for the Cape."

"It is strange," said the duchess, musingly; "I had the information from such good authority, too."

"There can be no better authority on the subject," said Lord Arleigh, laughingly, "than myself."

"You; I admit that. Well, as the ice is broken, Lord Arleigh, and we are old friends, I may ask, why do you not marry?"

"Simply because of marriage, and of love that ends in marriage, I have not thought," he answered lightly.

"It is time for you to begin," observed the duchess; "my own impression is that a man does no good in the world until he is married." And then she added: "I suppose you have an ideal of womanhood?"

Lord Arleigh's face flushed.

"Yes," he acknowledged, "I have an ideal of my own, derived from poetry I have read, from pictures I have seen—an ideal of perfect grace, loveliness, and purity. When I meet that ideal, I shall meet my fate."

"Then you have never yet seen the woman you would like to to marry?" pursued the duchess.

"No," he answered, quite seriously; "strange to say, although I have seen some of the fairest and noblest types of womanhood, I have not yet met with my ideal."

They were disturbed by a sudden movement—the flowers that Philippa held in her hand had fallen to the ground.

Chapter XI.

Captain Greshan sprang forward to lift the flowers which Miss L'Estrange had dropped.

"Nay," she said, "never mind them. A fresh flower is very nice. A flower that has once been in the dust has lost its beauty."

There was no trace of pain in the clear voice; it was rich and musical. Philippa L'Estrange, seated in the bright sunshine, heard the words that were to her a death-warrant, yet made no sign. "I have not yet met with my ideal," Lord Arleigh had said.

Captain Gresham picked up some of the fallen flowers.

"A dead flower from your hand, Miss L'Estrange," he observed "is worth a whole gardenful of living ones from any one else."

She laughed again that sweet musical laugh which seemed to come only from a happy heart; and then she looked round. The Duchess of Aytoun and Lord Arleigh were still in deep converse. Miss L'Estrange turned to Captain Gresham.

"I have been told," she said, "that there are some beautiful white hyacinths here; they are my favorite flowers. Shall we find them?"

He was only too pleased. She bade a laughing adieu to the duchess, and smiled at Lord Arleigh. There was no trace of pain or of sadness in her voice or face. They went away together and Lord Arleigh never even dreamed that she had heard his remark.

Then the duchess left him, and he sat under the spreading beech alone. His thoughts were not of the pleasantest nature; he did not like the general belief in his approaching marriage; it was fair neither to himself nor to Philippa—yet how was he to put an end to such gossip? Another idea occurred to him. Could it be possible that Philippa herself shared the idea? He would not believe it. Yet many things made him pause and think. She certainly evinced great preference for his society; she was never so happy as when with him. She would give up any engagement, any promised gayety or pleasure to be with him. She dressed to please him; she consulted him on most things; she seemed to identify her interests with his. But all this might be the result of their old friendship—it might have nothing to do with love.

Could it be possible that she still remembered the childish nonsense that had passed between them—that she considered either herself or him bound by a foolish tie that neither of them had contracted? Could it be possible that she regarded herself as engaged to him? The bare idea of it seemed absurd to him; he could not believe it. Yet many little things that he could not explain to himself made him feel uncomfortable and anxious. Could it be that she, the most beautiful and certainly the most popular woman in London, cared so much for him as to hold him by so slender a tie as their past childish nonsense?

He reproached himself for the thought, yet, do what he would, he could not drive it away. The suspicion haunted him; it made him miserable. If it was really so, what was he to do?

He was a gentleman, not a coxcomb. He could not go to this fair woman and ask her if it was really true that she loved him, if she really cared for him, if she held him by a tie contracted in childhood. He could not do it. He had not sufficient vanity. Why should he think that Philippa, who had some of the noblest men in England at her feet—why should life think that she would renounce all her brilliant prospects for him? Yet, if the mistake had really occurred— if she really thought the childish nonsense binding—if she really believed that he was about to make her his wife—it was high time that she was undeceived, that she knew the truth. And the truth was that although he had a great liking, a kindly affection for her, he was not in love with her. He admired her beauty—nay, he went further; he thought her the most beautiful woman he had ever seen, the most gifted, the most graceful. But he was not in love with her—never would be. She was not his type of woman, not his ideal. If she had been his sister, he would have loved her exceedingly—a brotherly affection was what he felt for her.

Yet how could he go to this fair woman with the ungracious words that he did not love her, and had no thought of marrying her? His face flushed hotly at the thought—there was something in it against which his whole manhood rose in hot rebellion Still it must be done; there must be no such shadow between them as this—there must be no such fatal mistake. If the report of their approaching marriage were allowed to remain much longer uncontradicted, why, then he would be in honor compelled to fulfill public expectations; and this he had no intention, no desire to do. The only thing therefore was to speak plainly to her.

How he hated the thought! How he loathed the idea! It seemed to him unmanly, most ignoble—and yet there was no help for it. There was one gleam of comfort for him, and only one. She was so quick, so keen, that she would be sure to understand him at once, without his entering into any long explanation. Few words would suffice, and those words he must choose as best he could. If it were possible, he would speak to her to-day—the sooner the better-and then all uncertainty would be ended. It seemed to him, as he pondered these things, that a cloud had fallen over the sunshine. In his heart he blamed the folly of that gentle mother who had been the cause of all this anxiety.

"Such matters are always best left alone," he said to himself, "If I should ever have children of my own, I will never interfere in their love affairs."

Think as he would ponder as he would, it was no easy task that lay before him—to tell her in so many words that he did not love her. Surely no man had ever had anything so ungracious to do before.

He looked round the grounds, and presently saw her the center of a brilliant group near the lake. The Duke of Ashwood was by her side, the *élite* of the guests had gathered round her. She—beautiful, bright, animated—was talking, as he could see, with her usual grace and ease. It struck him suddenly as absurd that this beautiful woman should care—as people said she did care—for him.

Let him get it all over. He longed to see the bright face shine on him with sisterly kindness, and to feel himself at ease with her; he longed to have all misunderstanding done away with.

He went up to the little group, and again the same peculiarity struck him—they all made way for him—even the Duke of Ashwood, although he did it with a frown on his face and an angry look in his eyes. Each one seemed to consider that he had some special right to be by the side of the beautiful Miss L'Estrange; and she, as usual when he was present, saw and heard no one else.

It was high time the world was disabused. Did she herself join in the popular belief? He could not tell. He looked at the bright face; the dark eyes met his, but he read no secret in them.

"Philippa," he said, suddenly, "the water looks very tempting—would you like a row?"

"Above everything else," she replied. And they went off in the little pleasure-boat together.

It was a miniature lake, tall trees bordering it and dipping their green branches into the water. The sun shone on the feathered spray that fell from the sculls, the white swans raised their graceful heads as the little boat passed by, and Philippa lay back languidly, watching the shadow of the trees. Suddenly an idea seemed to occur to her. She looked at Lord Arleigh.

"Norman," she said, "let the boat drift—I want to talk to you, and I cannot while you are rowing."

He rested on his sculls, and the boat drifted under the drooping branches of a willow-tree. He never forgot the picture that then presented itself—the clear deep water, the green trees, and the beautiful face looking at him. "Norman," she said, in a clear, low voice, "I want to tell you that I overheard all that you said to the Duchess of Aytoun. I could not help it—I was so near to you."

She was taking the difficulty into her own hands! He felt most thankful.

"Did you, Philippa? I thought you were engrossed with the gallant captain."

"Did you really and in all truth mean what you said to her?" she asked.

"Certainly; you know me well enough to be quite sure that I never say what I do not mean."

"You have never yet seen the woman whom you would ask to be your wife?" she said.

There was a brief silence, and then he replied:

"No, in all truth, I have not, Philippa."

A little bird was singing on a swaying bough just above them—to the last day of her life it seemed to her that she remembered the notes. The sultry silence seemed to deepen. She broke it.

"But, Norman," she said, in a low voice, "have you not seen me?"

He tried to laugh to hide his embarrassment, but it was a failure.

"I have seen you—and I admire you. I have all the affection of a brother for you, Philippa—" and then he paused abruptly.

"But," she supplied, "you have never thought of making me your wife? Speak to me quite frankly, Norman."

"No, Philippa, I have not."

"As matters stand between us, they require explanation," she said; and he saw her lips grow pale. "It is not pleasant for me to have to mention it, but I must do it. Norman, do you quite forget what we were taught to believe when we were children—that our lives were to be passed together?"

"My dearest Philippa, pray spare yourself and me. I did not know that you even remembered that childish nonsense."

She raised her dark eyes to his face, and there was something in them before which he shrank as one who feels pain.

"One word, Norman—only one word. That past which has been so much to me—that past in which I have lived, even more than in the present or the future—am I to look upon it as what you call nonsense?"

He took her hand in his.

"My dear Philippa," he said, "I hate myself for what I have to say—it makes me detest even the sound of my own voice. Yet you are right—there is nothing for us but perfect frankness; anything else would be foolish. Neither your mother nor mine had any right to try to bind us. Such things never answer, never prosper. I cannot myself imagine how they, usually so sensible, came in this instance to disregard all dictates of common sense. I have always looked upon the arrangement as mere nonsense; and I hope you have done the same. You are free as air—and so am I."

She made no answer, but, after a few minutes, when she had regained her self-possession, she said:

"The sun is warm on the water—I think we had better return;" and, as they went back, she spoke to him carelessly about the new rage for garden-parties.

"Does she care or not?" thought Lord Arleigh to himself. "Is she pleased or not? I cannot tell; the ways of women are inscrutable. Yet a strange idea haunts me—an uncomfortable suspicion."

As he watched her, there seemed to him no trace of anything but light-hearted mirth and happiness about her. She laughed and talked; she was the center of attraction, the life of the *fête*. When he spoke to her, she had a careless jest, a laughing word for him; yet he could not divest himself of the idea that there was something behind all this. Was it his fancy, or did the dark eyes wear every now and then an expression of anguish? Was it his fancy, or did it really happen that when she believed herself unobserved, the light died out of her face?

He was uncomfortable, without knowing why—haunted by a vague, miserable suspicion he could not explain, by a presentiment he could not understand—compelled against his will to watch her, yet unable to detect anything in her words and manner that justified his doing so. It had been arranged that after the *fête* he should return to Verdun House with Lady Peters and Philippa. He had half promised to dine and spend the evening there, but now he wondered if that arrangement would be agreeable to Philippa. He felt that some degree of restraint had arisen between them.

He was thinking what excuse he could frame, when Philippa sent for him. He looked into the fresh young face; there was no cloud on it.

"Norman," she said, "I find that Lady Peters has asked Miss Byrton to join us at dinner—will you come now? It has been a charming day, but I must own that the warmth of the sun has tired me."

Her tone of voice was so calm, so unruffled, he could have laughed at himself for his suspicions, his fears.

"I am quite ready," he replied. "If you would like the carriage ordered, we will go at once."

He noticed her going home more particularly than he had ever done before. She was a trifle paler, and there was a languid expression in her dark eyes which might arise from fatigue, but she talked lightly as usual. If anything, she was even kinder to him than usual, never evincing the least consciousness of what had happened. Could it have been a dream? Never was man so puzzled as Lord Arleigh.

They talked after dinner about a grand fancy ball that Miss Byrton intended giving at her mansion in Grosvenor Square. She was one of those who believed implicitly in the engagement between Lord Arleigh and Miss L'Estrange.

"I have a Waverley quadrille already formed," said Miss Byrton— "that is *de rigueur*. There could not be a fancy ball without a Waverley quadrille. How I should like two Shakesperian ones! I thought of having one from 'As You Like It' and another from 'Romeo and Juliet;' and, Miss L'Estrange, I wish you would come as *Juliet*. It seems rude even to suggest a character to any one with such perfect taste as yours—still I should like a beautiful *Juliet*—*Juliet* in white satin, and glimmer of pearls."

"I am quite willing," returned Philippa. "*Juliet* is one of my favorite heroines. How many *Romeos* will you have?"

"Only one, if I can so manage it," replied Miss Byrton—"and that will be Lord Arleigh."

She looked at him as she spoke; he shook his head, laughingly.

"No—I yield to no one in reverence for the creations of the great poet," he said; "but, to tell the truth, I do not remember that the character of *Romeo* ever had any great charm for me."

"Why not?" asked Miss Byrton.

"I cannot tell you; I am very much afraid that I prefer *Othello*—the noble Moor. Perhaps it is because sentiment has not any great attraction for me. I do not think I could ever kill myself for love. I should make a sorry *Romeo*, Miss Byrton."

With a puzzled face she looked from him to Miss L'Estrange.

"You surprise me," she said, quickly. "I should have thought *Romeo* a character above all others to please you."

Philippa has listened with a smile—nothing had escaped her. Looking up, she said, with a bright laugh:

"I cannot compliment you on being a good judge of character, Miss Byrton. It may be perhaps that you have not known Lord Arleigh well enough. But he is the last person in the world to make a good *Romeo*. I know but one character in Shakespeare's plays that would suit him."

"And that?" interrogated Lord Arleigh.

"That," replied Philippa, "is *Petruchio;*" and amidst a general laugh the conversation ended.

Miss Byrton was the first to take her departure. Lord Arleigh lingered for some little time—he was still unconvinced. The wretched, half-formed suspicion that there was something hidden beneath Philippa's manner still pursued him; he wanted to see if she was the same to him. There was indeed no perceptible difference. She leaned back in her favorite chair with an air of relief, as though she were tired of visitors.

"Now let us talk about the *fête*, Norman," she said. "You are the only one I care to talk with about my neighbors."

So for half an hour they discussed the *fête*, the dresses, the music, the different flirtations—Philippa in her usual bright, laughing, half-sarcastic fashion, with the keen sense of humor that was peculiar to her. Lord Arleigh could not see that there was any effort in her conversation; he could not see the least shadow on her brightness; and at heart he was thankful.

When he was going away, she asked him about riding on the morrow just as usual. He could not see the slightest difference in her manner. That unpleasant little conversation on the lake might never have taken place for all the remembrance of it that seemed to trouble her. Then, when he rose to take his leave, she held out her hand with a bright, amused expression.

"Good-night, *Petruchio*," she said. "I am pleased at the name I have found for you."

"I am not so sure that it is appropriate," he rejoined. "I think on the whole I would rather love a *Juliet* than tame a shrew."

"It may be in the book of fate that you will do both," she observed; and they parted, laughing at the idea.

To the last the light shone in her eyes, and the scarlet lips were wreathed in smiles; but, when the door had closed behind him and she was alone, the haggard, terrible change that fell over the young face was painful to see. The light, the youth, the beauty seemed all to fade from it; it grew white, stricken, as though the pain of death were upon her. She clasped her hands as one who had lost all hope.

"How am I to bear it?" she cried. "What am I to do?" She looked round her with the bewildered air of one who had lost her way—with the dazed appearance of one from beneath whose feet the plank of safety had been withdrawn. It was all over—life was all over; the love that had been her life was suddenly taken from her. Hope was dead—the past in which she had lived was all a plank—he did not love her.

She said the words over and over again to herself. He did not love her, this man to whom she had given the passionate love of her whole heart and soul—he did not love her, and never intended to ask her to be his wife.

Why, she had lived for this! This love, lying now in ruins around her, had been her existence. Standing there, in the first full pain of her despair, she realized what that love had been—her life, her hope, her world. She had lived in it; she had known no other wish, no other desire. It had been her all and now it was less than nothing.

"How am I to live and bear it?" she asked herself again; and the only answer that came to her was the dull echo of her own despair.

That night, while the sweet flowers slept under the light of the stars, and the little birds rested in the deep shade of the trees—while the night wind whispered low, and the moon sailed in the sky—Philippa L'Estrange, the belle of the season, one of the most beautiful women in London, one of the wealthiest heiresses in England, wept through the long hours—wept for the overthrow of her hope and her love, wept for the life that lay in ruins around her.

She was of dauntless courage—she knew no fear; but she did tremble and quail before the future stretching out before her—the future that was to have no love, and was to be spent without him.

How was she to bear it? She had known no other hope in life, no other dream. What had been childish nonsense to him had been to her a serious and exquisite reality. He had either forgotten it, or had thought of it only with annoyance; she had made it the very corner-stone of her life.

It was not only a blow of the keenest and cruelest kind to her affections, but it was the cruelest blow her vanity could have possibly received. To think that she, who had more admirers at her feet than any other woman in London, should have tried so hard to win this one, and have failed—that her beauty, her grace, her wit, her talent, should all have been lavished in vain.

Why did she fail so completely? Why had she not won his love? It was given to no other—at least she had the consolation of knowing that. He had talked about his ideal, but he had not found it; he had his own ideal of womanhood, but he had not met with it.

"Are other women fairer, more lovable than I am?" she asked herself. "Why should another win where I have failed?"

So through the long hours of the starlit night she lamented the love and the wreck of her life, she mourned for the hope that could never live again, while her name was on the lips of men who praised her as the queen of beauty, and fair women envied her as one who had but to will and to win.

She would have given her whole fortune to win his love—not once, but a hundred times over.

It seemed to her a cruel mockery of fate that she who had everything the world could give—beauty, health, wealth, fortune—should ask but this one gift, and that it should be refused her.

She watched the stars until they faded from the skies and then she buried her face in the pillow and sobbed herself to sleep.

Chapter XII.

It was when the sun, shining into her room, reached her that an idea occurred to Philippa which was like the up-springing of new life to her. All was not yet lost. He did not love her—he had not thought of making her his wife; but it did not follow that he would never do so. What had not patience and perseverance accomplished before now? What had not love won?

He had acknowledged that she was beautiful; he had owned to her often how much he admired her. So much granted, was it impossible that he should learn to love her? She told herself that she would take courage—that she would persevere—that her great love must in time prevail, and that she would devote her life unweariedly to it.

She would carefully hide all traces of pique or annoyance. She would never let him find her dull or unhappy. Men liked to be amused. She would do her best to entertain him; he would never have a moment's vacancy in her society. She would find sparkling anecdotes, repartees, witty, humorous stories, to amuse him. He liked her singing; she would cultivate it more and more. She would study him, dress for him, live for him, and him alone; she would have no other end, aim, thought, or desire. She would herself be the source of all his amusement, so that he should look for the every-day pleasures of his life to her—and, such being the case, she would win him; she felt sure of it. Why had she been so hopeless, so despairing? There was no real cause for it. Perhaps, after all, he had looked upon the whole affair, not as a solemn engagement, but as a childish farce. Perhaps he had never really thought of her as his wife; but there would be an end to that thoughtlessness now. What had passed on the previous day would arouse his attention, he could never know the same indifference again.

So she rose with renewed hope. She shrank from the look of her face in the glass. "Cold water and fresh air," she said to herself, with a smile, "will soon remedy such paleness." And thus on that very day began for her the new life—the life in which, no longer sure of her love, she was to try to win it.

He would have loved her had he been able; but his own words were true—"Love is fate."

There was nothing in common between them—no sympathy—none of those mystical cords that, once touched, set two human hearts throbbing, and never rest until they are one. He could not have been fonder of her than he was, in a brotherly sense; but as for lover's love, from the first day he had seen her, a beautiful, dark-eyed child, until the last he had never felt the least semblance of it.

It was a story of failure. She strove as perhaps woman never before had striven, and she succeeded in winning his truest admiration, his warmest friendship; he felt more at home with her than any one else in the wide world. But there it ended—she won no more.

It was not his fault; it was simply because the electric spark called love had never been and never could be elicited between his soul and hers. He would have done anything for her—he was her truest, best friend; but he was not her lover.

She hoped against hope. Each day she counted the kind words he had said to her; she noted every glance, every look, every expression. But she could not find that she made any progress—nothing that indicated any change from brotherly friendship to love. Still she hoped against hope, the chances are that she would have died of a broken heart.

Then the season ended. She went back to Verdun Royal with Lady Peters, and Lord Arleigh to Beechgrove. They wrote to each other at Christmas, and met at Calverley, the seat of Lord Rineham. She contrived, even when away from him, to fill his life. She was always consulting him on matters of interest to her; she sought his advice continually, and about everything, from the renewal of a lease to the making of a new acquaintance. "I cannot do wrong," she would say to him, "if I follow your advice." He was pleased and happy to be able to help the daughter of his mother's dearest friend.

Her manner completely deceived him. If she had evinced the least pique or discontent—if she had by word or look shown the least resentment—he would have suspected that she cared for him, and would have been on his guard. As it was, he would not have believed any one who had told him she loved him.

The explanation had been made; there was no longer even a shadow between them; they both understood that the weak, nonsensical tie was broken. That they were the dearest of friends, and quite happy, would have been Lord Arleigh's notion of matters. Philippa L'Estrange might have told a different story.

The proposed party at Beechgrove did not come off. There were some repairs needed in the eastern wing, and Lord Arleigh himself had so many engagements, that no time could be found for it; but when the season came round Philippa and he met again.

By this time some of Miss L'Estrange's admirers had come to the conclusion that there was no truth in the report of the engagement between herself and Lord Arleigh. Among these was his grace the Duke of Hazlewood. He loved the beautiful, queenly girl who had so disdainfully refused his coronet—the very refusal had made him care more than ever for her. He was worldly-wise enough to know that there were few women in London who would have refused him; and he said to himself that, if she would not marry him, he would go unmarried to the grave. He was one of the first to feel sure that there was no truth in the rumors that had grieved him so the previous year. Miss L'Estrange and Lord Arleigh were by force of circumstances great friends—nothing more, and this season he determined to make a friend of the man he had detested as a rival.

When the Duke of Hazlewood made up his mind, he generally accomplished his desire; he sought Lord Arleigh with such assiduity, he made himself so pleasant and agreeable to him, that the master of Beechgrove soon showed him his most cordial and sincere liking.

Then they became warm friends. The duke confided in Lord Arleigh—he told him the whole story of his love for Miss L'Estrange.

"I know," he said, "that no one has so much influence over her as you. I do not believe in the absurd stores told about an engagement between you, but I see plainly that she is your friend, and that you are hers; and I want you to use your influence with her in my favor."

Lord Arleigh promised to do so—and he intended to keep his promise; they were on such intimate and friendly terms that he could venture upon saying anything of that kind to her. She would not be displeased—on the contrary, she would like his advice; it might even be that before now she had wished to ask for it, but had not liked to do so—so completely did these two play at cross-purposes and misunderstand each other.

It was easier to say to himself that he would speak to her as the duke wished than to do it. He saw that any allusion to her lovers or admirers made her ill at ease—she did not like it; even his laughing comments on the homage paid to her did not please her.

"I do not like lovers," she said to him one day, "and I am tired of admirers—I prefer friends."

"But," he opposed, laughingly, "if all that wise men and philosophers tell us is correct, there are no true friends."

He never forgot the light that shone in her face as she raised it to his.

"I do not believe that," she returned; "there are true friends—you are one to me."

The tenderness of her manner struck him forcibly. Something kinder and softer stirred in his heart than had ever stirred before for her; he raised her hand to his lips and kissed it.

"You are right, Philippa" he said. "If ever a woman had a true, stanch friend, I am and will be one to you."

From her heart to her lips rose the words: "Shall you never be more?" Perhaps even her eyes asked the question more eloquently than her lips could have done, for his face flushed, and she turned away with some slight embarrassment.

"I shall try and keep your friendship," she said; "but that will be easily done, Norman."

"Yes," he replied; "one of the traditions of our house is 'truth in friendship, trust in love, honor in war.' To be a true friend and a noble foe is characteristic of the Arleighs."

"I hope that you will never be a foe of mine," she rejoined, laughingly. And that evening, thinking over the events of the day she flattered herself that she had made some little progress after all.

Chapter XIII.

The opportunity that Lord Arleigh looked for came at last. Philippa had some reason to doubt the honesty of a man whom she had been employing as agent. She was kind of heart, and did not wish to punish him, yet she felt sure that he had not done his duty by her. To speak to her solicitors about it would be, she felt, injurious to him, whether innocent or guilty. If innocent, it would create a prejudice against him; if guilty, they would wish to punish him. She resolved upon laying the matter before Lord Arleigh, and seeing what he thought of it.

He listened very patiently, examined the affair, and then told her that he believed she had been robbed.

"What shall I do?" she asked, looking at him earnestly.

"I know what you ought to do, Philippa. You ought to punish him."

"But he has a wife, Norman, and innocent little children; in exposing him I shall punish them, and they are innocent."

"That is one of the strangest of universal laws to me," said Lord Arleigh—"why the innocent always do, and always must, suffer for the guilty; it is one of the mysteries I shall never understand. Common sense tells me that you ought to expose this man—that he ought to be punished for what he has done. Yet, if you do, his wife and children will be dragged down into an abyss of misery. Suppose you make a compromise of matters and lecture him well."

He was half smiling as he spoke, but she took every word in serious earnest.

"Philippa," he continued, "why do you not marry? A husband would save you all this trouble; he would attend to your affairs, and shield you from annoyances of this kind."

"The answer to your question, 'Why do I not marry?' Would form a long story," she replied, and then she turned the conversation.

But he was determined to keep his word, and pleaded with her for the duke. Another opportunity came that evening. It was Lady Peters' birthday, and Philippa had invited some of her most intimate friends; not young people, but those with whom she thought her *chaperon* would enjoy herself best. The result was a very pleasant dinner-party, followed by a very pleasant evening. Lord Arleigh could not be absent, for it was, in some measure, a family *fête*.

The guests did not remain very late, and Lady Peters, professing herself tired with the exertions she had made, lay down on a couch, and was soon asleep. Philippa stood by the window with the rose-silk hangings drawn.

"Come out on the balcony," she said to Lord Arleigh, "the room is very warm."

It was night, but the darkness was silver-gray, not black. The sky above was brilliant with the gleam of a thousand stars, the moon was shining behind some silvery clouds, the great masses of foliage in the park were just stirred with the whisper of the night, and sweetest odors came from heliotrope and mignonnette; the brooding silence of the summer night lay over the land.

Philippa sat down, and Lord Arleigh stood by her side.

The moonlight falling on her beautiful face softened it into wondrous loveliness—it was pale, refined, with depths of passion in the dark eyes, and tender, tremulous smiles on the scarlet lips. She wore some material of white and gold. A thin scarf was thrown carelessly over her white shoulders. When the wind stirred it blew the scarf against her face.

She might have been the very goddess of love, she looked so fair out in the starlight. If there had been one particle of love in Lord Arleigh's heart, that hour and scene must have called it into life. For a time they sat in perfect silence. Her head was thrown back against a pillar round which red roses clustered and clung, and the light of the stars fell full upon her face; the dark eyes were full of radiance.

"How beautiful it is, Norman," she said, suddenly. "What music has ever equaled the whispers of the night-wind? It seems a sad pity after all that we are obliged to lead such conventional lives, and spend the greater part of them in warm, close rooms."

"You have a great love for out-of-door freedom," he remarked, laughingly.

"Yes, I love the fresh air. I think if any one asked me what I loved best on earth, I should say wind. I love it in all its moods—rough, caressing, tender, impetuous, calm, stormy. It is always beautiful. Listen to it now, just sighing in the branches of those tall trees. Could any music be sweeter or softer?"

"No," he replied, and then added, "The time and the scene embolden me, Philippa; there is something that I wish to say to you—something that I long have wished to say. Will you hear it now?"

A tremor like that of the leaves in the wind seemed to pass over her. There was a startled expression in the dark eyes, a quiver of the crimson lips. Was it coming at last—this for which she had longed all her life? She controlled all outward signs of emotion and turned to him quite calmly.

"I am always ready to listen to you, Norman, and to hear what you have to say."

"You see, Philippa, the starlight makes me bold. If we were in that brilliantly-lighted drawing-room of yours, I should probably hesitate long before speaking plainly, as I am going to do now."

He saw her clasp her hands tightly, but he had no key to what was passing in her mind. He drew nearer to her.

"You know, Philippa," he began, "that I have always been fond of you. I have always taken the same interest in you that I should have taken in a dearly-beloved sister of my own, if Heaven had given me one."

She murmured some few words which he did not hear.

"I am going to speak to you now," he continued, "just as though you were my own sister, have I your permission to do so, Philippa?"

"Yes," she replied.

"And you promise not to be angry about any thing that I may say?"

"I could never be angry with you, Norman," she answered.

"Then I want you to tell me why you will not marry the Duke of Hazlewood. You have treated me as your brother and your friend. The question might seem impertinent from another; from me it will not appear impertinent, not curious—simply true and kindly interest. Why will you not marry him, Philippa?"

A quick sharp spasm of pain passed over her face. She was silent for a minute before she answered him, and then she said:

"The reason is very simple, Norman—because I do not love him."

"That is certainly a strong reason; but, Philippa, let me ask you now another question—why do you not love him?"

She could have retorted, "Why do you not love me?" but prudence forbade it.

"I cannot tell you. I have heard you say that love is fate. I should imagine it must be because the Duke of Hazlewood is not my fate."

He did not know what answer to make to that, it was so entirely his own way of thinking.

"But, Philippa," he resumed after a pause, "do you not think that you might love him if you tried?"

"I have never thought about it," was the quiet reply.

Lord Arleigh continued:

"In my idea he is one of the most charming men in England; I have never seen a more perfect type of what an English gentleman should be—he is noble, generous, brave, chivalrous. What fault do you find with him, Philippa?"

"I?" she asked, looking up at him in wonder. "My dear Norman, I have never found fault with the duke in my life."

"Then why can you not love him?"

"That is a very different thing. I find no fault with him; on the contrary, I agree with you that he is one of the noblest of men, yet I have never thought of marrying him."

"But, Philippa"—and with kindly impressiveness he laid one hand on her shoulder—"why do you not think of marrying him? Between you and myself there can be no compliments, no flattery. I tell you that of all the women in England you are the most fitted to be the Duchess of Hazlewood—and you would be a beautiful duchess, too. Think of the position you would occupy—second only to royalty. I should like to see you in such a position—you would fill it grandly. Think of the power, the influence, the enormous amount of good you could do; think of it all, Philippa?"

He did not see the sudden, sharp quiver of pain that passed over the beautiful face, nor how pale it grew in the starlight.

"I am thinking," she answered, quietly—"I am listening attentively to all that you say."

She drew the light scarf more closely around her shoulders and shuddered as though a chill breeze had passed over her.

"Are you cold, dear?" he asked kindly.

"Cold! How could I be on this warm starlit night? Go on, Norman; let me hear all that you have to say."

"I am trying to persuade you to accept what seems to me one of the happiest lots ever offered to woman. I want to see you the Duke of Hazlewood's wife. I cannot imagine any man more calculated to win a woman's love, or to please her fancy, than he is. He is young, handsome, noble in face and figure as he is in heart and soul; and he is clever and gifted."

"Yes," she allowed, slowly, "he is all that, Norman."

"Some day or other he will be the leading spirit in the land; he will be the head of a great party."

"That I believe," she agreed.

"And he loves you so well, Philippa; I have never seen a man more devoted. How many years has he loved you now—two or three? And he tells me that he shall go unmarried to the grave unless you consent to be his wife."

"Did he tell you that? He must indeed be attached to me," she observed. "Norman, did he ask you to say all this to me?"

"He asked me to plead his cause," replied Lord Arleigh.

"Why did he ask you to do so?"

"Because—believing us to be what we really are, Philippa, tried and true friends—he thought I should have some influence over you."

"Clever duke!" she said. "Norman, are you well versed in modern poetry?"

He looked up in blank surprise at the question—it was so totally unexpected.

"In modern poetry?" he repeated. "Yes, I think I am. Why, Philippa?"

"I will tell you why," she said, turning her beautiful face to him. "If you will be patient, I will tell you why."

She was silent for a few minutes, and then Lord Arleigh said:

"I am patient enough, Philippa; will you tell me why?"

The dark eyes raised to his had in them a strange light—a strange depth of passion.

"I want to know if you remember the beautiful story of Priscilla, the Puritan maiden," she said, in a tremulous voice—the loveliest maiden of Plymouth?"

"You mean the story of Miles Standish," he corrected. "Yes, I remember it, Philippa."

"That which a Puritan maiden could do, and all posterity sing her praises for, surely I—a woman of the world—may do without blame. Do you remember, Norman, when John Alden goes to her to do the wooing which the stanch soldier does not do for himself—do you remember her answer? Let me give you the verse—

"'But, as he warmed and glowed in his simple and eloquent language, Quite forgetful of self, and full of the praise of his rival, Archly the maiden smiled, and with eyes overrunning with laughter, Said in a tremulous voice, "Why don't you speak for yourself, John?"'"

The sweet musical voice died away in the starlight, the wind stirred the crimson roses—silence, solemn and deep, fell over Lord Arleigh and his companion. Philippa broke it.

"Surely you, in common with all of us, admire the Puritan maiden, Norman?"

"Yes, I do admire her," he answered; "she is one of my favorite heroines."

"So she is of mine; and I love her the more for the womanly outburst of honest truth that triumphed over all conventionality. Norman, what she, the 'loveliest maiden in Plymouth,' the beloved of Miles Standish, said to John Alden, I say to you—'Why don't you speak for yourself?'"

There was infinite tenderness in his face as he bent over her—infinite pain in his voice as he spoke to her.

"John Alden loved Priscilla," he said, slowly—"she was the one woman in all the world for him—his ideal—his fate, but I—oh Philippa, how I hate myself because I cannot answer you differently! You are my friend, my sister, but not the woman I must love as my wife."

"When you urged me a few minutes since to marry your friend, you asked me why I could not love him, seeing that he had all lovable qualities. Norman, why can you not love me?"

"I can answer you only in the same words—I do not know. I love you with as true an affection as ever man gave to woman; but I have not for you a lover's love. I cannot tell why, for you are one of the fairest of fair women."

"Fair, but not your 'ideal woman,'" she said, gently.

"No, not my 'ideal woman,'" he returned; "my sister, my friend—not my love."

"I am to blame," she said, proudly; "but again I must plead that I am like Priscilla. While you are pleading the cause of another, the truth came uppermost; you must forgive me for speaking so forcibly. As the poem says:

"'There are moments in life when the heart is so full of emotions
That if, by chance, it be shaken, or into its depths, like a pebble,
Drops some careless word, it overflows, and its secret,
Spilt on the ground like water, can never be gathered together.'"

"My dearest Philippa, you have not been to blame," he said; "you judge yourself so hardly always." "It is the fate of a woman to be silent," she said again. "Still, I am glad that I have spoken. Norman, will you tell me what your ideal of woman is like, that I may know her when I see her?"

"Nay," he objected, gently, "let us talk of something else."

But she persisted.

"Tell me," she urged, "that I may know in what she differs from me."

"I do not know that I can tell you," he replied. "I have not thought much of the matter."

"But if any one asked you to describe your ideal of what a woman should be, you could do it," she pursued.

"Perhaps so, but at best it would be but an imperfect sketch. She must be young, fair, gentle, pure, tender of heart, noble in soul, with a kind of shy, sweet grace; frank, yet not outspoken; free from all affectation, yet with nothing unwomanly; a mixture of child and woman. If I love an ideal, it is something like that."

"And she must be fair, like all the ladies Arleigh, with eyes like the hyacinth, and hair tinged with gold, I suppose, Norman?" "Yes; I saw a picture once in Borne that realized my notion of true womanly loveliness. It was a very fair face, with something of the innocent wonder of a child mixed with the dawning love and passion of noblest womanhood."

"You admire an *ingénue*. We have both our tastes; mine, if I were a man, would incline more to the brilliant and handsome."

She would have added more, but at that moment Lady Peters drew aside the silken hanging.

"My dear children," she said, "I should ill play my part of chaperon if I did not remind you of the hour. We have been celebrating my birthday, but my birthday is past and gone—it is after midnight."

Lord Arleigh looked up in wonder.

"After midnight? Impossible! Yet I declare my watch proves that it is. It is all the fault of the starlight, Lady Peters; you must blame that."

Lady Peters went out to them.

"I do not wonder at your lingering here," she said. "How calm and sweet the night is! It reminds me of the night in 'Romeo and Juliet.' It was on such a night *Jessica*—"

Philippa held up her hands in horror.

"No more poetry to-night, dear Lady Peters; we have had more than enough."

"Is that true, Lord Arleigh? Have you really had more than enough?"

"I have not found it so," he replied. "However, I must go. I wish time would sometimes stand still; all pleasant hours end so soon. Good-night, Lady Peters."

But that most discreet of *chaperons* had already re-entered the drawing-room—it was no part of her business to be present when the two friends said good-night.

"Good-night, Philippa," he said, in a low, gentle voice, bending over her.

The wind stirred her perfumed hair until it touched his cheek, the leaves of the crimson roses fell in a shower around her. She raised her beautiful pale face to his—the unspeakable love, the yearning sorrow on it, moved him greatly. He bent down and touched her brow with his lips.

"Good-night, Philippa, my sister—my friend," he said.

Even by the faint starlight he saw a change pass over her face.

"Good-night," she responded. "I have more to say to you, but Lady Peters will be horrified if you remain any longer. You will call to-morrow, and then I can finish my conversation?"

"I will come," he replied, gravely.

He waited a moment to see if she would pass into the drawing-room before him, but she turned away and leaned her arms on the stone balustrade.

It was nearly half an hour afterward when Lady Peters once more drew aside the hangings.

"Philippa," she said, gently, "you will take cold out there."

She wondered why the girl paused some few minutes before answering; then Miss L'Estrange said, in a low, calm voice:

"Do not wait for me, Lady Peters; I am thinking and do not wish to be interrupted."

But Lady Peters did not seem quite satisfied.

"I do not like to leave you sitting there," she said, "the servants will think it strange."

"Their thoughts do not concern me," she returned, haughtily. "Good-night, Lady Peters; do not interrupt me again, if you please."

And the good-tempered *chaperon* went away, thinking to herself that perhaps she had done wrong in interrupting the *tete-a-tete*.

"Still I did it for the best," she said to herself; "and servants will talk."

Philippa L'Estrange did not move. Lady Peters thought she spoke in a calm, proud voice. She would have been surprised could she have seen the beautiful face all wet with tears; for, Philippa had laid her head on the cold stone, and was weeping such tears as women weep but once in life. She sat there not striving to subdue the tempest of emotion that shook her, giving full vent to her passion of grief, stretching out her hands and crying to her lost love.

It was all over now. She had stepped down from the proud height of her glorious womanhood to ask for his love, and he had told her that he had none to give her. She had thrown aside her pride, her delicacy. She had let him read the guarded secret of her heart, only to hear his reply—that she was not his ideal of womanhood. She had asked for bread—he had given her a stone. She had lavished her love at his feet—he had coolly stepped aside. She had lowered her pride, humiliated herself, all in vain.

"No woman," she said to herself, "would ever pardon such a slight or forgive such a wrong."

At first she wept as though her heart would break—tears fell like rain from her eyes, tears that seemed to burn as they fell; then after a time pride rose and gained the ascendancy. She, the courted, beautiful woman, to be so humiliated, so slighted! She, for whose smile the noblest in the land asked in vain, to have her almost offered love so coldly refused! She, the very queen of love and beauty, to be so spurned!

When the passion of grief had subsided, when the hot angry glow of wounded pride died away, she raised her face to the night-skies.

"I swear," she said, "that I will be revenged—that I will take such vengeance on him as will bring his pride down far lower than he has brought mine. I will never forgive him. I have loved him with a devotion passing the love of woman. I will hate more than I have loved him. I would have given my life to make him happy. I now consecrate it to vengeance. I swear to take such revenge on him as shall bring the name of Arleigh low indeed."

And that vow she intended to keep.

"If ever I forget what has passed here," she said to herself, "may Heaven forget me!"

To her servants she had never seemed colder or haughtier than on this night, when she kept them waiting while she registered her vow.

What shape was her vengeance to take?

"I shall find out," she thought; "it will come in time."

Chapter XIV.

Miss L'Estrange was standing alone in the small conservatory on the morning following her eventful conversation with Lord Arleigh, when the latter was announced. How she had passed the hours of the previous night was known only to herself. As the world looks the fairer and fresher for the passing of a heavy storm, the sky more blue, the color of flowers and trees brighter so she on this morning, after those long hours of agony, looked more beautiful than ever. Her white morning dress, made of choice Indian muslin, was relieved by faint touches of pink; fine white lace encircled her throat and delicate wrists. Tall and slender, she stood before a large plant with scarlet blossoms when he came in.

Lord Arleigh looked as he felt—ill at ease. He had not slept through thinking of the conversation in the balcony—it had made him profoundly wretched. He would have given much not to renew it; but she had asked him to come, and he had promised.

Would she receive him with tears and reproaches? Would she cry out that he was cold and cruel? Would she torture himself and herself by trying to find out why he did not love her? Or would she be sad, cold, and indifferent?

His relief was great when she raised a laughing, radiant face to his and held out her hand in greeting.

"Good-morning, Norman," she said, in a pleasant voice. "Now confess that I am a clever actress, and that I have given you a real fright."

He looked at her in wonder.

"I do not understand you," he returned.

"It is so easy to mislead a man," she said, laughingly.

"I do not understand, Philippa," he repeated.

"Did you really take all my pretty balcony scene in earnest last night?" she asked.

"I did indeed," he replied; and again the clear musical laugh, seemed to astonish him.

"I could not have believed it, Norman," she said. "Did you really think I was in earnest?"

"Certainly I did. Were you not?"

"No," she answered.

"Then I thank Heaven for it," he said, "for I have been very unhappy about you. Why did you say so much if you did not mean it, Philippa?"

"Because you annoyed me by pleading the cause of the duke. He had no right to ask you to do such a thing, and you were unwise to essay such a task. I have punished you by mystifying you—I shall next punish him."

"Then you did not mean all that you said?" he interrogated, still wondering at this unexpected turn of events.

"I should have given you credit for more penetration, Norman," she replied. "I to mean such nonsense—I to avow a preference for any man! Can you have been so foolish as to think so? It was only a charade, acted for your amusement."

"Oh, Philippa," he cried, "I am so pleased, dear! And yet—yet, do you know, I wish that you had not done it. It has given me a shock. I shall never be quite sure whether you are jesting or serious. I shall never feel that I really understand you."

"You will, Norman. It did seem so ridiculous for you, my old playfellow, to sit lecturing me so gravely about matrimony. You took it so entirely for granted that I did not care for the duke."

"And do you care for him, Philippa?" he asked.

"Can you doubt it, after the description you gave of him, Norman?"

"You are mocking me again, Philippa," he said.

"But you were very eloquent, Norman," she persisted. "I have never heard any one more so. You painted his Grace of Hazlewood in such glowing colors that no one could help falling in love with him."

"Did I? Well, I do think highly of him, Philippa. And so, after all, you really care for him?"

"I do not think I shall tell you, Norman. You deserve to be kept in the dark. Would you tell me if you found your ideal woman?"

"I would. I would tell you at once," he replied, eagerly.

"If you could but have seen your face!" she cried. "I feel tempted to act the charade over again. Why, Norman, what likeness can you see between Philippa L'Estrange, the proud, cold woman of the world, and that sweet little Puritan maiden at her spinning wheel?"

"I should never have detected any likeness unless you yourself had first pointed it out," he said. "Tell me, Philippa, are you really going to make the duke happy at last?"

"It may be that I am going to make him profoundly miserable As punishment for your lecture, I shall refuse to tell you anything about it," she replied; and then she added: "You will ride with me this morning, Norman?"

"Yes. I will ride with you, Philippa. I cannot tell you how thankful and relieved I am."

"To find that you have not made quite so many conquests as you thought," she said. "It was a sorry jest to play after all; but you provoked me to it, Norman. I want you to make me a promise."

"That I will gladly do," he replied. Indeed he was so relieved so pleased, so thankful to be freed from the load of self-reproach that he would have promised anything.

Her face grew earnest. She held out her hand to him.

"Promise me this, Norman," she said—"that, whether I remain Philippa L'Estrange or become Duchess of Hazlewood—no matter what I am, or may be—you will always be the same to me as you are now—my brother, my truest, dearest, best friend. Promise me."

"I do promise, Philippa, with all my heart," he responded. "And I will never break my promise."

"If I marry, you will come to see me—you-will trust in me—you will be just what you are now—you will make my house your home, as you do this?"

"Yes—that is, if your husband consents," replied Lord Arleigh.

"Rely upon it, my husband—if I ever have one—will not dispute my wishes," she said. "I am not the model woman you dream of. She, of course, will be submissive in everything; I intend to have my own way."

"We are friends for life, Philippa," he declared; "and I do not think that any one who really understands me will ever cavil at our friendship."

"Then, that being settled, we will go at once for our ride. How those who know me best would laugh, Norman, if they heard of the incident of the Puritan maiden! If I go to another fancy ball this season, I shall go as *Priscilla* of Plymouth and you had better go as *John Alden*."

He held up his hands imploringly.

"Do not tease me about it any more, Philippa," he remarked, "I cannot quite tell why, but you make me feel both insignificant and vain; yet nothing would have been further from my mind than the ideas you have filled it with."

"Own you were mistaken, and then I will be generous and forgive you," she said, laughingly.

"I was mistaken—cruelly so—weakly so—happily so," he replied. "Now you will be generous and spare me."

He did not see the bitter smile with which she turned away, nor the pallor that crept even to her lips. Once again in his life Lord Arleigh was completely deceived.

A week afterward he received "a note in Philippa's handwriting it said, simply:

"Dear Norman: You were good enough to plead the duke's cause. When you meet him next, ask him if he has anything to tell you.

Philippa L'Estrange."

What the Duke of Hazlewood had to tell was that Miss L'Estrange had promised to be his wife, and that the marriage was to take place in August. He prayed Lord Arleigh to be present as his "best man" on the occasion.

On the same evening Lady Peters and Miss L'Estrange sat in the drawing-room at Verdun House, alone. Philippa had been very restless. She had been walking to and fro; she had opened her piano and closed it; she had taken up volume after volume and laid it down again, when suddenly her eyes fell on a book prettily bound in crimson and gold, which Lady Peters had been reading.

"What book is that?" she asked, suddenly.

"Lord Lytton's 'Lady of Lyons,'" replied Lady Peters.

Philippa raised it, looked through it, and then, with a strange smile and a deep sigh, laid it down.

"At last," she said—"I have found it at last!"

"Found what, my dear?" asked Lady Peters, looking up.

"Something I have been searching for," replied Philippa, as she quitted the room, still with the strange smile on her lips.

Chapter XV.

The great event of the year succeeding was the appearance of the Duchess of Hazlewood. Miss L'Estrange the belle and the heiress, had been very popular; her Grace of Hazlewood was more popular still. She was queen of fashionable London. At her mansion all the most exclusive met. She had resolved upon giving her life to society, upon cultivating it, upon making herself its mistress and queen. She succeeded. She became essentially a leader of society. To belong to the Duchess of Hazlewood's "set" was to be the *créme de la créme*. The beautiful young duchess had made up her mind upon two things. The first was that she would be a queen of society; the second, that she would reign over such a circle as had never been gathered together before. She would have youth, beauty, wit, genius; she would not trouble about wealth. She would admit no one who was not famous for some qualification or other—some grace of body or mind—some talent or great gift. The house should be open to talent of all kinds, but never open to anything commonplace. She would be the encourager of genius, the patroness of the fine arts, the friend of all talent.

It was a splendid career that she marked out for herself, and she was the one woman in England especially adapted for it The only objection to it was that while she gave every scope to imagination— while she provided for all intellectual wants and needs—she made no allowance for the affections; they never entered into her calculations.

In a few weeks half London was talking about the beautiful Duchess of Hazlewood. In all the "Fashionable Intelligence" of the day she had a long paragraph to herself. The duchess had given a ball, had had a grand *réunion*, a *soirée*, a garden-party; the duchess had been at such an entertainment; when a long description of her dress or costume would follow. Nor was it only among the upper ten thousand that she was so pre-eminently popular. If a bazar, a fancy fair, a ball, were needed to aid some charitable cause, she was always chosen as patroness; her vote, her interest, one word from her, was all-sufficient.

Her wedding had been a scene of the most gorgeous magnificence. She had been married from her house at Verdun Royal, and half the county had been present at what was certainly the most magnificent ceremonial of the year. The leading journal, the *Illustrated Intelligence*, produced a supplement on the occasion, which was very much admired. The duke gave the celebrated artist, M. Delorme, a commission to paint the interior of the church at Verdun Royal as it appeared while the ceremony was proceeding. That picture forms the chief ornament now of the grand gallery at the Court.

The wedding presents were something wonderful to behold; it was considered that the duchess had one of the largest fortunes in England in jewels alone. The wedding-day was the fourth of August, and it had seemed as though nature herself had done her utmost to make the day most brilliant.

It was not often that so beautiful a bride was seen as the young duchess. She bore her part in the scene very bravely. The papers toll how Lord Arleigh was "best man" on the occasion but no one guessed even ever so faintly of the tragedy that came that morning to a crisis. The happy pair went off to Vere Court, the duke's favorite residence, and there for a short time the public lost sight of them.

If the duke had been asked to continue the history of his wedding-day, he would have told a strange story—how, when they were in the railway-carriage together, he had turned to his beautiful young wife with some loving words on his lips, and she had cried out that she wanted air, to let no one come near her—that she had stretched out her hands wildly, as though beating off something terrible.

He believed that she was overcome by excitement or the heat of the day; he soothed her as he would have soothed a child; and when they readied Vere Court he insisted that they should rest. She did so. Her dark hair fell round her white neck and shoulders, her beautiful face was flushed, the scarlet lips trembled as though she were a grieving child; and the young duke stood watching her, thinking how fair she was and what a treasure he had won. Then he heard her murmur some words in her sleep—what were they? He could not quite distinguish them; it was something about a Puritan maiden *Priscilla* and *John*—he could not catch the name—something that did not concern him, and in which he had no part. Suddenly she held out her arms, and, in a voice he never forgot, cried, "Oh, my love, my love!" That of course meant himself. Down on his knees by her side went the young duke—he covered her hands with kisses.

"My darling," he said, "you are better now, I have been alarmed about you, Philippa; I feared that you were ill. My darling, give me a word and a smile."

She had quite recovered herself then; she remembered that she was Duchess of Hazlewood—wife of the generous nobleman who was at her side. She was mistress of herself in a moment.

"Have I alarmed you?" she said. "I did feel ill; but I am better now— quite well, in fact." She said to herself that she had her new life to begin, and the sooner she began it the better; so she made herself very charming to the young duke, and he was in ecstasies over the prize he had won.

Thenceforward they lived happily enough. If the young duke found his wife less loving, less tender of heart, than he had believed her to be, he had no complaint.

"She is so beautiful and gifted," he would say to himself. "I cannot expect everything. I know that she loves me, although she does not say much about it. I know that I can trust her in all things, even though she makes no protestations."

They fell into the general routine of life. One loved—the other allowed herself to be loved. The duke adored his wife, and she accepted his adoration.

They were never spoken of as a model couple, although every one agreed that it was an excellent match—that they were very happy. The duke looked up with wondering admiration to the beautiful stately lady who bore his name. She could not do wrong in his eyes, everything she said was right, all she did was perfect. He never dreamed of opposing her wishes. There was no lady in England so completely her own mistress, so completely mistress of every one and everything around her, as her Grace of Hazlewood.

When the season came around again, and the brilliant life which she had laid out for herself was hers, she might have been the happiest of women but for the cloud which darkened, her whole existence. Lord Arleigh had kept his promise—he, had been her true friend, with her husband's full permission. The duke was too noble and generous himself to feel any such ignoble passion as jealousy—he was far too confiding. To be jealous of his wife would never have entered his mind; nor was there the least occasion for it. If Lord Arleigh had been her own brother, their relationship could not have been of a more blameless kind; even the censorious world of fashion, so quick to detect a scandal, so merciless in its enjoyment of one, never presumed to cast an aspersion on this friendship. There was something so frank, so open about it, that blame was an impossibility. If the duke was busy or engaged when his wife wanted to ride or drive, he asked her cousin Lord Arleigh to take his place, as he would have asked his own brother. If the duke could not attend opera or ball, Lord Arleigh was at hand. He often said it was a matter of perplexity to him which was his own home—whether he liked Beechgrove, Verdun Royal or Vere Court best.

"No one was ever so happy, so blessed with true friends as I am," he would say; at which speech the young duchess would smile that strange fathomless smile so few understood.

If they went to Vere Court, Lord Arleigh was generally asked to go with them; the Duke really liked him—a great deal for his own sake, more still for the sake of his wife. He could understand the childish friendship having grown with their growth; and he was too noble to expect anything less than perfect sincerity and truth.

The duchess kept her word. She made no further allusion to the Puritan maiden—that little episode had, so it appeared, completely escaped her memory. There was one thing to be noticed—she often read the "Lady of Lyons," and appeared to delight in it. When she had looked through a few pages, she would close the book with a sigh and a strange, brooding smile. At times, too, she would tease Lord Arleigh about his ideal woman but that was always in her husband's presence.

"You have not found the ideal woman yet, Norman?" she would ask him, laughingly; and he would answer. "No, not yet."

Then the duke would wax eloquent, and tell him that he really knew little of life—that if he wanted to be happy he must look for a wife.

"You were easily contented," the duchess would say. "Norman wants an ideal. You were content with a mere mortal—he will never be."

"Then find him an ideal, Philippa," would be the duke's reply "You know some of the nicest girls in London; find him an ideal among them."

Then to the beautiful face would come the strange, brooding smile.

"Give me time," would her Grace of Hazlewood say; "I shall find just what I want for him—in time."

Chapter XVI.

It was a beautiful, pure morning. For many years there had not been so brilliant a season in London; every one seemed to be enjoying it; ball succeeded ball; *fête* succeeded *fête*. Lord Arleigh had received a note from the Duchess of Hazlewood, asking him if he would call before noon, as she wished to see him.

He went at once to Verdun House, and was told that the duchess was engaged, but would see him in a few minutes. Contrary to the usual custom, he was shown into a pretty morning-room, one exclusively used by the duchess—a small, octagonal room, daintily furnished, which opened on to a small rose-garden, also exclusively kept for the use of the duchess. Into this garden neither friend nor visitor ever ventured; it was filled with rose-trees, a little fountain played in the midst, and a small trellised arbor was at one side. Why had he been shown into the duchess' private room? He had often heard the duke tease his wife about her room, and say that no one was privileged to enter it; why, then, was such a privilege accorded him?

He smiled to himself, thinking that in all probability it was some mistake of the servants; he pictured to himself the expression of Philippa's face when she should find him there. He looked round; the room bore traces of her presence—around him were some of her favorite flowers and books.

He went to the long French window, wondering at the rich collection of roses, and there he saw a picture that never forsook his memory again—there he met his fate—saw the ideal woman of his dreams at last. He had treated all notions of love in a very off-hand, cavalier kind of manner; he had contented himself with his own favorite axiom—"Love is fate;" if ever it was to come to him it would come, and there would be an end of it. He had determined on one thing—this same love should be his slave, his servant, never his master; but, as he stood looking out, he was compelled to own his kingship was over.

Standing there, his heart throbbing as it had never done before, every nerve thrilling, his face flushed, a strange, unknown sensation filling him with vague, sweet wonder, Lord Arleigh met his fate.

This was the picture he saw—a beautiful but by no means a common one. In the trellised arbor, which contained a stand and one or two chairs, was a young girl of tall, slender figure, with a fair, sweet face, inexpressibly lovely, lilies and roses exquisitely blended—eyes like blue hyacinths, large, bright, and starlight, with white lids and dark long lashes, so dark that they gave a peculiar expression to the eyes—one of beauty, thought, and originality. The lips were sweet and sensitive, beautiful when smiling, but even more beautiful in repose. The oval contour of the face was perfect; from the white brow, where the veins were so clearly marked, rose a crown of golden hair, not brown or auburn, but of pure pale gold—a dower of beauty in itself.

The expression of the face was one of shy virgin beauty. One could imagine meeting it in the dim aisles of some cathedral, near the shrine of a saint, as an angel or a Madonna; one could imagine it bending over a sick child, lighting with its pure loveliness the home of sorrow; but one could never picture it in a ball-room. It was a face of girlish, saintly purity, of fairest loveliness—a face where innocence, poetry, and passion all seemed to blend in one grand harmony. There was nothing commonplace about it. One could not mistake it for a plebeian face; "patrician" was written on every feature.

Lord Arleigh looked at her like one in a dream.

"If she had an aureole round her head, I should take her for an angel," he thought to himself, and stood watching her.

The same secret subtle harmony pervaded every action; each new attitude seemed to be the one that suited her best. If she raised her arms, she looked like a statue. Her hands were white and delicate, as though carved in ivory. He judged her to be about eighteen. But who was she, and what had brought her there? He could have stood through the long hours of the sunny day watching her, so completely had she charmed him, fascinated his very senses.

"Love is fate!" How often had he said that to himself, smiling the while? Now here his fate had come to him all unexpectedly—this most fair face had found its way to the very depths of his heart and nestled there.

He could not have been standing there long, yet it seemed to him that long hours parted him from the life he had known before. Presently he reproached himself for his folly. What had taken place? He had seen a fair face, that was all—a face that embodied his dream of loveliness. He had realized his ideal, he had suddenly, and without thinking of it, found his fate—the figure, the beauty that he had dreamed of all his life.

Nothing more than that; yet the whole world seemed changed. There was a brighter light in the blue skies, a new beauty had fallen on the flowers; in his heart was strange, sweet music; everything was idealized—glorified. Why? Because he had seen the face that had always filled his thoughts.

It seemed to him that he had been there long hours, when the door suddenly opened, and her Grace of Hazlewood entered.

"Norman," she said, as though in sudden wonder, "why did they show you in here?"

"I knew they were doing wrong," he replied. "This is your own special sanctum, Philippa?"

"Yes, it is indeed; still, as you are here, you may stay. I want to speak to you about that Richmond dinner. My husband does not seem to care about it. Shall we give it up?"

They talked for a few minutes about it, and then the duchess said, suddenly:

"What do you think about my roses, Norman?"

"They are wonderful," he replied, and then, in a low voice, he asked, "Philippa, who is that beautiful girl out there among your flowers?"

She did not smile, but a sudden light came into her eyes.

"It would be a great kindness not to tell you," she answered. "You see what comes of trespassing in forbidden places. I did not intend you to see that young lady."

"Why not?" he asked, abruptly.

"The answer to your question would be superfluous," she replied.

"But, Philippa, tell me at least who she is."

"That I cannot do," she replied, and then the magnificent face was lighted with a smile. "Is she your ideal woman, Norman?" she asked.

"My dear Philippa," he answered, gravely, "she is the idea," woman herself neither more nor less."

"Found at last!" laughed the duchess. "For all that, Norman, you must not look it her."

"Why not? Is she married—engaged?"

"Married? That girl! Why, she has only just left school. If you really wish to know who she is I will tell you; but you must give me your word not to mention it."

"I promise," he replied.

He wondered why the beautiful face grew crimson and the dark eyes dropped.

"She is a poor relative of ours," said the duchess, "poor, you understand—nothing else."

"Then she is related to the duke?" he interrogated.

"Yes, distantly; and, after a fashion, we have adopted her. When she marries we shall give her a suitable dot. Her mother married unfortunately."

"Still, she was married?" said Lord Arleigh.

"Yes, certainly; but unhappily married. Her daughter, however, has received a good education, and now she will remain with us. But, Norman, in this I may trust you, as in everything else?"

"You may trust me implicitly," he replied.

"The duke did not quite like the idea of having her to live with us at first—and I do not wish it to be mentioned to him. If he speaks of it to you at all, it will be as my caprice. Let it pass—do not ask any questions about her; it only annoys her—it only annoys him. She is very happy with me. You see," she continued, "women can keep a secret. She has been here three weeks, yet you have never seen her before, and now it is by accident."

"But," said Norman, "what do you intend to do with her?"

The duchess took a seat near him, and assumed quite a confidential air.

"I have been for some time looking out for a companion," she said; "Lady Peters really must live at Verdun Royal—a housekeeper is not sufficient for that large establishment—it requires more than that. She has consented to make it her home, and I must have some one to be with me."

"You have the duke," he put in, wonderingly.

"True, and a husband most, perforce, be all that is adorable; still, having been accustomed to a lady-companion, I prefer keeping one; and this girl, so beautiful, so pure, so simple, is all that I need, or could wish for."

"So I should imagine," he replied. "Will you introduce her into society, Philippa?"

"I think not; she is a simple child, yet wonderfully clever. No, society shall not have her. I will keep her for my own."

"What is her name?" asked Lord Arleigh.

The duchess laughed.

"Ah, now, man-like, you are growing curious! I shall not tell you. Yes, I will; it is the name above all others for an ideal—Madaline."

"Madaline," he repeated; "it is very musical—Madaline."

"It suits her," said the duchess; "and now, Norman, I must go. I have some pressing engagements to-day."

"You will not introduce me then, Philippa?"

"No—why should I? You would only disturb the child's dream."

Chapter XVII.

Lord Arleigh could not rest for thinking of the vision he had seen; the face of the duchess' companion haunted him as no other face had ever done. He tried hard to forget it, saying to himself that it was a fancy, a foolish imagination, a day-dream; he tried to believe that in a few days he should have forgotten it.

It was quite otherwise. He left Vere House in a fever of unrest; he went everywhere he could think of to distract his thoughts. But the fair face with its sweet, maidenly expression, the tender blue eyes with their rich poetic depths, the sweet, sensitive lips were ever present. Look where he would he saw them. He went to the opera, and they seemed to smile at him from the stage; he walked home in the starlight—they were smiling at him from the stars; he tried to sleep—they haunted him; none had followed him as those eyes did.

"I think my heart and brain are on fire," he said to himself. "I will go and look once again at the fair young face; perhaps if she smiles at me or speaks to me I shall be cured."

He went; it was noon when he reached the Duke of Hazlewood's mansion. He inquired for the duchess, and was told she had gone to Hampton Court. He repeated the words in surprise.

"Hampton Court!" he said. "Are you quite sure?"

"Yes, my lord," was the footman's reply. "Her grace has gone there, for I heard her talking about the pictures this morning."

He could hardly imagine the duchess at Hampton Court. He felt half inclined to follow, and then he thought that perhaps it would be an intrusion; if she had wanted his society, she would certainly have asked for it. No, he would not go. He stood for a few minutes irresolute, wondering if he could ask whether the duchess had taken her young companion with her, and then he remembered that he did not even know her name.

How was the day to pass? Matters were worse than ever. If he had seen her, if he could have spoken to her, he might perhaps have felt better; as it was, the fever of unrest had deepened.

He was to meet the duchess that evening at the French Embassy; he would tell her she must relax some of her rigor in his favor. She was talking to the ambassador when he entered, but with a smiling gesture she invited him to her side.

"I hear that you called to-day," she said. "I had quite forgotten to tell you that we were going to Hampton Court."

"I could hardly believe it," he replied. "What took you there?"

"You will wonder when I tell you, Norman," she replied, laughingly. "I have always thought that I have a great capacity for spoiling people. My fair Madaline, as I have told you, is both poet and artist. She begged so hard to see the pictures at Hampton Court that I could not refuse her."

"I should not think the history of the belles of the court of Charles II. would be very useful to her," he said; and she was quick to detect the jealousy in his voice.

"Norman, you are half inclined to be cross, I believe, because I did not ask you to go with us."

"I should have enjoyed it, Philippa, very much."

"It would not have been prudent," she observed, looking most bewitchingly beautiful in her effort to look matronly and wise.

He said no more; but if her grace had thought of a hundred plans for making him think of Madaline, she could not have adopted one more to the purpose.

From the moment Lord Arleigh believed that the young duchess intended to forbid all acquaintance with her fair *protégée*, he resolved to see her and to make her like him.

The day following he went again to the mansion; the duchess was at home, and wished to see him, but at that moment she was engaged. He was shown into the library, where in a few minutes she joined him.

"My dear Norman," she said, with a bright smile of greeting, "Vere told me, if you came, to keep you for luncheon; he wants to see you particularly. The horse that won the Derby, he has been told, is for sale, and he wants you to see it with him."

"I shall be very pleased," replied Lord Arleigh. "You seem hurried this morning, Philippa."

"Yes; such a *contretemps*! Just as I was anticipating a few hours with you, the Countess of Farnley came in, with the terrible announcement that she was here to spend the morning. I have to submit to fate, and listen to the account of Clara's last conquests, of the infamous behavior of her maid, of Lord Darnley's propensity for indiscreet flirtations. I tell her there is safety in number. I have to look kind and sympathetic while I am bored to death."

"Shall I accompany you and help you to amuse Lady Farnley?"

She repeated the words with a little laugh.

"Amuse Lady Farnley? I never undertake the impossible. You might as well ask me to move the monument, it would be quite as easy."

"Shall I help her to amuse you, then?" he said.

"No, I will not impose on your friendship. Make yourself as comfortable as you can, and I will try to hasten her departure."

Just as she was going away Lord Arleigh called to her.

"Philippa!" she turned her beautiful head half impatiently to him.

"What is it, Norman? Quick! The countess will think I am lost."

"May I go into your pretty rose-garden?" he asked.

She laughed.

"What a question! Certainly; you my go just where you please."

"She has forgotten her companion," he said to himself, "or she is not about."

He went into the morning-room and through the long, open French window; there were the lovely roses in bloom, and there—oh, kind, blessed fate!—there was his beautiful Madaline, seated in the pretty trellised arbor, busily working some fine point-lace, looking herself like the fairest flower that ever bloomed.

The young girl looked up at him with a startled glance—shy, sweet, hesitating—and then he went up to her.

"Do not let me disturb you," he said. "The duchess is engaged and gave me permission to wait for her here."

She bowed, and he fancied that her white fingers trembled.

"May I introduce myself to you?" he continued. "I am Lord Arleigh."

A beautiful blush, exquisite as the hue of the fairest rose, spread over her face. She looked at him with a smile.

"Lord Arleigh," she repeated—"I know the name very well."

"You know my name very well—how is that?" he asked, in surprise.

"It is a household word here," she said; "I hear it at least a hundred times a day."

"Do you? I can only hope that you are not tired of it."

"No, indeed I am not;" and then she drew back with a sudden hesitation, as though it had just occurred to her that she was talking freely to a stranger.

He saw her embarrassment, and did his best to remove it.

"How beautiful these roses are!" he said, gently. "The duchess is fortunate to have such a little paradise here."

"She ought to be surrounded by everything that is fairest and most beautiful on earth," she declared, "for there is no one like her."

"You are fond of her?" he said.

She forgot all her shyness, and raised her blue eyes to his.

"Fond of her? I love her better than any one on earth—except perhaps, my mother. I could never have dreamed of any one so fair, so bewitching, so kind as the duchess."

"And she seems attached to you," he said, earnestly.

"She is very good to me—she is goodness itself;" and the blue eyes, with their depth of poetry and passion, first gleamed with light, and then filled with tears.

"We must be friends," said Lord Arleigh, "for I, too, love the duchess. She has been like a sister to me ever since I can remember;" and he drew nearer to the beautiful girl as he spoke. "Will you include me among your friends?" he continued. "This is not the first time that I have seen you. I stood watching you yesterday; you were among the roses, and I was in the morning-room. I thought then, and

I have thought ever since, that I would give anything to be included among your friends."

His handsome face flushed as he spoke, his whole soul was in his eyes.

"Will you look upon me as one of your friends?" he repeated, and his voice was full of softest music. He saw that even her white brow grew crimson.

"A friend of mine, my lord?" she exclaimed. "How can I? Surely you know I am not of your rank—I am not one of the class from which you select your friends."

"What nonsense!" he exclaimed. "If that is your only objection I can soon remove it. I grant that there may be some trifling difference. For instance, I may have a title; you—who are a thousand times more worthy of one—have none. What of that? A title does not make a man. What is the difference between us? Your beauty—nay, do not think me rude or abrupt—- my heart is in every word that I say to you—your grace would ennoble any rank, as your friendship would ennoble any man."

She looked up at him, and said, gently:

"I do not think you quite understand."

"Yes, I do," he declared, eagerly; "I asked the duchess yesterday who you were, and she told me your whole story."

It was impossible for him not to see how she shrank with unutterable pain from the words. The point-lace fell on the grass at her feet—she covered her face with her hands.

"Did she? Oh, Lord Arleigh, it was cruel to tell it!"

"It was not cruel to tell me," he returned. "She would not tell any one else, I am quite sure. But she saw that I was really anxious—that I must know it—that it was not from curiosity I asked."

"Not from curiosity!" she repeated, still hiding her burning face with her hands.

"No, it was from a very different motive." And then he paused abruptly. What was he going to say? How far had he already left all conventionality behind? He stopped just in time, and then continued, gravely: "The Duchess of Hazlewood and myself are such true and tried friends that we never think of keeping any secrets from each other. We have been, as I told you before, brother and sister all our lives—it was only natural that she should tell me about you."

"And, having heard my story, you ask me to be one of your friends?" she said, slowly. There were pain and pathos in her voice as she spoke.

"Yes," he replied, "having heard it all, I desire nothing on earth so much as to win your friendship."

"My mother?" she murmured.

"Yes—your mother's unfortunate marriage, and all that came of it. I can repeat the story."

"Oh, no!" she interrupted. "I do not wish to hear it. You know it, and you would still be my friend?"

"Answer me one question," he said, gently. "Is this sad story the result of any fault of yours? Are you in any way to blame for it?"

"No; not in the least. Still, Lord Arleigh, although I do not share the fault, I share the disgrace—nothing can avert that from me."

"Nothing of the kind," he opposed; "disgrace and yourself are as incompatible as pitch and a dove's wing."

"But," she continued, wonderingly, "do you quite understand?"

"Yes; the duchess told me the whole story. I understand it, and am truly grieved for you; I know the duke's share in it and all."

He saw her face grow pale even to the lips.

"And yet you would be my friend—you whom people call proud—you whose very name is history! I cannot believe it, Lord Arleigh."

There was a wistful look in her eyes, as though she would fain believe that it were true, yet that she was compelled to plead even against herself.

"We cannot account for likes or dislikes," he said; "I always look upon them as nature's guidance as to whom we should love, and whom we should avoid. The moment I saw you I—liked you. I went home, and thought about you all day long."

"Did you?" she asked, wonderingly. "How very strange!"

"It does not seem strange to me," he observed. "Before I had looked at you three minutes I felt as though I had known you all my life. How long have we been talking here? Ten minutes, perhaps—yet I feel as though already there is something that has cut us off from the rest of the world, and left us alone together. There is no accounting for such strange feelings as these."

"No," she replied, dreamily, "I do not think there is."

"Perhaps," he continued, "I may have been fanciful all my life; but years ago, when I was a boy at school, I pictured to myself a heroine such as I thought I should love when I came to be a man."

She had forgotten her sweet, half sad shyness, and sat with faint flush on her face, her lips parted, her blue eyes fixed on his.

"A heroine of my own creation," he went on; "and I gave her an ideal face—lilies and roses blended, rose-leaf lips, a white brow, eyes the color of hyacinths, and hair of pale gold."

"That is a pretty picture," she said, all unconscious that it was her own portrait he had sketched.

His eyes softened and gleamed at the *naïveté* of the words.

"I am glad you think so. Then my heroine had, in my fancy, a mind and soul that suited her face—pure, original, half sad, wholly sweet, full of poetry."

She smiled as though charmed with the picture.

"Then I grew to be a youth, and then to be a man," he continued. "I looked everywhere for my ideal among all the fair women I knew. I looked in courts and palaces, I looked in country houses, but I could not find her. I looked at home and abroad, I looked at all times and all seasons, but I could not find her."

He saw a shadow come over the sweet, pure face as though she felt sorry for him.

"So time passed, and I began to think that I should never find my ideal, that I must give her up, when one day, quite unexpectedly, I saw her."

There was a gleam of sympathy in the blue eyes.

"I found her at last," he continued. "It was one bright June morning; she was sitting out among the roses, ten thousand times fairer and sweeter than they."

She looked at him with a startled glance; not the faintest idea had occurred to her that he was speaking of her.

"Do you understand me?" he asked.

"I—I am frightened, Lord Arleigh."

"Nay, why should you fear? What is there to fear? It is true. The moment I saw you sitting here I knew that you were my ideal, found at last."

"But," she said, with the simple wonder of a child. "I am not like the portrait you sketched."

"You are unlike it only because you are a hundred times fairer," he replied; "that is why I inquired about you—why I asked so many questions. It was because you were to me a dream realized. So it came about that I heard your true history. Now will you be my friend?"

"If you still wish it, Lord Arleigh, yes; but, if you repent of having asked me, and should ever feel ashamed of our friendship, remember that I shall not reproach you for giving me up."

"Giving you up?" cried Lord Arleigh. "Ah, Madaline—let me call you Madaline, the name is so sweet—I shall never give you up! When a man has been for many years looking for some one to fill his highest and brightest dreams, he knows how to appreciate that some one when found."

"It seems all so strange," she said, musingly.

"Nay, why strange? You have read that sweetest and saddest of all love stories—'Romeo and Juliet?' Did *Juliet* think it strange that, so soon after seeing her, *Romeo* should be willing to give his life for her?"

"No, it did not seem strange to them," she replied, with a smile; "but it is different with us. This is the nineteenth century, and there are no *Juliets*."

"There are plenty of *Romeos*, though," he remarked, laughingly. "The sweetest dreams in my life are the briefest. Will you pluck one of those roses for me and give it to me, saying, 'I promise to be your friend?'"

"You make me do things against my will," she said; but she plucked a rose, and held it toward him in her hand. "I promise to be your friend," she said, gently.

Lord Arleigh kissed the rose. As he did so their eyes met; and it would have been hard to tell which blushed the more deeply. After that, meetings between them became more frequent. Lord Arleigh made seeing her the one great study of his life—and the result was what might be imagined.

Chapter XVIII.

The yacht of Mr. Conyers, one of the richest commoners in England—a yacht fitted as surely no yacht ever before had been fitted—was for sale. He was a wealthy man, but to keep that sea-palace afloat was beyond his means. The Duchess of Hazlewood was sole mistress of a large fortune in her own right; the duke had made most magnificent settlements upon her. She had a large sum of money at her command; and the idea suddenly occurred to her to purchase Mr. Conyers' yacht unknown to her husband and present him with it. He was fond of yachting—it was his favorite amusement. She herself was a wretched sailor, and would not be able to accompany him; but that would not matter. It was not of her own pleasure that the Duchess of Hazlewood was thinking, while the old strange brooding smile lingered on her beautiful face and deepened on her perfect lips.

"It would be the very thing," she said to herself, "it would afford to me the opportunity I am seeking—nothing could be better."

She purchased the yacht and presented it to the duke, her husband. His pleasure and astonishment were unbounded. She was, as a rule, so undemonstrative that he could not thank her sufficiently for what seemed to him her great interest in his favorite pursuit.

"The only drawback to the splendid gift, Philippa, is that you can never enjoy it; it will take me away from you."

"Yes, I do indeed deplore that I am a wretched sailor, for I can imagine nothing pleasanter than life on board such a yacht as that. But, while you are cruising about, Vere, I shall go to Verdun Royal and take Madaline with me; then I shall go to Vere Court—make a kind of royal progress, set everything straight and redress all wrongs, hold a court at each establishment I shall enjoy that more than yachting."

"But I shall miss you so much, Philippa," said the young husband.

"We have the remainder of our lives to spend together," she rejoined; "if you are afraid of missing me too much, you had better get rid of the yacht."

But he would not hear of that—he was delighted with the beautiful and valuable present. The yacht was christened "Queen Philippa"; and it was decided that, when the end of the season had come, the duke should take his beautiful wife to Verdun Royal, and, after having installed her there, should go at once to sea. He had invited a party of friends—all yachtsmen like himself—and they had agreed to take "Queen Philippa" to the Mediterranean, there to cruise during the autumn months.

As it was settled so it was carried out; before the week had ended the duke, duchess, and Madeline were all at Verdun Royal. Perhaps the proud young wife had never realized before how completely her husband loved her. This temporary parting was to him a real pain.

A few days before it took place he began to look pale and ill. She saw that he could not eat, that he did not sleep or rest. Her heart was touched by his simple fidelity, his passionate love, although the one fell purpose of her life remained unchanged.

"If you dislike going, Vere," she said to him one day, "do not go—stay at Verdun Royal."

"The world would laugh if I did that, Philippa," he returned; "it would guess at once what was the reason, because every one knows how dearly I love you. We should be called *Darby* and *Joan*."

"No one would ever dare to call me *Joan*," she said, "for I have nothing of *Joan* in me."

The duke sighed—perhaps he thought that it would be all the better if she had; but, fancying there was something, after all, slightly contemptuous in her manner, as though she thought it unmanly in him to repine about leaving her, he said no more.

One warm, brilliant day he took leave of her and she was left to work out her purpose. She never forgot the day of his departure—it was one of those hot days when the summer skies seemed to be half obscured by a copper-colored haze, when the green leaves hang languidly, and the birds seek the coolest shade, when the flowers droop with thirst, and never a breath of air stir their blossoms, when there is no picture so refreshing to the senses as that of a cool deep pool in the recesses of a wood.

She stood at the grand entrance, watching him depart, and she knew that with all her beauty, her grace, her talent, her sovereignty, no one had ever loved her as this man did. Then, after he was gone, she stood still on the broad stone terrace, with that strange smile on her face, which seemed to mar while it deepened her beauty.

"It will be a full revenge," she said to herself. "There could be no fuller. But what shall I do when it is all known?"

She was not one to flinch from the course of action she had marked out for herself, nor from the consequences of that course; but she shuddered even in the heat, as she thought what her life would be when her vengeance was taken.

"He will never forgive me," she said, "he will look upon me as the wickedest of women. It does not matter; he should not have exasperated me by slighting me."

Then the coppery haze seemed to gather itself together—great purple masses of clouds piled themselves in the sky, a lurid light overspread the heavens, the dense oppressive silence was broken by a distant peal of thunder, great rain-drops fell—fierce, heavy drops. The trees seemed to stretch out their leaves to drink in the moisture, the parched flowers welcomed the downpour; and still the Duchess of Hazlewood stood out on the terrace, so deeply engrossed in her thoughts that she never heeded the rain.

Madaline hastened out to her with a shawl.

"Dear duchess," she cried, "it is raining; and you are so absorbed in thought that you do not notice it."

She laughed a strange, weird laugh, and raised her beautiful face with its expression of gloom.

"I did not notice it, Madaline," she said; "but there is no need for anxiety about me," she added, proudly.

They re-entered the house together. Madaline believed that the duchess was thinking of and grieving over the departure of the duke. Lady Peters thought the same. They both did their best to comfort her—to amuse her and distract her thoughts. But the absent expression did not die from her dark eyes. When they had talked to her some little time she took up the "Lady of Lyons."

"How much you admire that play," said Madaline; "I see you reading it so often."

"I have a fancy for it," returned the duchess; "it suits my taste. And I admire the language very much."

"Yet it is a cruel story," observed Madaline; "the noblest character in it is *Pauline*."

"She was very proud; and pride, I suppose, must suffer," said the duchess, carelessly.

"She was not too proud, after all, to love a noble man, when she once recognized him, duchess."

"She learned to love the prince—she would never have loved the gardener," remarked Philippa; "it was a terrible vengeance."

"I do not like stories of vengeance," said Madaline. "After all, though, I love the *Claude* of the story, and find much true nobility in him—much to admire. When reading the play I am tempted all the time to ask myself, How could he do it? It was an unmanly act."

There was a strange light in the dark eyes, a quiver on the scarlet lips, as Philippa said:

"Do you think so? Suppose some one had offended you as *Pauline* offended *Claude*—laughing at the love offered, scorned, mocked, despised you—and that such vengeance as his lay in your power; would you not take it?"

The sweet face flushed.

"No, I would rather die," Madaline replied, quickly.

"I would take it, and glory in it," said the duchess, firmly

"If I were wounded, insulted, and slighted as *Claude* was, I would take the cruelest revenge that I could."

Madeline took one of the jeweled hands in her own and kissed it.

"I should never be afraid of you," she said; "you can never hurt any one. Your vengeance would end in the bestowal of a favor."

"Do you think so highly of me, Madaline?" asked Philippa, sadly.

"Think highly of you! Why, you would laugh if you knew how I loved you—how I adore you. If all the world were to swear to me that you could do the least thing wrong, I should not believe them."

"Poor child!" said the duchess, sadly.

"Why do you call me 'poor child?'" she asked, laughingly.

"Because you have such implicit faith, and are sure to be so cruelly disappointed."

"I would rather have such implicit faith, and bear the disappointment, than be without both," said Madaline.

Chapter XIX.

On the day of his departure the duke had said to his wife: "I have invited Norman to spend a few weeks with you; have some pleasant people to meet him. He tells me he shall not go to Scotland this year."

"I will ask Miss Byrton and Lady Sheldon," Philippa had promised.

"Only two ladies!" the duke had laughed. "He will want some one to smoke his cigar with."

"I will trust to some happy inspiration at the time, then," she had replied; and they had not mentioned the matter again.

Early in August Lord Arleigh wrote that if it were convenient he should prefer paying his promised visit at once. He concluded his letter by saying:

"My dear Philippa, your kind, good husband has said something to me about meeting a pleasant party. I should so much prefer one of my old style visits—no parties, no ceremonies. I want to see you and Verdun Royal, not a crowd of strange faces. Lady Peters is *chaperon*, if you have any lingering doubt about the 'proprieties.'"

So it was agreed that he should come alone, and later on, if the duchess cared to invite more friends, she could do so.

The fact was that Lord Arleigh wanted time for his wooing. He had found that he could not live without Madaline. He had thought most carefully about everything, and had decided on asking her to be his wife. True, there was the drawback of her parentage—but that was not grievous, not so terrible. Of course, if she had been lowly-born— descended from the dregs of the people, or the daughter of a criminal—he would have trampled his love under foot. He would have said to himself "*Noblesse oblige,*" and rather than tarnish the honor of his family, he would have given her up.

This was not needed. Related to the Duke of Hazlewood, there could not be anything wrong. The duchess had told him distinctly that Madaline's mother had married beneath her, and that the whole family on that account had completely ignored her. He did not remember that the duchess had told him so in as many words, but he was decidedly of the opinion that Madaline's mother was a cousin of the duke's, and that she had married a drawing-master, who had afterward turned out wild and profligate. The drawing-master was dead. His darling Madaline had good blood in her veins—was descended from an ancient and noble family. That she had neither fortune nor position was immaterial to him. He had understood from the duchess that the mother of his fair young love lived in quiet retirement. He could not remember in what words all this had been told to him, but this was the impression that was on his mind. So he had determined on making Madaline his wife if he could but win her consent. The only thing to be feared was her own unwillingness. She was fair and fragile, but she had a wonderful strength of will.

He had thought it all over. He remembered well what the duchess had said about the duke's not caring to hear the matter mentioned. Lord Arleigh could understand that, with all his gentleness, Hazlewood was a proud man, and that, if there had been a *mésalliance* in his family, he would be the last to wish it discussed. Still Lord Arleigh knew that he would approve of the marriage. It was plain, however, that it would be better for it to take place while he was away from England, and then it would not, could not in any way compromise him. A quiet marriage would not attract attention.

If he could only win Madeline's consent. She had been so unwilling to promise him her friendship, and then so unwilling to hear that he loved her. He could form no idea how she would receive the offer of marriage that he intended to make her.

That was why he wished to go alone. He would have time and opportunity then. As for Philippa, he did not fear any real objection from her; if she once believed or thought that his heart was fixed on marrying Madaline, he was sure she would help him.

Marry Madaline he must—life was nothing to him without her. He had laughed at the fever called love. He knew now how completely love had mastered him. He could think of nothing but Madaline.

He went down to Verdun Royal, heart and soul so completely wrapped in Madaline that he hardly remembered Philippa—hardly remembered that he was going as her guest; he was going to woo Madeline—fair, sweet Madeline—to ask her to be his wife, to try to win her for his own.

It was afternoon when he reached Verdun Royal. The glory of summer was over the earth. He laughed at himself, for he was nervous and timid; he longed to see Madaline, yet trembled at the thought of meeting her.

"So this is love?" said Lord Arleigh to himself, with a smile. "I used to wonder why it made men cowards, and what there was to fear; I can understand it now."

Then he saw the gray towers and turrets of Verdun Royal rising from the trees; he thought of his childish visits to the house, and how his mother taught him to call the child Philippa his little wife. Who would have thought in those days that Philippa would live to be a duchess, and that he should so wildly worship, so madly love a fairer, younger face?

He was made welcome at Verdun Royal. Lady Peters received him as though he were her own son. Then the duchess entered, with a glad light in her eyes, and a smile that was half wistful. She greeted him warmly; she was pleased to see him—pleased to welcome him; the whole house was at his service, and everything in it. He had never seen the duchess look better; she wore her favorite colors, amber and white.

"I have attended to your wishes, Norman," she said; "you must not blame me if you are dull. I have asked no one to meet you."

"There is no fear of my ever being dull here, Philippa," he returned. "You forget that I am almost as much at home as you are yourself. I can remember when I looked upon coming to Verdun Royal as coming home."

A shadow of pain crossed her face at this reference to those early, happy days. Then he summoned up courage, and said to her:

"Where is your fair companion, Philippa?"

"She is somewhere about the grounds," replied the duchess. "I can never persuade her to remain in-doors unless she has something to do. So you have not forgotten her?" added the duchess, after a short pause.

"I have not forgotten her, Philippa. I shall have something very important to say to you about her before I go away again."

She gave no sign that she understood him, but began to talk to him on a number of indifferent matters—the warmth of the weather, his journey down, the last news from her husband—and he answered her somewhat impatiently. His thoughts were with Madaline.

At last the signal of release came.

"We need not play at 'company,' Norman," said the duchess. "As you say, Verdun Royal has always been like home to you. Continue to make it so. We dine at eight—it is now nearly five. You will find plenty to amuse yourself with. Whenever you wish for my society, you will find me in the drawing-room or my *boudoir*."

He murmured some faint word of thanks, thinking to himself how considerate she was, and that she guessed he wanted to find Madaline. With a smile on her face, she turned to him as she was quitting the room.

"Vere seemed very uneasy, when he was going away, lest you should not feel at liberty to smoke when you liked," she said. "Pray do not let the fact of his absence prevent you from enjoying a cigar whenever you feel inclined for one."

"A thousand thanks, Philippa," returned Lord Arleigh, inwardly hoping that Madaline would give him scant time for the enjoyment of cigars.

Then he went across the lawn, wondering how she would look, where he should find her, and what she would say to him when she saw him. Once or twice he fancied he saw the glimmer of a white dress between the trees. He wondered if she felt shy at seeing him, as he did at seeing her. Then suddenly—it was as though a bright light had fallen from the skies—he came upon her standing under a great linden tree.

"Madaline!" he said, gently. And she came to him with outstretched hands.

Chapter XX.

Later on that afternoon the heat seemed to have increased, not lessened, and the ladies had declared even the cool, shaded drawing-room, with its sweet scents and mellowed light, to be too warm; so they had gone out on to the lawn, where a sweet western wind was blowing. Lady Peters had taken with her a book, which she made some pretense of reading, but over which her eyes closed in most suspicious fashion. The duchess, too, had a book, but she made no pretense of opening it—her beautiful face had a restless, half-wistful expression. They had quitted the drawing-room all together, but Madaline had gone to gather some peaches. The duchess liked them freshly gathered, and Madaline knew no delight so keen as that of giving her pleasure.

When she had been gone some few minutes, Lord Arleigh asked where she was, and the duchess owned, laughingly, to her fondness for ripe, sun-kissed peaches.

"Madaline always contrives to find the very best forms," she said. "She is gone to look for some now."

"I will go and help her," said Lord Arleigh, looking at Philippa's face. He thought the fair cheeks themselves not unlike peaches, with their soft, sweet, vivid coloring.

She smiled to herself with bitter scorn as he went away.

"It works well," she said; "but it is his own fault—Heaven knows, his own fault."

An hour afterward Lady Peters said to her, in a very solemn tone of voice:

"Philippa, my dear, it may not be my duty to speak, but I cannot help asking you if you notice anything?"

"No, nothing at this minute."

But Lady Peters shook her head with deepest gravity.

"Do you not notice the great attention that Lord Arleigh pays your beautiful young companion?"

"Yes, I have noticed it," said the duchess—and all her efforts did not prevent a burning, passionate flush rising to her face.

"May I ask you what you think of it, my dear?"

"I think nothing of it. If Lord Arleigh chooses to fall in love with her, he may. I warned him when she first came to live with me—I kept her most carefully out of his sight; and then, when I could no longer conveniently do so, I told him that he must not fall in love with her. I told him of her birth, antecedents, misfortunes—everything connected with her. His own mother or sister could not have warned him more sensibly."

"And what was the result?" asked Lady Peters, gravely.

"Just what one might have expected from a man," laughed the duchess. "Warn them against any particular thing, and it immediately possesses a deep attraction for them. The result was that he said she was his ideal, fairly, fully, and perfectly realized. I, of course, could say no more."

"But," cried Lady Peters, aghast, "you do not think it probable that he will marry her?"

"I cannot tell. He is a man of honor. He would not make love to her without intending to marry her."

"But there is not a better family in England than the Arleighs of Beechgrove, Philippa. It would be terrible for him—such a *mésalliance;* surely he will never dream of it."

"She is beautiful, graceful, gifted, and good," was the rejoinder. "But it is useless for us to argue about the matter. He has said nothing about marrying her; he has only called her his ideal."

"I cannot understand it," said poor Lady Peters. "It seems strange to me."

She would have thought it stranger still if she had followed them and heard what Lord Arleigh was saying.

He had followed Madaline to the southern wall, whereon the luscious peaches and apricots grew. He found her, as the duchess had intimated, busily engaged in choosing the ripest and best. He thought he had never seen a fairer picture than this golden-haired girl standing by the green leaves and rich fruit. He thought of Tennyson's "Gardener's daughter."

> "One arm aloft— — Gowned in pure white that fitted
> to the shape—
> Holding the bush, to fix it back, she stood.
> The full day dwelt on her brows and sunned
> Her violet eyes, and all her Hebe bloom,
> And doubled his own warmth against her lips,
> And on the beauteous wave of such a breast
> As never pencil drew. Half light, half shade,
> She stood, a sight to make an old man young."

He repeated the lines as he stood watching her, and then he went nearer and called:

"Madaline!"

Could he doubt that she loved him? Her fair face flushed deepest crimson; but, instead of turning to him, she moved half coyly, half shyly away.

"How quick you are," he said, "to seize every opportunity of evading me! Do you think you can escape me, Madaline? Do you think my love is so weak, so faint, so feeble, that it can be pushed aside lightly by your will? Do you think that, if you tried to get to the other end of the world, you could escape me?"

Half blushing, half laughing, trembling, yet with a happy light in her blue eyes, she said:

"I think you are more terrible than any one I know."

"I am glad that you are growing frightened, and are willing to own that you have a master—that is as it should be. I want to talk to you, Madaline. You evade me lest you should be compelled to speak to me; you lower those beautiful eyes of yours, lest I should be made happy by looking into them. If you find it possible to avoid my presence, to run away from me, you do. I am sure to woo you, to win you, to make you my sweet, dear wife—to make you happier, I hope, than any woman has ever been before—and you try to evade me, fair, sweet, cruel Madaline!"

"I am afraid of you, Lord Arleigh," she said, little dreaming how much the naïve confession implied.

"Afraid of me! That is because you see that I am quite determined to win you. I can easily teach you how to forget all fear."

"Can you?" she asked, doubtfully.

"Yes, I can, indeed, Madaline. Deposit those peaches in their green leaves on the ground. Now place both your hands in mine."

She quietly obeyed the first half of his request as though she were a child, and then she paused. The sweet face crimsoned again; he took her hands in his.

"You must be obedient," he said. "Now look at me."

But the white lids drooped over the happy eyes.

155

"Look at me, Madaline," he repeated, "and say, 'Norman, I do love you. I will forget all the nonsense I have talked about inequality of position, and will be your wife.'"

"In justice to yourself I cannot say it."

He felt the little hands tremble in his grasp, and he released them with a kiss.

"You will be compelled to say it some day, darling. You might as well try now. If I cannot win you for my wife, I will have no wife, Madaline. Ah, now you are sorry you have vexed me!

"'And so it was—half sly, half shy;
  You would and would not, little one,
Although I pleaded tenderly
  And you and I were all alone.'

Why are you so hard, Madaline? I am sure you like me a little; you dare not raise your eyes to mine and say, 'I do not love you, Norman.'"

"No," she confessed, "I dare not. But there is love and love; the lowest love is all self, the highest is all sacrifice. I like the highest."

And then her eyes fell on the peaches, and she gave a little cry of alarm.

"What will the duchess say?" she cried. "Oh, Lord Arleigh, let me go."

"Give me one kind word, then."

"What am I to say? Oh, do let me go!"

"Say, 'I like you, Norman.'"

"I like you, Norman," she said; and, taking up the peaches, she hastened away. Yet, with her flushed face and the glad light in her happy eyes, she did not dare to present herself at once before the duchess and Lady Peters.

Chapter XXI.

Was there some strange, magnetic attraction between Lord Arleigh and Madaline, or could it be that the *valet*, knowing or guessing the state of his master's affections, gave what he no doubt considered a timely hint? Something of the kind must have happened, for Madaline, unable to sleep, unable to rest, had risen in the early morning, while the dew was on the grass, and had gone out into the shade of the woods. The August sun shone brightly, a soft wind fanned her cheeks.

Madaline looked round before she entered the woods. The square turrets of Verdun Royal rose high above the trees. They were tall and massive, with great umbrageous boughs and massive rugged trunks, the boughs almost reaching down to the long, thick grass. A little brook went singing through the woods—a brook of clear, rippling water. Madaline sat down by the brook-side. Her head ached for want of sleep, her heart was stirred by a hundred varied emotions.

Did she love him? Why ask herself the question? She did love him— she trembled to think how much. It was that very love which made her hesitate. She hardly dared to think of him. In her great humility she overlooked entirely the fact of her own great personal loveliness, her rare grace and gifts. She could only wonder what there was in her that could attract him.

He was a descendant of one of the oldest families in England—he had a title, he was wealthy, clever, he had every great and good gift—yet he loved her; he stooped from his exalted position to love her, and she, for his own sake, wished to refuse his love. But she found it difficult.

She sat down by the brook-side, and, perhaps for the first time in her gentle life, a feeling of dissatisfaction rose within her; yet it was not so much that as a longing that she could be different from what she was—a wish that she had been nobly born, endowed with some great gift that would have brought her nearer to him. How happy she would have been then—how proud to love him—how glad to devote her sweet young life to him! At present it was different; the most precious thing that she could give him—which was her love—would be most prejudicial to him. And just as that thought came to her, causing the blue eyes to fill with tears, she saw him standing before her.

She was not surprised; he was so completely part and parcel of her thoughts and her life that she would never have felt surprised at seeing him. He came up to her quietly.

"My darling Madaline, your face is pale, and there are tears in your eyes. What is the matter? What has brought you out here when you ought to be in-doors? What is the trouble that has taken away the roses and put lilies in their place?"

"I have no trouble, Lord Arleigh," she replied. "I came here only to think."

"To think of what, sweet?"

Her face flushed.

"I cannot tell you," she answered. "You cannot expect that I should tell you everything."

"You tell me nothing, Madaline. A few words from you should make me the happiest man in the world, yet you will not speak them."

Then all the assumed lightness and carelessness died from his manner. He came nearer to her; her eyes drooped before the fire of his.

"Madaline, my love, let me plead to you," he said, "for the gift of your love. Give me that, and I shall be content. You think I am proud," he continued; "I am not one-half so proud, sweet, as you. You refuse to love me—why? Because of your pride. You have some foolish notions that the difference in our positions should part us. You are quite wrong—love knows no such difference."

"But the world does," she interrupted.

"The world!" he repeated, with contempt. "Thank Heaven it is not my master! What matters what the world says?"

"You owe more to the name and honor of your family than to the world," she said.

"Of that," he observed, "you must allow me to be the best judge."

She bowed submissively.

"The dearest thing in life to me is the honor of my name, the honor of my race," said Lord Arleigh. "It has never been tarnished and I pray Heaven that no stain may ever rest upon it. I will be frank with you, Madaline, as you are with me, though I love you so dearly that my very life is bound up in yours. I would not ask you to be my wife if I thought that in doing so I was bringing a shadow of dishonor on my race—if I thought that I was in even ever so slight a degree tarnishing my name; but I do not think so. I speak to you frankly. I know the story of your misfortunes, and, knowing it, do not deem it sufficient to part us. Listen and believe me, Madaline—if I stood with you before the altar, with your hand in mine, and the solemn words of the marriage service on my lips, and anything even then came to my knowledge which I thought prejudicial to the fame and honor of my race, I should without hesitation ask you to release me. Do you believe me?"

"Yes," she replied, slowly, "I believe you."

"Then why not trust me fully? I know your story—it is an old story after all. I know it by heart; I am the best judge of it. I have weighed it most carefully; it has not been a lightly-considered matter with me at all, and, after thinking it well over, I have come to the conclusion that it is not sufficient to part us. You see, sweet, that you may implicitly believe me. I have no false gloss of compliments. Frankly, as you yourself would do, I admit the drawback; but, unlike you, I affirm that it does not matter."

"But would you always think so? The time might come when the remembrance of my father's— —"

"Hush!" he said, gently. "The matter must never be discussed between us. I tell you frankly that I should not care for the whole world to know your story. I know it—the duke and duchess know it. There is no need for it to be known to others; and, believe me, Madaline, it will never be and need never be known—we may keep it out of sight. It is not likely that I shall ever repent, for it will never be of any more importance to me than it is now."

He paused abruptly, for her blue eyes were looking wistfully at him.

"What is it, Madaline?" he asked, gently.

"I wish you would let me tell you all about it—how my mother, so gentle and good, came to marry my father, and how he fell—how he was tempted and fell. May I tell you, Lord Arleigh?"

"No," he replied, after a short pause, "I would rather not hear it. The duchess has told me all I care to know. It will be better, believe me, for the whole story to die away. If I had wished to hear it, I should have asked you to tell it me."

"It would make me happier," she said; "I should know then that there was no mistake."

"There is no mistake, my darling—the duchess has told me; and it is not likely that she has made a mistake, is it?"

"No. She knows the whole story from beginning to end. If she has told you, you know all."

"Certainly I do; and, knowing all, I have come here to beg you to make me happy, to honor me with your love, to be my Wife. Ah, Madaline, do not let your pride part us!"

He saw that she trembled and hesitated.

"Only imagine what life must be for us, Madaline, if we part. You would perhaps go on living with the duchess all your life—for, in spite of your coyness and your fear, I believe you love me so well, darling, that, unless you marry me, you will marry no one—you would drag on a weary, tried, sad, unhappy existence, that would not have in it one gleam of comfort."

"It is true," she said, slowly.

"Of course it is true. And what would become of me? The sun would have no more brightness for me; the world would be as a desert; the light would die from my life. Oh, Madaline, make me happy by loving me!"

"I do love you," she said, unguardedly.

"Then why not be my wife?"

She drew back trembling, her face pale as death.

"Why not be my wife?" he repeated.

"It is for your own sake," she said. "Can you not see? Do you not understand?"

"For my sake. Then I shall treat you as a vanquished kingdom—I shall take possession of you, my darling, my love!"

Bending down, he kissed her face—and this time she made no resistance to his sovereign will.

"Now," said Lord Arleigh, triumphantly, "you are my very own, nothing can separate us—that kiss seals our betrothal; you must forget all doubts, all fears, all hesitation, and only say to yourself that you are mine—all mine. Will you be happy, Madaline?"

She raised her eyes to his, her face bedewed with happy tears.

"I should be most ungrateful if I were not happy," she replied; "you are so good to me, Lord Arleigh."

"You must not call me 'Lord Arleigh'—say 'Norman.'"

"Norman," she repeated, "you are so good to me."

"I love you so well, sweet," he returned.

The happy eyes were raised to his face.

"Will you tell me," she asked, "why you love me, Norman? I cannot think why it is. I wonder about it every day. You see girls a thousand times better suited to you than I am. Why do you love me so?"

"What a question to answer, sweet! How can I tell why I love you? I cannot help it; my soul is attracted to your soul, my heart to your heart, Madaline. I shall be unwilling to leave you again; when I go away from Verdun Royal, I shall want to take my wife with me."

She looked at him in alarm.

"I am quite serious," he continued. "You are so sensitive, so full of hesitation, that, if I leave you, you will come to the conclusion that you have done wrong, and will write me a pathetic little letter, and go away."

"No, I shall not do that," she observed.

"I shall not give you a chance, my own; I shall neither rest myself nor let any one else rest until you are my wife. I will not distress you now by talking about it. I shall go to the duchess to-day, and tell her that you have relented in my favor at last; then you will let us decide for you, Madaline, will you not?"

"Yes," she replied, with a smile; "it would be useless for me to rebel."

"You have made some very fatal admissions," he said, laughingly. "You have owned that you love me; after that, denial, resistance, coyness, shyness, nothing will avail. Oh, Madaline, I shall always love this spot where I won you! I will have a picture of this brook-side painted some day. We must go back to the house now; but, before we go, make me happy; tell me of your own free will that you love me."

"You know I do. I love you, Norman—I will say it now—I love you ten thousand times better than my life. I have loved you ever since I first saw you; but I was afraid to say so, because of—well, you know why."

"You are not afraid now, Madaline?"

"No, not now," she replied; "you have chosen me from all the world to be your wife. I will think of nothing but making you happy."

"In token of that, kiss me—just once—of your own free will."

"No," she refused, with a deep blush.

"You will, if you love me," he said; and then she turned her face to his. She raised her pure, sweet lips to his and kissed him, blushing as she did so to the very roots of her golden hair.

"You must never ask me to do that again," she said, gravely.

"No," returned he; "it was so remarkably unpleasant, Madaline, I could not wish for a repetition;" and then they went back to the house together.

"Norman," said Madaline, as they stood before the great Gothic porch, "will you wait until to-morrow before you tell the duchess?"

"No," he laughed, "I shall tell her this very day."

Chapter XXII.

It was almost noon before Lord Arleigh saw Philippa, and then it struck him that she was not looking well. She seemed to have lost some of her brilliant color, and he fancied she was thinner than she used to be. She had sent for him to her *boudoir*.

"I heard that you were inquiring for me, Norman," she said. "Had you any especial reason for so doing?"

"Yes," he replied, "I have a most important reason. But you are not looking so bright as usual, Philippa. Are you not well?"

"The weather is too warm for one to look bright," she said, "much sunshine always tires me. Sit down here, Norman; my room looks cool enough, does it not?"

In its way her room was a triumph of art; the hangings were of pale amber and white—there was a miniature fountain cooling the air with its spray, choice flowers emitting sweet perfume. The fair young duchess was resting on a couch of amber satin; she held a richly-jeweled fan in her hands, which she used occasionally. She looked very charming in her dress of light material, her dark hair carelessly but artistically arranged. Still there was something about her unlike herself; her lips were pale, and her eyes had in them a strange, wistful expression. Norman took his seat near the little conch.

"I have come to make a confession, Philippa," he began.

"So I imagined; you look very guilty. What is it?"

"I have found my ideal. I love her, she loves me, and I want to marry her."

The pallor of the lovely lips deepened. For a few minutes no sound was heard except the falling of the spray of the fountain and then the Duchess of Hazlewood looked up and said:

"Why do you make this confession to me, Norman?"

"Because it concerns some one in whom you are interested. It is Madaline whom I love, Madaline whom I wish to marry. But that is not strange news to you, I am sure, Philippa."

Again there was a brief silence; and then the duchess said, in a low voice:

"You must admit that I warned you, Norman, from the very first."

He raised his head proudly.

"You warned me? I do not understand."

"I kept her out of your sight. I told you it would be better for you not to see her. I advised you, did I not?"

She seemed rather to be pleading in self-defense than thinking of him.

"But, my dearest Philippa, I want no warning—I am very happy as to the matter I have nearest my heart. I thank you for bringing my sweet Madaline here. You do not seem to understand?"

She looked at him earnestly.

"Do you love her so very much, Norman?"

"I love her better than any words of mine can tell," he said. "The moment I saw her first I told you my dream was realized—I had found my ideal. I have loved her ever since."

"How strange!" murmured the duchess.

"Do you think it strange? Remember how fair and winsome she is—how sweet and gentle. I do not believe there is any one like her."

The white hand that, held the jeweled fan moved more vigorously.

"Why do you tell me this, Norman? What do you wish me to do?"

"You have always been so kind to me," he said, "you have ever been as a sister, my best, dearest, truest friend. I could not have a feeling of this kind without telling you of it. Do you remember how you used to tease me about my ideal. Neither of us thought in those days that I should find her under your roof."

"No," said the duchess, quietly, "it is very strange."

"I despaired of winning Madaline," he continued. "She had such strange ideas of the wonderful distance between us—she thought so much more of me than of herself, of the honor of my family and my name—that, to tell you the truth, Philippa, I thought I should never win her consent to be my wife."

"And you have won it at last," she put in, with quiet gravity.

"Yes—at last. This morning she promised to be my wife."

The dark eyes looked straight into his own.

"It is a miserable marriage for you, Norman. Granted that Madaline has beauty, grace, purity, she is without fortune, connection, position. You, an Arleigh of Beechgrove, ought to do better. I am speaking as the world will speak. It is really a wretched marriage."

"I can afford to laugh at the world to please myself in the choice of a wife. There are certain circumstances under which I would not have married any one; these circumstances do not surround my darling. She stands out clear and distinct as a bright jewel from the rest of the world. To-day she promised to be my wife, but she is so sensitive and hesitating that I am almost afraid I shall lose her even now, and I want to marry her as soon as I can."

"But why," asked the duchess, "do you tell me this?"

"Because it concerns you most nearly. She lives under your roof—she is, in some measure, your protégée."

"Vere will be very angry when he hears of it," said the duchess. And then Lord Arleigh looked up proudly.

"I do not see why he should. It is no business of his."

"He will think it so strange."

"It is no stranger than any other marriage," said Lord Arleigh. "Philippa, you disappoint me. I expected more sympathy at least from you."

The tone of his voice was so full of pain that she looked up quickly.

"Do you think me unkind, Norman? You could not expect any true friend of yours to be very delighted at such a marriage as this, could you?" It seemed as though she knew and understood that opposition made his own plan seem only the dearer to him. "Still I have no wish to fail in sympathy. Madaline is very lovely and very winning—I have a great affection for her—and I think—nay, I am quite sure—that she loves you very dearly."

"That is better—that is more like your own self, Philippa. You used to be above all conventionality. I knew that in the depths of your generous heart you would be pleased for your old friend to be happy at last—and I shall be happy, Philippa. You wish me well, do you not?"

Her lips seemed hard and dry as she replied:

"Yes, I wish you well."

"What I wished to consult you about is my marriage. It must not take place here, of course. I understand, and think it only natural, that the duke does not wish to have public attention drawn to Madaline. We all like to keep our little family secrets; consequently I have thought of a plan which I believe will meet all the difficulties of the case."

The pallor of the duchess' face deepened.

"Are you faint or ill, Philippa?" he asked, wondering at her strange appearance.

"No," she replied, "it is only the heat that affects me. Go on with your story, Norman; it interests me."

"That is like my dear old friend Philippa. I thought a marriage from here would not do—it would entail publicity and remark; that none of us would care for—besides, there could hardly be a marriage under your auspices during the absence of the duke."

"No, it would hardly be *en règle*," she agreed.

"But," continued Norman, "if Lady Peters would befriend me—if she would go away to some quiet sea-side place, and take Madaline with her—then, at the end of a fortnight, I might join them there, and we could be married, with every due observance of conventionality, but without calling undue public attention to the ceremony. Do you not think that a good plan, Philippa?"

"Yes," she said slowly.

"Look interested in it, or you will mar my happiness. Why, if it were your marriage, Philippa, I should consider every detail of high importance. Do not look cold or indifferent about it."

She roused herself with a shudder.

"I am neither cold nor indifferent," she said—"on the contrary I am vitally interested. You wish me, of course, to ask Lady Peters if she will do this?"

"Yep, because I know she will refuse you nothing."

"Then that is settled," said the duchess. "There is a pretty, quiet little watering-place called St. Mildred's—I remember hearing Vere speak of it last year—which would meet your wishes, I think, if Lady Peters and Madaline consent."

"I am sure they will consent," put in Lord Arleigh hopefully.

"There is another thing to be thought of," said the duchess—"a *trousseau* for the fair young bride."

"Yes, I know. She will have every fancy gratified after our marriage, but there will not be time for much preparations before it."

"Let me be fairy godmother," said the duchess. "In three weeks from to-day I engage to have such a *trousseau* as has rarely been seen. You can add dresses and ornaments to it afterward."

"You are very good. Do you know," he said, "that it is only now that I begin to recognize my old friend? At first you seemed so unsympathetic, so cold—now you are my sister Philippa the sharer of my joys and sorrows. We had no secrets when we were children."

"No," she agreed, mournfully, "none."

"And we have none now," he said, with a happy laugh. "How astonished Vere will be when he returns and finds that Madaline is married! And I think that, if it can be all arranged without any great blow to his family pride, he will not be ill-pleased."

"I should think not," she returned, listlessly.

"And you, Philippa—you will extend to my beloved wife the friendship and affection that you have given to me?"

"Yes," she replied, absently.

"Continue to be her fairy-godmother. There is no friend who can do as you can do. You will be Madaline's sheet-anchor and great hope."

She turned away with a shudder.

"Philippa," he continued, "will you let me send Lady Peters to you now, that I may know as soon as possible whether she consents?"

"You can send her if you will, Norman."

Was it his fancy, or did he really, as he stood at the door, hear a deep, heart-broken sigh? Did her voice, in a sad, low wail, come to him—"Norman, Norman!"

He turned quickly, but she seemed already to have forgotten him, and was looking through the open window.

Was it his fancy again, when the door had closed, or did she really cry—"Norman!" He opened the door quickly.

"Did you call me, Philippa?" he asked.

"No," she replied; and he went away.

"I do not understand it," he thought; "there is something not quite right. Philippa is not like herself."

Then he went in search of Lady Peters, whom he bewildered and astonished by telling her that it lay in her power to make him the happiest of men.

"That is what men say when they make an offer of marriage," she observed; "and I am sure you are not about to make one to me."

172

"No; but, dear Lady Peters, I want you to help me marry some one else. Will you go to the duchess? She will tell you all about it."

"Why not tell me yourself?" she asked.

"She has better powers of persuasion," he replied, laughingly.

"Then I am afraid, if so much persuasion is required, that something wrong is on the *tapis*," said Lady Peters. "I cannot imagine why men who have beautiful young wives go yachting. It seems to me a terrible mistake."

Lord Arleigh laughed.

"The duke's yachting has very little to do with this matter," he said. "Lady Peters, before you listen to the duchess, let me make one appeal to you. With all my heart I beseech you to grant the favor that she will ask."

He bent his handsome head, and kissed her hand, while emotion rose to the lady's eyes.

"Is it something for you, Lord Arleigh?" she asked.

"Yes," he replied, "for my own unworthy self."

"Then I will do it if possible," she replied.

But when the Duchess of Hazlewood had told her what was needed, and had placed the whole matter before her, Lady Peters looked shocked.

"My dear Philippa," she said, "this is terrible. I could not have believed it. She is a lovely, graceful, pure-minded girl, I know; but such a marriage for an Arleigh! I cannot believe it."

"That is unfortunate," said her grace, dryly, "for he seems very much in earnest."

"No money, no rank, no connections, while he is one of the finest matches in England."

"She is his ideal," was the mocking reply. "It is not for us to point out deficiencies."

"But what will the duke say?" inquired her ladyship, anxiously.

"I do not suppose that he will be very much surprised. Even if he is, he will have had time to recover from his astonishment before he returns. The duke knows that 'beauty leads man at its will.' Few can resist the charm of a pretty face"

"What shall I do?" asked Lady Peters, hopelessly. "What am I to say?"

"Decide for yourself. I decline to offer any opinion. I say simply that if you refuse he will probably ask the favor of some one else."

"But do you advise me to consent, Philippa?" inquired Lady Peters, anxiously.

"I advise you to please yourself. Had he asked a similar favor of me, I might have granted or I might have refused it; I cannot say."

"To think of that simple, fair-faced girl being Lady Arleigh!" exclaimed Lady Peters. "I suppose that I had better consent, or he will do something more desperate. He is terribly in earnest, Philippa."

"He is terribly in love," said the duchess, carelessly, and then Lady Peters decided that she would accede to Lord Arleigh's request.

Chapter XXIII.

More than once during the week that ensued after his proposal of marriage to Madaline, Lord Arleigh looked in wonder at the duchess. She seemed so unlike herself—absent, brooding, almost sullen. The smiles, the animation, the vivacity, the wit, the brilliant repartee that had distinguished her had all vanished. More than once he asked her if she was ill; the answer was always "No." More than once he asked her if she was unhappy; the answer was always the same—"No."

"You are miserable because your husband is not here," he said to her one day, compassionately. "If you had known how much you would have missed him, you would not have let him go."

There was a wondrous depth of pain in the dark eyes raised to his.

"I wish he had not gone," she said; "from the very depths of my heart I wish that." Then she seemed to recover her natural gayety. "I do not know, though, why I should have detained him," she said, half laughingly. "He is so fond of yachting."

"You must not lose all your spirits before he returns, Philippa, or he will say we have been but sorry guardians."

"No one has ever found fault with my spirits before," said the duchess. "You are not complimentary, Norman."

"You give me such a strange impression," he observed. "Of course it is highly ridiculous, but if I did not know you as well as I do, I should think that you had something on your mind, some secret that was making you unhappy—that there was a struggle always going on between something you would like to do and something you are unwilling to do. It is an absurd idea, I know, yet it has taken possession of me."

She laughed, but there was little music in the sound.

"What imaginative power you have, Norman! You would make your fortune as a novelist. What can I have to be unhappy about? Should you think that any woman has a lot more brilliant than mine? See how young I am for my position—how entirely I have my own way! Could any one, do you think, be more happy than I?"

"No, perhaps not," he replied.

So the week passed, and at the end of it Lady Peters went with Madaline to St. Mildred's. At first the former had been unwilling to go—it had seemed to her a terrible *mésalliance*, but, woman-like, she had grown interested in the love-story—she had learned to understand the passionate love that Lord Arleigh had for his fair-haired bride. A breath of her own youth swept over her as she watched them.

It might be a *mésalliance*, a bad match, but it was decidedly a case of true love, of the truest love she had ever witnessed; so that her dislike to the task before her melted away.

After all, Lord Arleigh had a perfect right to please himself—to do as he would; if he did not think Madaline's birth placed her greatly beneath him, no one else need suggest such a thing. From being a violent opponent of the marriage, Lady Peters became one of its most strenuous supporters. So they went away to St. Mildred's, where the great tragedy of Madaline's life was to begin.

On the morning that she went way, the duchess sent for her to her room. She told her all that she intended doing as regarded the elaborate and magnificent *trousseau* preparing for her. Madaline was overwhelmed.

"You are too good to me," she said—"you spoil me. How am I to thank you?"

"Your wedding-dress—plain, simple, but rich, to suit the occasion— will be sent to St. Mildred's," said the duchess—"also a handsome traveling costume; but all the rest of the packages can be sent to Beechgrove. You will need them only there."

Madaline kissed the hand extended to her.

"I shall never know how to thank you," she said.

A peculiar smile came over the darkly-beautiful face.

"I think you will," returned the duchess "I can imagine what blessings you will some day invoke on my name."

Then she withdrew her hand suddenly from the touch of the pure sweet lips.

"Good-by, Madaline," she said; and it was long before the young girl saw the fair face of the duchess again.

Just as she was quitting the room Philippa placed a packet in her hand.

"You will carefully observe the directions given in this?" she said; and Madaline promised to do so.

The time at St. Mildred's soon passed. It was a quiet, picturesque village, standing at the foot of a green hill facing the bay. There was little to be seen, except the shining sea and the blue sky. An old church, called St. Mildred's, stood on the hill-top. Few strangers ever visited the little watering-place. The residents were people who preferred quiet and beautiful scenery to everything else. There was a hotel, called the Queen's, where the few strangers that came mostly resided; and just facing the sea stood a newly-built terrace of houses called Sea View, where other visitors also sojourned.

It was just the place for lovers' dreams—a shining sea, golden sands, white cliffs with little nooks and bays, pretty and shaded walks on the hill-top.

Madaline's great happiness was delightful to see. The fair face grew radiant in its loveliness; the blue eyes shone brightly. There was the delight, too, every day of inspecting the parcels that arrived one after the other; but the greatest pleasure of all was afforded by the wedding-dress. It was plain, simple, yet, in its way, a work of art—a rich white silk with little lace or trimming, yet looking so like a wedding-dress that no one could mistake it. There were snowy gloves and shoes—in fact everything was perfect, selected by no common taste, the gift of no illiberal hand. Was it foolish of her to kiss the white folds while the tears filled her eyes, and to think of herself that she was the happiest creature under the sun? Was it foolish of her to touch the pretty bridal robes with soft, caressing fingers, as though they were some living thing that she loved—to place them where the sunbeams fell on them, to admire them in every different fold and arrangement?

Then the eventful day came—Lord Arleigh and Madaline were to be married at an early hour.

"Not," said Lord Arleigh, proudly, "that there is any need for concealment—why should there be?—but you see, Lady Peters if it were known that it was my wedding-day, I have so many friends, so many relatives, that privacy would be impossible for us; therefore the world has not been enlightened as to when I intended to claim my darling for my own."

"It is a strange marriage for an Arleigh," observed Lady Peters—"the first of its kind, I am sure. But I think you are right—your plan is wise."

All the outward show made at the wedding consisted in the rapid driving of a carriage from the hotel to the church—a carriage containing two ladies—one young, fair, charming as a spring morning, the other older, graver, and more sedate.

The young girl was fair and sweet, her golden hair shining through the marriage vail, her blue eyes wet with unshed tears, her face flushed with daintiest rose-leaf bloom.

It was a pleasant spectacle to see the dark, handsome face of her lover as he greeted her, the love that shone in his eyes, the pride of his manner, as though he would place her before the whole world, and defy it to produce one so graceful or so fair. Lady Peters' face softened and her heart beat as she walked up to the altar with them. This was true love.

So the grand old words of the marriage-service were pronounced—they were promised to each other for better for worse, for weal for woe—never to part until death parted them—to be each the other's world.

It was the very morning for a bride. Heaven and earth smiled their brightest, the sunshine was golden, the autumn flowers bloomed fair, the autumn foliage had assumed its rich hues of crimson and of burnished gold; there was a bright light over the sea and the hill-tops.

Only one little *contretemps* happened at the wedding. Madaline smiled at it. Lord Arleigh was too happy even to notice it, but Lady Peters grew pale at the occurrence; for, according to her old-fashioned ideas, it augured ill.

Just as Lord Arleigh was putting the ring on the finger of his fair young bride, it slipped and fell to the ground. The church was an old-fashioned one, and there were graves and vaults all down the aisle. Away rolled the little golden ring, and when Lord Arleigh stooped down he could not see it. He was for some minutes searching for it, and then he found it—it had rolled into the hollow of a large letter on one of the level grave-stones.

Involuntarily he kissed it as he lifted it from the ground; it was too cruel for anything belonging to that fair young bride to have been brought into contact with death. Lady Peters noted the little incident with a shudder, Madaline merely smiled. Then the ceremony was over—Lord Arleigh and Madaline were man and wife. It seemed to him that the whole world around him was transformed.

They walked out of the church together, and when they stood in the sunlight he turned to her.

"My darling, my wife," he said, in an impassioned voice, "may Heaven send to us a life bright as this sunshine, love as pure—life and death together! I pray Heaven that no deeper cloud may come over our lives than there is now in the sky above us."

These words were spoken at only eleven in the morning. If he had known all that he would have to suffer before eleven at night, Lord Arleigh, with all his bravery, all his chivalry, would have been ready to fling himself from the green hill-top into the shimmering sea.

Chapter XXIV.

It was the custom of the Arleighs to spend their honeymoon at home; they had never fallen into the habit of making themselves uncomfortable abroad. The proper place, they considered, for a man to take his young wife to was home; the first Lord Arleigh had done so, and each lord had followed this sensible example. Norman, Lord Arleigh, had not dreamed of making any change. True, he had planned with his fair young bride that when the autumn month had passed away they would go abroad, and not spend the winter in cold, foggy England. They had talked of the cities they would visit — and Madaline's sweet eyes had grown brighter with happy thoughts. But that was not to be yet; they were to go home first, and when they had learned something of what home-life would be together, then they could go abroad.

Lady Peters went back to Verdun Royal on the same morning; her task ended with the marriage. She took back with her innumerable messages for the duchess. As she stood at the carriage-door, she — so little given to demonstration — took the young wife into her arms.

"Good-by, Madaline — or I should say now, Lady Arleigh — good-by, and may Heaven bless you! I did not love you at first, my dear, and I thought my old friend was doing a foolish thing; but now I love you with all my heart; you are so fair and wise, so sweet and pure, that in making you his wife he has chosen more judiciously than if he had married the daughter of a noble house. That is my tribute to you, Madaline; and to it I add, may Heaven bless you, and send you a happy life!"

Then they parted; but, as she went home through all the glory of the sunlit day, Lady Peters did not feel quite at ease.

"I wish," she said to herself, "that he had not dropped the Wedding-ring; it has made me feel uncomfortable."

Bride and bridegroom had one of the blithest, happiest journeys ever made. What cloud could rise in such a sky as theirs. They were blessed with youth, beauty, health; there had been no one to raise the least opposition to their marriage; before them stretched a long golden future.

The carriage met them at the station, it was then three in the afternoon, and the day continued fair.

"We will have a long drive through the park, Madaline," said Lord Arleigh. "You will like to see your new home."

So, instead of going direct to the mansion, they turned off from the main avenue to make a tour of the park.

"Now I understand why this place is called Beechgrove," said Madaline, suddenly. "I have never seen such trees in my life."

She spoke truly. Giant beech-trees spread out their huge boughs on all sides. They were trees of which any man would have been proud, because of their beauty and magnificence. Presently from between the trees she saw the mansion itself, Lord Arleigh touched his young wife's arm gently.

"My darling," he said, "that is home."

Her face flushed, her eyes brightened, the sensitive lips quivered.

"Home!" she repeated. "How sweet the word sounds to me!" With a tremulous smile she raised her face to his. "Nor man," she said, "do you know that I feel very much as Lady Burleigh, the wife of Lord Burleigh, of Stamford-town, must have felt."

"But you, Madaline," he laughed, "are not quite the simple maiden—he wooed and won. You have the high-bred grace of a lady—nothing could rob you of that."

"She must have been lovely and graceful to have won Lord Burleigh," she remarked.

"Perhaps so, but not like you, Madaline—there has never been any one quite like you. I shall feel tempted to call you 'Lady Burleigh.' Here we are at home; and, oh, my wife, my darling, how sweet the coming home is!"

The carriage stopped at the grand entrance. Wishing to spare his young wife all fatigue and embarrassment, Lord Arleigh had not dispatched the news of his marriage home, so that no one at Beechgrove expected to see Lady Arleigh. He sent at once for the housekeeper, a tall, stately dame, who came into the dining-room looking in unutterable amazement at the beautiful, blushing young face.

"Mrs. Chatterton," he said, "I wish to introduce you to my wife, Lady Arleigh."

The stately dame curtesied almost to the ground.

"Welcome home, my Lady," she said, deferentially. "If I had known that your ladyship was expected I would have made more befitting preparations."

"Nothing could be better—you have everything in admirable order," responded Lord Arleigh, kindly.

Then the housekeeper turned with a bow to her master.

"I did not know that you were married, my lord," she said.

"No, Mrs. Chatterton; for reasons of my own, I hurried on my marriage. No one shall lose by the hurry, though"—which she knew meant a promise of handsome bounty.

Presently the housekeeper went with Lady Arleigh to her room.

The grandeur and magnificence of the house almost startled her. She felt more like Lady Burleigh than ever, as she went up the broad marble staircase and saw the long corridors with the multitude of rooms.

"His lordship wrote to tell me to have all the rooms in the western wing ready," said Mrs. Chatterton; "but he did not tell why. They are splendid rooms, my lady—large, bright and cheerful. They look over the beautiful beeches in the park, from which the place takes its name. Of course you will have what is called Lady Arleigh's suite."

As she spoke Mrs. Chatterton threw open the door, and Lady Arleigh saw the most magnificent rooms she had ever beheld in her life—a *boudoir* all blue silk and white lace, a spacious sleeping-chamber daintily hung with pink satin, a dressing-room that was a marvel of elegance, and a small library, all fitted with the greatest luxury.

"This is the finest suite of rooms in the house," said the housekeeper; "they are always kept for the use of the mistress of Beechgrove. Has your ladyship brought your maid?"

"No," replied Lady Arleigh; "the fact is I have not chosen one. The Duchess of Hazlewood promised to find one for me."

The illustrious name pleased the housekeeper. She had felt puzzled at the quiet marriage, and the sudden home-coming. If the new mistress of Beechgrove was an intimate friend of her Grace of Hazlewood's, as her words seemed to imply, then all must be well.

When Lady Arleigh had changed her traveling-dress, she went down-stairs. Her young husband looked up in a rapture of delight.

"Oh, Madaline," he said, "how long have you been away from me? It seems like a hundred hours, yet I do not suppose it has been one. And how fair you look, my love! That cloudy white robe suits your golden hair and your sweet face, which has the same soft, sweet expression as when I saw you first; and those pretty shoulders of yours gleam like polished marble through the lace. No dress could be more coquettish or prettier."

The wide hanging sleeves were fastened back from the shoulders with buttons of pearl, leaving the white, rounded arms bare; a bracelet of pearls—Lady Peters' gift—was clasped round the graceful neck; the waves of golden hair, half loose, half carelessly fastened, were like a crown on the beautiful head.

"I am proud of my wife," he said. "I know that no fairer Lady Arleigh has ever been at Beechgrove. When we have dined, Madaline, I will take you to the picture-gallery, and introduce you to my ancestors and ancestresses."

A *récherché* little dinner had been hastily prepared, and was served in the grand dining-room. Madaline's eyes ached with the dazzle of silver plate, the ornaments and magnificence of the room.

"Shall I ever grow accustomed to all this?" she asked herself. "Shall I ever learn to look upon it as my own? I am indeed bewildered."

Yet her husband admired her perfect grace and self-possession. She might have been mistress of Beechgrove all her life for any evidence she gave to the contrary. His pride in her increased every moment; there was no one like her.

"I have never really known what 'home' meant before, Madaline," he said. "Imagine sitting opposite to a beautiful vision, knowing all the time that it is your wife. My own wife—there is magic in the words."

And she, in her sweet humility, wondered why Heaven had so richly blessed her, and what she had done that the great, passionate love of this noble man should be hers. When dinner was ended he asked her if she was tired.

"No," she answered, laughingly; "I have never felt less fatigued."

"Then I should like to show you over the house," he said—"my dear old home. I am so proud of it, Madaline; you understand what I mean—proud of its beauty; its antiquity—proud that no shadow of disgrace has ever rested on it. To others these are simply ancient gray walls; to me they represent the honor, the stainless repute, the unshadowed dignity of my race. People may sneer if they will, but to me there seems nothing so sacred as love of race—jealousy of a stainless name."

"I can understand and sympathize with you," she said, "although the feeling is strange to me."

"Not quite strange, Madaline. Your mother had a name, dear, entitled to all respect. Now come with me, and I will introduce you to the long line of the Ladies Arleigh."

They went together to the picture-gallery, and as they passed through the hall Madaline heard the great clock chiming.

"Ah, Norman," she said, listening to the chimes, "how much may happen in one day, however short that day may be."

Chapter XXV.

The picture-gallery was one of the chief attractions of Beechgrove; like the grand old trees, it had been the work of generations. The Arleighs had always been great patrons of the fine arts; many a lord of Beechgrove had expended what was a handsome fortune in the purchase of pictures. The gallery itself was built on a peculiar principal; it went round the whole of the house, extending from the eastern to the western wing—it was wide, lofty, well-lighted, and the pictures were well hung. In wet weather the ladies of the house used it as a promenade. It was filled with art-treasures of all kinds, the accumulation of many generations. From between the crimson velvet hangings white marble statues gleamed, copies of the world's great masterpieces; there were also more modern works of art. The floor was of the most exquisite parquetry; the seats and lounges were soft and luxurious; in the great windows east and west there stood a small fountain, and the ripple of the water sounded like music in the quietude of the gallery. One portion of it was devoted entirely to family portraits. They were a wonderful collection perhaps one of the most characteristic in England.

Lord Arleigh and his young wife walked through the gallery.

"I thought the gallery at Verdun Royal the finest in the world," she said; "it is nothing compared to this."

"And this," he returned, "is small, compared with the great European galleries."

"They belong to nations; this belongs to an individual," she said—"there is a difference."

Holding her hand in his, he led her to the long line of fair-faced women. As she stood, the light from the setting sun falling on her fair face and golden hair, he said to himself that he had no picture in his gallery one-half so exquisite.

"Now," he said, "let me introduce you to the ladies of my race."

At that moment the sunbeams that had been shining on the wall died out suddenly. She looked up, half laughingly.

"I think the ladies of your race are frowning on me, Norman," she said.

"Hardly that; if they could but step down from their frames, what a stately company they would make to welcome you!"

And forthwith he proceeded to narrate their various histories.

"This resolute woman," he said, "with the firm lips and strong, noble face, lived in the time of the Roses; she held this old hall against her foes for three whole weeks, until the siege was raised, and the enemy retired discomfited."

"She was a brave woman," remarked Lady Arleigh.

"This was a heroine," he went on—"Lady Alicia Arleigh; she would not leave London when the terrible plague raged there. It is supposed that she saved numberless lives; she devoted herself to the nursing of the sick, and when all the fright and fear had abated, she found herself laden with blessings, and her name honored throughout the land. This is Lady Lola, who in time of riot went out unattended, unarmed, quite alone, and spoke to three or four hundred of the roughest men in the country; they had come, in the absence of her husband, to sack and pillage the Hall—they marched back again, leaving it untouched. This, Lady Constance, is a lineal descendant of Lady Nethsdale—the brave Lady Nethsdale." She clung to his arm as she stood there.

"Oh, Norman," she said, "do you mean that my portrait, too, will hang here?"

"I hope so, my darling, very soon."

"But how can I have a place among all these fair and noble women," she asked, with sad humility—"I whose ancestors have done nothing to deserve merit or praise? Why, Norman, in the long years to come, when some Lord Arleigh brings home his wife, as you have brought me, and they stand together before my picture as I stand before these, the young wife will ask: 'Who was this?' and the answer will be: 'Lady Madaline Arleigh.' She will ask again: 'Who was she?' And what will the answer be? 'She was no one of importance; she had neither money, rank, nor aught else.'"

He looked at the bent face near him.

"Nay, my darling, not so. That Lord Arleigh will be able to answer: 'She was the flower of the race; she was famed for her pure, gentle life, and the good example she gave to all around her; she was beloved by rich and poor.' That is what will be said of you, my Madaline."

"Heaven make me worthy!" she said, humbly. And then they came to a picture that seemed to strike her.

"Norman," she said, "that face is like the Duchess of Hazlewood's."

"Do you think so, darling? Well, there is perhaps a faint resemblance."

"It lies in the brow and in the chin," she said. "How beautiful the duchess is!" she continued. "I have often looked at her till her face seemed to dazzle me."

"I know some one who is far more beautiful in my eyes," he returned.

"Norman," she said, half hesitatingly, "do you know one thing that I have thought so strange?"

"No, I have not been trusted with many of your thoughts yet," he returned.

189

"I have wondered so often why you never fell in love with the duchess."

"Fate had something better in store for me," he said, laughing.

She looked surprised.

"You cannot mean that you really think I am better than she is, Norman?"

"I do think it, darling; ten thousand times better—ten thousand times fairer in my eyes."

"Norman," she said, a sudden gleam of memory brightening her face; "I had almost forgotten—the duchess gave me this for you; I was to be sure to give it to you before the sun set on our wedding-day."

She held out a white packet sealed securely, and he took it wonderingly. He tore off the outer cover, and saw, written on the envelope:

"A wedding present from Philippa, Duchess of to Lord Arleigh. To be read alone on his wedding-day."

Chapter XXVI.

Lord Arleigh stared at the packet which his wife had given him, and again and again read the words that were inscribed on it: "A wedding present from Philippa, Duchess of Hazlewood to Lord Arleigh. To be read alone on his wedding-day." What could it mean? Philippa at times took strange caprices into her head. This seemed to be one of the strangest. He held the letter in his hand, a strange presentiment of evil creeping over him which he could not account for. From the envelope came a sweet scent, which the duchess always used. It was so familiar to him that for a few minutes it brought her vividly before him—he could have fancied her standing near him. Then he remembered the strange words: "To be read alone." What could that mean? That the letter contained something that his young wife must not see or hear.

He looked at her. She had seemingly forgotten all about the packet, and stood now, with a smile on her face, before one of the finest pictures in the gallery, wrapt in a dream of delight. There could not be anything in the letter affecting her. Still, as Philippa had written so pointedly, it would be better perhaps for him to heed her words.

"Madaline, my darling," he said, sinking on to an ottoman, "you have taken no tea. You would like some. Leave me here alone for half an hour. I want to think."

She did what she had never done voluntarily before. She went up to him, and clasped her arms round his neck. She bent her blushing face over his, and the caress surprised as much as it delighted him— she was so shyly demonstrative.

"What are you going to think about, Norman? Will it be of me?"

"Of whom else should I think on my wedding-day, if not of my wife?" he asked.

"I should be jealous if your thoughts went anywhere else," replied Madaline. "There is a daring speech, Norman. I never thought I should make such a one."

"Your daring is very delightful, Madaline; let me hear more of it."

She laughed the low, happy, contented laugh that sounded like sweetest music in his ears. "I will dare to say something else, Norman, if you will promise not to think it uncalled for. I am very happy, my darling husband—I love you very much, and I thank you for your love."

"Still better," he said, kissing the beautiful, blushing face. "Now go, Madaline. I understand the feminine liking for a cup of tea."

"Shall I send one to you?" she asked.

"No," he replied, laughingly. "You may teach me to care about tea in time. I do not yet."

He was still holding the letter in his hand, and the faint perfume was like a message from Philippa, reminding him that the missive was still unread.

"I shall not be long," said Madaline. She saw that for some reason or other he wanted to be alone.

"You will find me here," he returned. "This is a favorite Book of mine. I shall not leave it until you return."

The nook was a deep bay window from which there was a magnificent view of the famous beeches. Soft Turkish cushions and velvet lounges filled it, and near it hung one of Titian's most gorgeous pictures—a dark-eyed woman with a ruby necklace. The sun's declining rays falling on the rubies, made them appear like drops of blood. It was a grand picture, one that had been bought by the lords of Beechgrove, and the present Lord Arleigh took great delight in it.

He watched the long folds of Madaline's white dress, as she passed along the gallery, and then the hangings fell behind her. Once more he held up the packet.

"A wedding present from Philippa, Duchess of Hazlewood, to Lord Arleigh."

Whatever mystery it contained should be solved at once. He broke the seal; the envelope contained a closely-written epistle. He looked at it in wonder. What could Philippa have to write to him about? The letter began as follows:

"A wedding present from Philippa, Duchess of Hazlewood, to Norman, Lord Arleigh. You will ask what it is? My answer is, my revenge—well planned, patiently awaited.

"You have read the lines:

"'Heaven has no rage like love to hatred turned,
Nor hell a fury like a woman scorned.'

They are true. Fire, fury, and hatred rage now in my heart as I write this to you. You have scorned me—this is my revenge. I am a proud woman—I have lowered my pride to you. My lips have never willfully uttered a false word; still they have lied to you. I loved you once, Norman, and on the day my love died I knew that nothing could arise from its ashes. I loved you with a love passing that of most women; and it was not all my fault. I was taught to love you—the earliest memory of my life is having been taught to love you.

"You remember, too. It may have been injudicious, imprudent, foolish, yet while I was taught to think, to read, to sing, I was also taught to consider myself your 'little wife.' Hundreds of times have you given me that name, while we walked together as children—you with your arm about my neck, I proud of being called your 'little wife.'

193

"As a child, I loved you better than anything else in the wide world—better than my mother, my home, my friends; and my love grew with my growth. I prided myself on my unbroken troth to you. I earned the repute of being cold and heartless, because I could think of no one but you. No compliments pleased me, no praise flattered me; I studied, learned, cultivated every gift Heaven had given me— all for your sake. I thought of no future, but with you, no life but with you, no love but for you; I had no dreams apart from you. I was proud when they talked of my beauty; that you should have a fair wife delighted me.

"When you returned home I quite expected that you were coming to claim me as your wife—I thought that was what brought you to England. I remember the day you came. Ah, well, revenge helps me to live, or I should die! The first tones of your voice, the first clasp of your hand, the first look of your eyes chilled me with sorrow and disappointment. Yet I hoped against hope. I thought you were shy, perhaps more reserved than of yore. I thought everything and anything except that you had ceased to love me; I would have believed anything rather than that you were not going to fulfill our ancient contract, and make me your wife. I tried to make you talk of old times—you were unwilling; you seemed confused, embarrassed I read all those signs aright; still I hoped against hope. I tried to win you—I tried all that love, patience, gentleness, and consideration could do.

"What women bear, and yet live on! Do you know that every moment of that time was full of deadly torture to me, deadly anguish? Ah, me, the very memory of it distresses me! Every one spoke to me as though our engagement was a certainty, and our marriage settled. Yet to me there came, very slowly, the awful conviction that you had ignored, or had forgotten the old ties. I fought against that conviction. I would not entertain it. Then came for me the fatal day when I heard you tell the Duchess of Aytoun that you had never seen the woman you would care to make your wife. I heard your confession, but would not give in; I clung to the idea of winning your love, even after I had hoped against hope, and tried to make you care for me. At last came the night out on the balcony, when I resolved to risk all, to ask you for your love—do you remember it? You were advocating the cause of another; I asked you why you did not speak for yourself. You must have known that my woman's heart was on fire—you must have seen that my whole soul was in my speech, yet you told me in cold, well-chosen words that you had only a brother's affection for me. On that night, for the first time, I realized the truth that, come what might, you would never love me—that you had no idea of carrying out the old contract—that your interest in me was simply a kindly, friendly one. On that night, when I realized that truth, the better part of me died; my love—the love of my life—died; my hopes—the life-long hopes—died; the best, truest, noblest part of me died.

"When you had gone away, when I was left alone, I fell on my knees and swore to be revenged. I vowed vengeance against you, no matter what it might cost. Again let me quote to you the lines:

"'Heaven has no rage like love to hatred turned,
Nor hell a fury like a woman scorned.'

You scorned me—you must suffer for it. I swore to be revenged, but how was I to accomplish my desire? I could not see any way in which it was possible for me to make you suffer. I could not touch your heart, your affections, your fortune. The only thing that I could touch was your pride. Through your pride, your keen sensitiveness I decided to stab you; and I have succeeded! I recovered my courage and my pride together, made you believe that all that had passed had been jest, and then I told you that I was going to marry the duke. "I will say no more of my love or my sorrow. I lived only for vengeance, but how my object was to be effected I could not tell. I thought of many plans, they were all worthless—they could not hurt you as you had hurt me. At last, one day, quite accidentally I took up 'The Lady of Lyons,' and read it through. That gave me an idea of what my revenge should be like. Do you begin to suspect what this present is that the Duchess of Hazlewood intends making to you on your wedding-day?"

195

As he read on his face grew pale. What could it mean—this reference to "The Lady of Lyons?" That was the story of a deceitful marriage—surely all unlike his own.

"You are wondering. Turn the page and you shall read that, when an idea once possesses a woman's mind, she has no rest until it is carried out. I had none. My vengeance was mapped out for me—it merely required filling in. Let me show you how it was filled up—how I have lied to you, who to another have never uttered a false word.

"Years ago we had a maid whom my mother liked very much. She was gentle, well-mannered, and well-bred for her station in life. She left us, and went to some other part of England. She married badly—a handsome, reckless ne'er-do-well, who led her a most wretched life.

"I know not, and care nothing for the story of her married life, her rights and wrongs. How she becomes of interest to you lies in the fact that shortly after my marriage she called to see me and ask my aid. She had been compelled to give up her home in the country and come to London, where, with her husband and child, she was living in poverty and misery. While she was talking to me the duke came in. I think her patient face interested him. He listened to her story, and promised to do something for her husband. You will wonder how this story of Margaret Dornham concerns you. Read on. You will know in time.

"My husband having promised to assist this man, sent for him to the house; and the result of that visit was that the man seeing a quantity of plate about, resolved upon helping himself to a portion of it. To make my story short, he was caught, after having broken into the house, packed up a large parcel of plate, and filled his pockets with some of my most valuable jewels. There was no help for it but to prosecute him, and his sentence was, under the circumstances, none too heavy, being ten years' penal servitude.

"Afterward I went to see his wife Margaret, and found her in desperate circumstances; yet she had one ornament in her house—a beautiful young girl, her daughter, so fair of face that she dazzled me. The moment I saw her I thought of your description of your ideal—eyes like blue hyacinths, and hair of gold. Forthwith a plan entered my mind which I have most successfully carried out.

"I asked for the girl's name, and was told that it was Madaline—an uncommon name for one of her class—but the mother had lived among well-to-do people, and had caught some of their ideas. I looked at the girl—her face was fair, sweet, pure. I felt the power of its beauty, and only wondered that she should belong to such people at all; her hands were white and shapely as my own, her figure was slender and graceful. I began to talk to her, and found her well educated, refined, intelligent—all, in fact, that one could wish.

"Little by little their story came out—it was one of a mother's pride and glory in her only child. She worshiped her—literally worshiped her. She had not filled the girl's mind with any nonsensical idea about being a lady, but she had denied herself everything in order that Madaline might be well educated. For many years Madaline had been what is called a governess-pupil in a most excellent school. 'Let me die when I may,' said the poor, proud mother, 'I shall leave Madaline with a fortune in her own hands; her education will always be a fortune to her.'

"I asked her one day if she would let me take Madaline home with me for a few hours; she seemed delighted, and consented at once. I took the girl home, and with my own hands dressed her in one of my most becoming toilets. Her beauty was something marvelous. She seemed to gain both grace and dignity in her new attire. Shortly afterward, with her mother's permission, I sent her for six months to one of the most fashionable schools in Paris. The change wrought in her was magical; she learned as much in that time as some girls would have learned in a couple of years. Every little grace of manner seemed to come naturally to her; she acquired a tone that twenty years spent in the best of society does not give to some. Then I persuaded Vere, my husband, to take me to Paris for a few days, telling him I wanted to see the daughter of an old friend, who was at school there. In telling him that I did not speak falsely—Madaline's mother had been an old friend of mine. Then I told him that my whim was to bring Madaline home and make a companion of her; he allowed me to do just as I pleased, asking no questions about her parents, or anything else. I do not believe it ever occurred to him as strange that the name of my *protégée* and of the man who had robbed him was the same—indeed, he seemed to have forgotten all about the robbery. So I brought Madaline home to Vere Court, and then to London, where I knew that you would see her. My husband never asked any questions about her; he made no objection, no remark— everything that I did was always well done in his eyes.

"But you will understand clearly that to you I told a lie when I said that Madaline's mother was a poor relative of the duke's—you know now what relationship there is between them. Even Lady Peters does not know the truth. She fancies that Madaline is the daughter of some friend of mine who, having fallen on evil days, has been glad to send her to me.

"Knowing you well, Norman, the accomplishment of my scheme was not difficult. If I had brought Madaline to you and introduced her, you might not have been charmed; the air of mystery about her attracted you. My warning against your caring for her would, I knew, also help to allure you. I was right in every way. I saw that you fell in love with her at once—the first moment you saw her— and then I knew my revenge was secured.

"I bought my husband the yacht on purpose that he might go away and leave me to work out my plans. I knew that he could not resist the temptation I offered. I knew also that if he remained in England he would want to know all about Madaline before he allowed you to marry her. If the marriage was to take place at all, it must be during his absence. You seemed, of your own free will, Norman, to fall naturally into the web woven for you.

"I write easily, but I found it hard to be wicked—hard to see my lost love, my dear old companion, drift on to his ruin.

"More than once I paused, longing to save you; more than once I drew back, longing to tell you all. But the spirit of revenge within me was stronger than myself—my love had turned to hate. Yet I could not quite hate you, Norman—not quite. Once, when you appealed to my old friendship, when you told me of your plans, I almost gave way. 'Norman!' I cried, as you were leaving me; but when you turned again I was dumb.

"So I have taken my revenge. I, Philippa, Duchess of Hazlewood on this your wedding-day, reveal to you the first stain on the name of Arleigh—unvail the first blot on one of the noblest escutcheons in the land. You have married not only a low-born girl, but the daughter of a felon—a felon's daughter is mistress of proud Beechwood! You who scorned Philippa L'Estrange, who had the cruelty to refuse the love of a woman who loved you—you who looked for your ideal in the clouds, have found it near a prison cell! The daughter of a felon will be the mistress of the grand old house where some of the noblest ladies of the land have ruled—the daughter of a felon will be mother of the heirs of Arleigh. Could I have planned, prayed for, hoped for, longed for a sweeter revenge?

"I am indifferent as to what you may do in return. I have lived for my revenge, and now that I have tasted it life is indifferent to me. You will, of course, write to complain to the duke, and he, with his honest indignation justly aroused, will perhaps refuse to see me again. I care not; my interest in life ended when my love died.

"Let me add one thing more. Madaline herself has been deceived. I told her that you knew all her history, that I had kept nothing from you, and that you loved her in spite of it, but that she was never to mention it to you."

He read the letter with a burning flush on his face, which afterward grew white as with the pallor of death; a red mist was before his eyes, the sound of surging waters in his ears, his heart beat loud and fast. Could it be true—oh, merciful Heaven, could it be true? At first he had a wild hope that it was a cruel jest that Philippa was playing with him on his wedding-day. It could not be true—his whole soul rose in rebellion against it. Heaven was too just, too merciful—it could not be. It was a jest. He drew his breath with a long quivering sigh—his lips trembled; it was simply a jest to frighten him on his wedding day.

Then, one by one—slowly, sadly, surely—a whole host of circumstances returned to his mind, making confirmation strong. He remembered well—only too well—the scene in the balcony. He remembered the pale starlight, the light scarf thrown over Philippa's shoulders, even the very perfume that came from the flowers in her hair; he remembered how her voice had trembled, how her face had shown in the faint evening light. When she had quoted the words of *Priscilla*, the loveliest maiden of Plymouth, she had meant them as applicable to her own case—"Why don't you speak for yourself, John?" They came back to him with a fierce, hissing sound, mocking his despair. She had loved him through all—this proud, beautiful, brilliant woman for whom men of highest rank had sighed in vain. And, knowing her pride, her haughtiness, he could guess exactly what her love had cost her, and that all that followed had been a mockery. On that night her love had changed to hate. On that night she had planned this terrible revenge. Her offering of friendship had been a blind. He thought to himself that he had been foolish not to see it. A thousand circumstances presented themselves to his mind. This, then, was why Madaline had so persistently—and, to his mind, so strangely—refused his love. This was why she had talked incessantly of the distance between them—of her own unworthiness to be his wife. He bad thought that she alluded merely to her poverty, whereas it was her birth and parentage she referred to.

How cleverly, how cruelly Philippa had deceived them both— Philippa, his old friend and companion, his sister in all but name! He could see now a thousand instances in which Madaline and himself had played at cross purposes—a thousand instances in which the poor girl had alluded to her parent's sin, and he had thought she was speaking of her poverty. It was a cruel vengeance, for, before he had read the letter through, he knew that if the story were correct, she could be his wife in name only—that they must part. Poverty, obscurity, seemed as nothing now—but crime? Oh, Heaven, that his name and race should be so dishonored! If he had known the real truth, he would have died rather than have uttered one word of love to her.

The daughter of a felon—and he had brought her to Beechgrove as successor to a roll of noble women, each one of whom had been of noble birth! She was the daughter of a felon—no matter how fair, how graceful, how pure. For the first time the glory of Beechgrove was tarnished. But it would not be for long—it could not be for long; she must not remain. The daughter of a felon to be the mother of his children—ah, no, not if he went childless to the grave! Better that his name were extinct, better that the race of Arleigh should die out, than that his children should be pointed at as children with tainted blood! It could never be. He would expect the dead and gone Arleighs to rise from their graves in utter horror, he would expect some terrible curse to fall on him, were so terrible a desecration to happen. They must part. The girl he loved with all the passionate love of his heart, the fair young wife whom he worshiped must go from him, and he must see her no more. She must be his wife in name only.

He was young, and he loved her very dearly. His head fell forward on his breast, and as bitter a sob as ever left man's lips died on his. His wife in name only! The sweet face, the tender lips were not for him—yet he loved her with the whole passion and force of his soul. Then he raised his head—for he heard a sound, and knew that she was returning. Great drops of anguish fell from his brow—over his handsome face had come a terrible change; it had grown fierce with pain, haggard with despair, white with sorrow.

Looking up, he saw her—she was at the other end of the gallery; he saw the tall, slender figure and the sweeping dress—he saw the white arms with their graceful contour, the golden hair, the radiant face—and he groaned aloud; he saw her looking up at the pictures as she passed slowly along—the ancestral Arleighs of whom he was so proud. If they could have spoken, those noble women, what would they have said to this daughter of a felon?

She paused for a few minutes to look up at her favorite, Lady Alicia, and then she came up to him and stood before him in an the grace of her delicate loveliness, in all the pride of her dainty beauty. She was looking at the gorgeous Titian near him.

"Norman," she said, "the sun has turned those rubies into drops of blood—- they looked almost terrible on the white throat. What a strange picture! What a tragical face!"

Suddenly with outstretched arms she fell on her knees at his side.

"Oh, my darling, what has happened? What is the matter?"

She had been away from him only half an hour, yet it seemed to him ages since he had watched her leave the gallery with a smile on her lips.

"What is it, my darling?" she cried again. "Dear Norman, you look as though the shadow of death had passed over you. What is it?"

In another moment she had flung herself on his breast, clasped her arms round his neck, and was kissing his pale changed face as she had never done before.

"Norman, my darling husband, you are ill," she said—"ill, and you will not tell me. That is why you sent me away."

He tried to unclasp her arms, but she clung the more closely to him.

"You shall not send me away. You wish to suffer in silence? Oh, my darling, my husband, do you forget that I am your wife, for better, for worse, in sickness and in health? You shall not suffer without my knowledge."

"I am not ill, Madaline," he said, with a low moan. "It is not that."

"Then something has happened—you have been frightened."

He unclasped her arms from his neck—their caress was a torture to him.

"My poor darling, my poor wife, it is far worse than that. No man has ever seen a more ghastly specter than I have seen of death in life."

She looked round in quick alarm.

"A specter!" she cried fearfully; and then something strange in his face attracted her attention. She looked at him. "Norman," she said, slowly, "is it—is it something about me?"

How was he to tell her? He felt that it would be easier to take her out into the glorious light of the sunset and slay her than kill her with the cruel words that he must speak. How was he to tell her? No physical torture could be so great as that which he must inflict; yet he would have given his life to save her from pain.

"It is—I am quite sure," she declared, slowly—"something about me. Oh, Norman, what is it? I have not been away from you long. Yet no change from fairest day to darkest night could be so great as the change in you since I left you. You will not tell me what it is—you have taken my arms from your neck—you do not love me!"

"Do not torture me, Madaline," he said. "I am almost mad. I cannot bear much more."

"But what is it? What have I done? I who you send from you now am the same Madaline whom you married this morning—whom you kissed half an hour since. Norman, I begin to think that I am in a terrible dream."

"I would to Heaven it were a dream. I am unnerved—unmanned—I have lost my strength, my courage, my patience, my hope. Oh, Madaline, how can I tell you?"

The sight of his terrible agitation seemed to calm her; she took his hand in hers.

"Do not think of me," she said—"think of yourself. I can bear what you can bear. Let me share your trouble, whatever it may be, my husband."

He looked at the sweet, pleading face. How could he dash the light and brightness from it? How could he slay her with the cruel story he had to tell. Then, in a low, hoarse voice, he said:

"You must know all, and I cannot say it. Read this letter, Madeline, and then you will understand."

Chapter XXVII.

Slowly, wonderingly, Lady Arleigh took the Duchess of Hazlewood's letter from her husband's hands and opened it.

"Is it from the duchess?" she asked.

"Yes, it is from the duchess," replied her husband.

He saw her sink slowly down upon a lounge. Above her, in the upper panes of the window beneath which they were sitting, were the armorial bearings of the family in richest hues of stained glass. The colors and shadows fell with strange effects on her white dress, great bars of purple and crimson crossing each other, and opposite to her hung the superb Titian, with the blood-red rubies on the white throat.

Lord Arleigh watched Madaline as she read. Whatever might be the agony in his own heart, it was exceeded by hers. He saw the brightness die out of her face, the light fade from her eyes, the lips grow pale. But a few minutes before that young face had been bright with fairest beauty, eloquent with truest love, lit with passion and with poetry—now it was like a white mask.

Slowly, and as though it was with difficulty that she understood Lady Arleigh read the letter through, and then—she did not scream or cry out—she raised her eyes to his face. He saw in them a depth of human sorrow and human woe which words are powerless to express.

So they looked at each other in passionate anguish. No words passed—of what avail were they? Each read the heart of the other. They knew that they must part. Then the closely-written pages fell to the ground, and Madaline's hands clasped each other in helpless anguish. The golden head fell forward on her breast. He noticed that in her agitation and sorrow she did not cling to him as she had clung before—that she did not even touch him. She seemed by instinct to understand that she was his wife now in name only.

So for some minutes they sat, while the sunset glowed in the west. He was the first to speak.

"My dear Madaline," he said, "my poor wife"—his voice seemed to startle her into new life and new pain—"I would rather have died than have given you this pain."

"I know it—I am sure of it," she said, "but, oh, Norman, how can I release you?"

"There is happily no question about that," he answered.

He saw her rise from her seat and stretch out her arms.

"What have I done," she cried, "that I must suffer so cruelly? What have I done?"

"Madaline," said Lord Arleigh, "I do not think that so cruel a fate has ever befallen any one as has befallen us. I do not believe that any one has ever suffered so cruelly, my darling. If death had parted us, the trial would have been easier to bear."

She turned her sad eyes to him.

"It is very cruel," she said, with a shudder. "I did not think the duchess would be so cruel."

"It is more than that—it is infamous!" he cried. "It is vengeance worthier of a fiend than of a woman."

"And I loved her so!" said the young girl, mournfully. "Husband, I will not reproach you—your love was chivalrous and noble; but why did you not let me speak freely to you? I declared to you that no doubt ever crossed my mind. I thought you knew all, though I considered it strange that you, so proud of your noble birth, should wish to marry me. I never imagined that you had been deceived. The duchess told me that you knew the whole history of my father's crime, that you were familiar with every detail of it, but that you wished me never to mention it—never even ever so remotely to allude to it. I thought it strange, Norman, that one in your position should be willing to overlook so terrible a blot; but she told me your love for me was so great that you could not live without me. She told me even more—that I must try to make my own life so perfect that the truest nobility of all, the nobility of virtue, might be mine."

"Did she really tell you that?" asked Lord Arleigh wonderingly.

"Yes; and, Norman, she said that you would discuss the question with me once, and once only—that would be on my wedding-day. On that day you would ask for and I should tell the whole history of my father's crime; and after that it was to be a dead-letter, never to be named between us."

"And you believed her?" he said.

"Yes, as I believe you. Why should I have doubted her? My faith in her was implicit. Why should I have even thought you would repent? More than once I was on the point of running away. But she would not let me go. She said that I must not be cruel to you—that you loved me so dearly that to lose me would prove a death-blow. So I believed her, and, against my will, staid on."

"I wish you had told me this," he said, slowly.

She raised her eyes to his.

"You would not let me speak, Norman. I tried so often, dear, but you would not let me."

"I remember," he acknowledged; "but, oh, my darling, how little I knew what you had to say! I never thought that anything stood between us except your poverty."

They remained silent for a few minutes—such sorrow as theirs needed no words. Lord Arleigh was again the first to speak.

"Madaline," he said, "will you tell me all you remember of your life."

"Yes; it is not much. It has been such a simple life, Norman, half made up of shadows. First, I can remember being a child in some far off woodland house. I am sure it was in the woods; for I remember the nuts growing on the trees, the squirrels, and the brown hares. I remember great masses of green foliage, a running brook, and the music of wild birds. I remember small latticed windows against which the ivy tapped. My father used to come in with his gun slung across his shoulders—he was a very handsome man, Norman, but not kind to either my mother or me. My mother was then, as she is now, patient, kind, gentle, long-suffering. I have never heard her complain. She loved me with an absorbing love. I was her only comfort. I did my best to deserve her affection. I loved her too. I cannot remember that she ever spoke one unkind word to me, and I can call to mind a thousand instances of indulgence and kindness. I knew that she deprived herself of almost everything to give it to me. I have seen her eat dry bread patiently, while for me and my father there was always some little dainty. The remembrance of the happiness of my early life begins and ends with my mother. My memories of her are all pleasant." She continued as though recalling her thoughts with difficulty. "I can remember some one else. I do not know who or what he was, except that he was, I think, a doctor. He used to see me, and used to amuse me. Then there came a dark day. I cannot tell what happened, but after that day I never saw my friend again."

He was looking at her with wondering eyes.

"And you remember no more than that about him, Madaline?"

"No," she replied. "Then came a time," she went on, "when it seemed to me that my mother spent all her days and nights in weeping. There fell a terrible shadow over us, and we removed. I have no recollection of the journey—not the faintest; but I can remember my sorrow at leaving the bright green woods for a dull, gloomy city lodging. My mother was still my hope and comfort. After we came to London she insisted that, no matter what else went wrong I should have a good education; she toiled, saved, suffered for me. 'My darling must be a lady,' she used to say. She would not let me work, though I entreated her with tears in my eyes. I used to try to deceive her even, but I never could succeed. She loved me so, my poor mother. She would take my hands in hers and kiss them. 'Such dainty hands, dear,' she would say, 'must not be spoiled.' After a great deal of trouble and expense, she contrived to get me an engagement as governess-pupil in a lady's school; there I did receive a good education. One failing of my mother always filled me with wonder—she used to fancy that people watched me. 'Has any one spoken to you, darling?' she would ask. 'Has any stranger seen you?' I used to laugh, thinking it was parental anxiety; but it has struck me since as strange. While I was at the ladies' school my father committed the crime for which I—alas!—am suffering now."

"Will you tell me what the crime was?" requested Lord Arleigh.

A dreary hopelessness, inexpressibly painful to see, came over her face, and a deep-drawn sigh broke from her lips.

"I will tell you all about it," she said—"would to Heaven that I had done so before! My mother, many years ago, was in the service of Lady L'Estrange; she was her maid then. Miss L'Estrange married the Duke of Hazlewood, and, when my mother was in great difficulties, she went to the duchess to ask for employment. The duchess was always kind," continued Madaline, "and she grew interested in my mother. She came to see her, and I was at home. She told me afterward that when she first saw me she conceived a liking for me. I know now that I was but the victim of her plot."

She stopped abruptly, but Lord Arleigh encouraged her.

"Tell me all, Madaline," he said, gently; "none of this is your fault, my poor wife. Tell me all."

"The duchess was very kind to my mother, and befriended her in many ways. She interested the duke in her case, and he promised to find employment for my unfortunate father, who went to his house to see him. Whether my father had ever done wrong before, I cannot tell. Sometimes I fear that he had done so, for no man falls suddenly into crime. In few words—oh, Norman, how hard they are to say!—what he saw in the duke's mansion tempted him. He joined some burglars, and they robbed the house. My unfortunate father was found with his pockets filled with valuable jewelry. My mother would not let me read the history of the trial, but I learned the result—he was sentenced to ten years' penal servitude."

She paused again; the dreary hopelessness of her face, the pain in her voice, touched him inexpressibly.

"None of this is your fault, my darling," he said. "Go on."

"Then," she continued "the duchess was kinder than ever to my mother. She furnished her with the means of gaining her livelihood; she offered to finish my education and adopt me. My mother was at first unwilling; she did not wish me to leave her. But the duchess said that her love was selfish—that it was cruel to stand in my light when such an offer was made. She consented and I, wondering much what my ultimate fate was to be, was sent to school in Paris. When I had been there for some time, the duke and duchess came to see me. I must not forget to tell you, Norman, that she saw me herself first privately. She said he was so forgetful that he would never remember having heard the name of Dornham. She added that the keeping of the secret was very important, for, if it became known, all her kind efforts in our favor must cease at once. I promised to be most careful. The duke and duchess arranged that I was to go home with them and live as the duchess' companion. Again she warned me never upon any account to mention who I was, or anything about me. She called me the daughter of an old friend—and so I was, although that friend was a very humble one. From the first, Norman, she talked so much about you; you were the model of everything chivalrous and noble, the hero of a hundred pleasant stories. I had learned to love you long even before I saw you—to love you after a fashion, Norman, as a hero. I can see it all now. She laid the plot—we were the victims. I remember that the very morning on which you saw me first the duchess sent me into the trellised arbor; I was to wait there until she summoned me. Rely upon it, Norman, she also gave orders that you were to be shown into the morning-room, although she pretended to be annoyed at it. I can see all the plot now plainly. I can only say— — Oh, Norman, you and I were both blind! We ought to have seen through her scheme. Why should she have brought us together if she had not meant that we should love each other? What have we in common—I, the daughter of a felon; you, a nobleman, proud of your ancestry, proud of your name? Oh, Norman, if I could but die here at your feet, and save you from myself!"

Even as she spoke she sank sobbing, no longer on to his breast, no longer with her arms clasped round his neck, but at his feet.

He raised her in his arms—for he loved her with passionate love.

"Madaline," he said, in a low voice, "do not make my task harder for me. That which I have to do is indeed bitter to me—do not make it harder."

His appeal touched her. For his sake she must try to be strong.

Slowly he looked up at the long line of noblemen and women whose faces shone down upon him; slowly he looked at her graceful figure and bowed head of his wife, the daughter of a felon—the first woman who had ever entered those walls with even the semblance of a stain upon her name. As he looked at her the thought came to him that, if his housekeeper had told him that she had inadvertently placed such a person—the daughter of a felon—in his kitchen, he would never have rested until she had been sent away.

He must part from her—this lovely girl-wife whom he loved with such passionate love. The daughter of a criminal could not reign at Beechgrove. If the parting cost his life and hers it must take place. It was cruel. The strong man trembled with agitation; his lips quivered, his face was pale as death. He bent over his weeping wife.

"Madaline," he said, gently, "I do not understand the ways of destiny. Why you and I have to suffer this torture I cannot say. I can see nothing in our lives that deserves such punishment. Heaven knows best. Why we have met and loved, only to undergo such anguish, is a puzzle I cannot solve. There is only one thing plain to me, and that is that we must part."

He never forgot how she sprang away from him, her colorless face raised to his.

"Part, Norman!" she cried. "We cannot part now; I am your wife!"

"I know it; but we must part."

"Part!" repeated the girl. "We cannot; the tie that binds us cannot be sundered so easily."

"My poor Madaline, it must be."

She caught his hand in hers.

"You are jesting, Norman. We cannot be separated—we are one. Do you forget the words—'for better for worse,' 'till death us do part?'— You frighten me!" And she shrank from him with a terrible shudder.

"It must be as I have said," declared the unhappy man. "I have been deceived—so have you. We have to suffer for another's sin."

"We may suffer," she said, dully, "but we cannot part. You cannot send me away from you."

"I must," he persisted. "Darling, I speak with deepest love and pity, yet with unwavering firmness. You cannot think that, with that terrible stain resting on you, you can take your place here."

"But I am your wife!" she cried, in wild terror.

"You are my wife," he returned, with quivering lips; "but you must remain so in name only." He paused abruptly, for it seemed to him that the words burned his lips as they passed them. "My wife," he muttered, "in name only."

With a deep sob she stretched out her arms. "But I love you, Norman—you must not send me away! I love you—I shall die if I have to leave you!"

The words seemed to linger on her lips.

"My darling," he said, gently, "it is even harder for me than for you."

"No, no," she cried, "for I love you so dearly, Norman—better than my life! Darling, my whole heart went out to you long ago—you cannot give it back to me."

"If it kills you and myself too," he declared, hoarsely, "I must send you away."

"Send me away? Oh, no, Norman, not away! Let me stay with you, husband, darling. We were married only this morning My place is here by your side—I cannot go."

Looking away from her, with those passionate accents still ringing in his ears, his only answer was:

"Family honor demands it."

"Norman," she implored, "listen to me, dear! Do not send me away from you. I will be so good, so devoted. I will fulfill my duties so well, I will bear myself so worthily that no one shall remember anything against me; they shall forget my unhappy birth, and think only that you have chosen well. Oh, Norman, be merciful to me! Leaving you would be a living death!"

"You cannot suffer more than I do," he said—"and I would give my life to save you pain; but, my darling, I cannot be so false to the traditions of my race, so false to the honor of my house, so untrue to my ancestors and to myself, as to ask you to stay here. There has never been a blot on our name. The annals of our family are pure and stainless. I could not ask you to remain here and treat you as my wife, even to save my life!"

"I have done no wrong, Norman; why should you punish me so cruelly?"

"No, my darling, you have done no wrong—and the punishment is more mine than yours. I lose the wife whom I love most dearly—I lose my all."

"And what do I lose?" she moaned.

"Not so much as I do, because you are the fairest and sweetest of women. You shall live in all honor, Madaline. You shall never suffer social degradation, darling—the whole world shall know that I hold you blameless; but you can be my wife in name only."

She was silent for a few minutes, and then she held out her arms to him again.

"Oh, my love, relent!" she cried. "Do not be so hard on me—indeed, I have done no wrong. Be merciful! I am your wife; your name is so mighty, so noble, it will overshadow me. Who notices the weed that grows under the shadow of the kingly oak? Oh, my husband, let me stay! I love you so dearly—let me stay!"

The trial was so hard and cruel that great drops fell from his brow and his lips trembled.

"My darling, it is utterly impossible. We have been deceived. The consequences of that deceit must be met. I owe duties to the dead as well as to the living. I cannot transgress the rules of my race. Within these time-honored walls no woman can remain who is not of stainless lineage and stainless repute. Do not urge me further."

"Norman," she said, in a trembling voice, "you are doing wrong in sending me away. You cannot outrage Heaven's laws with impunity. It is Heaven's law that husband and wife should cleave together. You cannot break it."

"I have no wish to break it. I say simply that I shall love you until I die, but that you must be my wife in name only."

"It is bitterly hard," she observed; and then she looked up at him suddenly. "Norman," she said, "let me make one last appeal to you. I know the stigma is terrible—I know that the love-story must be hateful to you—I know that the vague sense of disgrace which clings to you even now is almost more than you can bear; but, my darling, since you say you love me so dearly, can you not bear this trial for my sake, if in everything else I please you—if I prove myself a loving, trustful, truthful wife, if I fulfill all my duties so as to reflect honor on you; if I prove a worthy mistress of your household?"

"I cannot," he replied, hoarsely; but there must have been something in his face from which she gathered hope, for she went on, with a ring of passionate love in her voice.

"If, after we had been married, I had found out that you had concealed something from me, do you think that I should have loved you less?"

"I do not think you would, Madaline; but the present case is different—entirely different; it is not for my own sake, but for the honor of my race. Better a thousand times that my name should die out than that upon it there should be the stain of crime!"

"But, Norman—this is a weak argument, I know—a woman's argument—still, listen to it, love—who would know my secret if it were well kept?"

"None; but I should know it," he replied, "and that would be more than sufficient. Better for all the world to know than for me. I would not keep such a secret. I could not. It would hang over my head like a drawn sword, and some day the sword would fall. My children, should Heaven send any to me, might grow up, and then, in the height of some social or political struggle, when man often repeats against his fellow man all that he knows of the vilest and the worst, there might be thrown into their faces the fact that they were descended from a felon. It must not be; a broken heart is hard to bear—injured honor is perhaps harder."

She drew up her slender figure to its full height, her lovely face glowed with a light he did not understand.

"You may be quite right," she said. "I cannot dispute what you say. Your honor may be a sufficient reason for throwing aside the wife of less than twelve hours, but I cannot see it. I cannot refute what you have said, but my heart tells me you are wrong."

"Would to Heaven that I thought the same!" he rejoined, quickly. "But I understand the difficulties of the case, my poor Madaline, and you do not."

She turned away with a low, dreary sigh, and the light died from her face.

"Madaline," said Lord Arleigh, quietly, "do not think, my darling, that you suffer most—indeed, it is not so. Think how I love you—think how precious you are to me—and then ask yourself if it is no pain to give you up."

"I know it is painful," she continued, sadly, "but, Norman, if the decision and choice rested with me as they do with you, I should act differently."

"I would, Heaven knows, if I could," he said, slowly.

"Such conduct is not just to me," she continued, her face flushing with the eagerness of her words. "I have done no wrong, no harm, yet I am to be driven from your house and home—I am to be sent away from you, divorced in all but name. I say it is not fair, Norman—not just. All my womanhood rises in rebellion against such a decree. What will the world say of me? That I was weighed in the balance and found wanting—that I was found to be false or light, due doubtless to my being lowly born. Do you think I have no sense of honor—no wish to keep my name and fame stainless? Could you do me a greater wrong, do you think, than to put me away, not twelve hours after our marriage, like one utterly unworthy?"

He made no answer. She went on in her low, passionate, musical voice.

"When I read in history the story of Anne of Cleves, I thought it cruel to be sought in marriage, brought over from another land, looked at, sneered at, and dismissed; but, Norman, it seems to me her fate was not so cruel as mine."

"You are wrong," he cried. "I hold you in all reverence, all honor, in deepest respect. You are untouched by the disgrace attached to those nearest to you. It is not that. You know that, even while I say we must part, I love you from the very depths of my heart."

"I can say no more," she moaned, wringing her hands. "My own heart, my woman's instinct, tells me you are wrong. I cannot argue with you, nor can I urge anything more."

She turned from him. He would have given much to take her into his arms, and kissing her, bid her stay.

"You remember the old song, Madaline?

"'I could not love thee, dear, so much,
Loved I not honor more.'

217

If I could be false to the dead, Madaline, I should be untrue to the living. That I am not so is your security for my faith. If I could be false to the traditions of my race, I could be false to my vows of love."

"I can say no more—I can urge no more. You are a man—wise, strong, brave. I submit."

It was a cruel fate. He looked round on his pictured ancestors Would they have suffered, have sacrificed as much for the honor of their house as he was about to sacrifice now? Yes, he knew they would, for love of race and pride of name had always been unspeakably dear to them.

Chapter XXVIII.

Lord Arleigh raised his head from his breast. His wife was kneeling sobbing at his feet.

"Norman," she said, in a broken voice, "I yield, I submit. You know best, dear. In truth, I am not worthy to be your wife. I urge no claim on you; but, my darling, must I leave you? You are the very light of my life, heart of my heart, soul of my soul—must I leave you? Could I not remain here as your servant, your slave, the lowliest in your house—somewhere near, where I may hear the tones of your voice, the sound of your footsteps—where I may stand sometimes at the window and see you ride away—where I may render you little attentions such as loving wives render? Oh, Norman, be merciful and grant me that at least!"

"My darling, I cannot—do not tempt me. You do not understand I love you with a fierce, passionate love. If you were near me, I should be compelled to show that love to you every hour of the day—to treat you as my dear and honored wife. If you were near me, I might forget my resolves and remember only my love."

"No one should know," she whispered, "that I was your wife. I should take the guise of the humblest servant in the place. No one should know, love. Oh, darling, let it be so!"

She saw great drops of agony on his brow; she saw a world of pain in his eyes which alarmed her.

"It cannot be," he replied, hoarsely. "You must urge me no more—you are torturing me."

Then she rose, humbly enough, and turned away.

"I will say no more, Norman. Now do with me what you please."

There was silence for a few minutes. The sun was sinking low in the western sky, the chirp of the birds was growing faint in the trees. She raised her colorless face to his.

"I submit, Norman," she said. "You have some plan to propose. Do with me just as you will."

It was cruel—no crueler fate had ever fallen to a man's lot—but honor obliged him to act as he did. He took her hand in his.

"Some day, dear wife," he said, "you will understand what suffering this step has cost me."

"Yes," she murmured, faintly; "I may understand in time."

"While I have been sitting here," he went on, "I have been thinking it all over, and I have come to a decision as to what will be best for you and for me. You are Lady Arleigh of Beechgrove—you are my wife; you shall have all the honor and respect due to your position."

She shuddered as though the words were a most cruel mockery.

"You will honor," she questioned, bitterly, "the daughter of a felon?"

"I will honor my wife, who has been deceived even more cruelly than myself," he replied. "I have thought of a plan," he continued, "which can be easily carried out. On our estate not twenty miles from here—there is a little house called the Dower House—a house where the dowagers of the family have generally resided. It is near Winiston, a small country town. A housekeeper and two servants live in the house now, and keep it in order. You will be happy there, my darling, I am sure, as far as is possible. I will see that you have everything you need or require."

She listened as one who hears but dimly.

"You have no objection to raise, have you, Madaline?"

"No," she replied, "it matters little where I live; I only pray that my life may be short."

"Hush, my darling. You pain me."

"Oh, Norman, Norman," she cried, "what will they think of me— what will they say—your servants, your friends?"

"We must not trouble about that," said Norman; "we must not pause to consider what the world will say. We must do what we think is right."

He took out his watch and looked at it.

"It is eight o'clock," he said; "we shall have time to drive to Winiston to-night."

There was a world of sorrowful reproach in the blue eyes raised to his.

"I understand," she said, quietly; "you do not wish that the daughter of a felon should sleep, even for one night, under your roof."

"You pain me and you pain yourself; but it is, if you will bear the truth, my poor Madaline, just as you say. Even for these ancient walls I have such reverence."

"Since my presence dishonors them," she said, quietly, "I will go. Heaven will judge between us, Norman. I say that you are wrong. If I am to leave your house, I should like to go at once. I will go to my room and prepare for the journey."

He did not attempt to detain her, for he well knew that, if she made another appeal to him, he could not resist the impulse to clasp her in his arms, and at the cost of what he thought his honor to bid her stay.

She lingered before him, beautiful, graceful, sorrowful.

"Is there anything more you would like to say to me?" she asked, with sad humility.

"I dare not," he uttered, hoarsely; "I cannot trust myself."

He watched her as with slow, graceful steps she passed down, the long gallery, never turning her fair face or golden head back to him, her white robes trailing on the parquetry floor. When she had reached the end, he saw her draw aside the hangings and stand for a minute looking at the pictured faces of the Arleighs; then she disappeared, and he was left alone.

He buried his face in his hands and wept bitterly.

"I could curse the woman who has wrought this misery!" he exclaimed, presently.

And then the remembrance of Philippa, as he had known her years before—Philippa as a child, Philippa, his mother's favorite—restrained him.

"Perhaps I too was to blame," he thought; "she would not have taken such cruel vengeance had I been more candid."

Lady Arleigh went to her room. The pretty traveling-costume lay where she had left it; the housekeeper had not put away anything. Hastily taking off her white dress and removing the jewels from her neck, and the flowers from her hair, Madaline placed them aside, and then having attired herself for the journey, she went down stairs, meeting no one.

Some little surprise was created among the servants when orders came for the carriage to be got ready.

"Going out at this time of night. What can it mean?" asked one of them.

"They are going to the Dower House," answered a groom.

"Ah, then his lordship and her ladyship will not remain at the Abbey! How strange! But there—rich people have nothing to do but indulge in whims and caprices!" said the under house-maid, who was immediately frowned down by her superiors in office.

Not a word was spoken by husband and wife as Lady Arleigh took her seat in the carriage. Whatever she felt was buried in her own breast. Her face shone marble-white underneath her vail, and her eyes were bent downward. Never a word did she speak as the carriage drove slowly through the park, where the dews were falling and the stars were bright.

Once her husband turned to her and tried to take her hand in his, but she drew back.

"It will be better not to talk, Norman," she said. "I can bear it best in silence."

So they drove on in unbroken quietude. The dew lay glistening on the grass and trees; all nature was hushed, tranquil, sweet, and still. It was surely the strangest drive that husband and wife had ever taken together. More than once, noting the silent, graceful figure, Lord Arleigh was tempted to ask Madaline to fly with him to some foreign land, where they could live and die unknown—more than once he was tempted to kiss the beautiful lips and say to her, "Madaline, you shall not leave me;" but the dishonor attaching to his name caused him to remain silent.

They had a rapid drive, and reached Winiston House—as it was generally called—before eleven. Great was the surprise and consternation excited by so unexpected an arrival. The house was in the charge of a widow whose husband had been the late, lord's steward. She looked somewhat dubiously at Lord Arleigh and then at his companion, when they had entered. Madaline never opened her lips. Lord Arleigh was strangely pale and confused.

"Mrs. Burton," he said, "I can hardly imagine that you have heard of my marriage. This is my wife—Lady Arleigh."

All the woman's doubt and hesitation vanished then—she became all attention; but Lord Arleigh inwardly loathed his fate when he found himself compelled to offer explanations that he would have given worlds to avoid.

"I am not going to remain here myself," he said, in answer to the inquiries about rooms and refreshments. "Lady Arleigh will live at Winiston House altogether; and, as you have always served the family faithfull and well, I should like you to remain in her service."

The woman looked up at him in such utter bewilderment and surprise that he felt somewhat afraid of what she might say; he therefore hastened to add:

"Family matters that concern no one but ourselves compel me to make this arrangement. Lady Arleigh will be mistress now of Winiston House. She will have a staff of servants here. You can please yourself about remaining—either as housekeeper or not—just as you like."

"Of course, my lord, I shall be only too thankful to remain, but it seems so very strange—"

Lord Arleigh held up his hand.

"Hush!" he said. "A well-trained servant finds nothing strange."

The woman took the hint and retired. Lord Arleigh turned to say farewell to his wife. He found her standing, white and tearless, by the window.

"Oh, my darling," he cried, "we must now part! Yet how can I leave you—so sad, so silent, so despairing? Speak to me, my own love—one word—just one word."

Her woman's heart, so quick to pity, was touched by his prayer. She stalled as sad, as sweet a smile as ever was seen on woman's lips.

"I shall be better in time, Norman," she said, "and shall not always be sad."

"There are some business arrangements which must be made," he continued, hurriedly—"but it will be better for us not to meet again just yet, Madaline—I could not bear it. I will see that all is arranged for your comfort. You must have every luxury and—"

"Luxury!" she repeated, mockingly. "Why, I would rather be the sorriest beggar that ever breathed than be myself! Luxury! You mock me, Lord Arleigh."

"You will be less bitter against me in time, my darling," he said. "I mean just what I say—that you will have everything this world can give you—"

"Except love and happiness," she interposed.

"Love you have, sweet; you have mine—the fervent, true, honest, deep love of my heart and soul. Happiness comes in time to all who do their duty. Think of Carlyle's words—'Say unto all kinds of happiness, "I can do without thee"—with self-renunciation life begins.'"

"Carlyle had no such fate as mine in his thoughts," she said, "when he wrote that. But, Lord Arleigh, I do not wish to complain. I am sorry that I have interrupted you. I have accepted my fate. Say all you wish—I will be silent."

"I have only to add, my darling, that if money, luxury, comfort can give you happiness, you shall have them all. You shall have respect and honor too, for I will take care that the whole world knows that this separation arises from no fault of yours. Promise me, darling wife—oh, Heaven help me, how hard it is!—promise me, when the first smart of the pain is over, that you will try to be happy."

She bent her head, but spoke no word.

"Promise me too, Madaline, that, if sickness and sorrow should come to you, you will send for me at once."

"I promise," she said.

"A few words more, and I have done. Tell me what course you wish me to pursue toward the duchess."

"I have no wish in the matter," she replied, directly. "She was kind to me once; for the sake of that kindness I forgive her. She forgot that I must suffer in her wish to punish you. I shall leave her to Heaven."

"And I," he said, "will do the same; voluntarily I will never see her or speak to her again."

There remained for him only to say farewell. He took her little white hand; it was as cold as death.

"Farewell, my love," he said—"farewell!"

He kissed her face with slow, sweet reverence, as he would have kissed the face of a dead woman whom he loved; and then he was gone.

Like one in a dream, she heard the wheel of a carriage rolling away. She stretched out her hands with a faint cry.

"Norman—my husband—my love!" she called; but from the deep silence of the night there came no response. He was gone.

Madaline passed the night in watching the silent skies. Mrs. Burton, after providing all that was needful, had retired quickly to rest. She did not think it "good manners" to intrude upon her ladyship.

All night Madaline watched the stars, and during the course of that night the best part of her died—youth, love, hope, happiness.

Strange thoughts came to her—thoughts that she could hardly control. Why was she so cruelly punished? What had she done? She had read of wicked lives that had met with terrible endings. She had read of sinful men and wicked women whose crimes, even in this world, had been most bitterly punished. She had read of curses following sin. But what had she done? No woman's lot surely had ever been so bitter. She could not understand it, while the woman who had loved her husband, who had practiced fraud and deceit, and lied, went unpunished.

Yet her case was hardly that, for Norman did not love her. Daughter of a felon as she—Madaline—was—poor, lowly, obscure—he had given her his heart, although he could never make her the mistress of his home. There was some compensation for human suffering, some equality in the human lot, after all. She would be resigned. There were lots in life far worse than hers. What if she had learned to love Norman, and he had never cared for her? What if she had learned to love him, and had found him less noble than he was? What if, in the bitterness of his disappointment and passion, he had vented his anger upon her? After all, she could not but admire his sense of honor, his respect for his name, his devotion to his race; she could not find fault with his conduct, although it had cost her so dear.

"I think," she admitted to herself, "that in his place I should have done the same thing. If my parent's crime has brought sorrow and disgrace to me, who have no name, no fame, no glory of race to keep up, what must it have brought to him? In his place I should have done as he has done."

Then, after a time, she clasped her hands.

"I will submit," she said. "I will leave my fate to Providence."

When morning dawned she went to her room; she did not wish the household to know that she had sat up and watched the night through.

Once out of the house, Lord Arleigh seemed to realize for the first time what had happened; with a gesture of despair he threw himself back in the carriage. The footman came to him.

"Where to, my lord—to Beechgrove?"

"No," replied Lord Arleigh—"to the railway station. I want to catch the night-mail for London."

Lord Arleigh was just in time for the train. The footman caught a glimpse of his master's face as the train went off—it was white and rigid.

"Of all the weddings in this world, well, this is the queerest!" he exclaimed to himself.

When he reached Beechgrove, he told his fellow-servants what had happened, and many were the comments offered about the marriage that was yet no marriage—the wedding that was no wedding—the husband and wife who were so many miles apart. What could it mean?

Chapter XXIX.

Three days after Lord Arleigh's most inauspicious marriage. The Duchess of Hazlewood sat in her drawing-room alone. Those three days had changed her terribly; her face had lost its bloom, the light had died from her dark eyes, there were great lines of pain round her lips. She sat with her hands folded listlessly, her eyes, full of dreamy sorrow, fixed on the moving foliage of the woods. Presently Lady Peters entered with an open newspaper in her hand.

"Philippa, my dear," she said, "I am very uncomfortable. Should you think this paragraph refers to Lord Arleigh? It seems to do so—yet I cannot believe it."

The deadly pallor that was always the sign of great emotion with the duchess spread now even to her lips.

"What does it say?" she asked.

Lady Peters held the paper out to her; but her hands trembled so that she could not take it.

"I cannot read it," she said, wearily. "Read it to me."

And then Lady Peters read:

"Scandal in High Life.—Some strange revelations are shortly expected in aristocratic circles. A few days since a noble lord, bearing one of the most ancient titles in England, was married. The marriage took place under circumstances of great mystery; and the mystery has been increased by the separation of bride and bridegroom on their wedding-day. What has led to a separation is at present a secret, but it is expected that in a few days all particulars will be known. At present the affair is causing a great sensation."

A fashionable paper which indulged largely in personalities, also had a telling article on Lord Arleigh's marriage. No names were mentioned, but the references were unmistakable. A private marriage, followed by a separation on the same day, was considered a fair mark for scandal. This also Lady Peters read, and the duchess listened with white, trembling lips.

"It must refer to Lord Arleigh," said Lady Peters.

"It cannot," was the rejoinder. "He was far too deeply in love with his fair-faced bride to leave her."

"I never did quite approve of that marriage," observed Lady Peters.

"The scandal cannot be about him," declared the duchess. "We should have heard if there had been anything wrong."

The next day a letter was handed to her. She recognized the handwriting—it was Lord Arleigh's. She laid the note down, not daring to read it before Lady Peters. What had he to say to her?

When she was alone she opened it.

"You will be pleased to hear, duchess, that your scheme has entirely succeeded. You have made two innocent people who have never harmed you as wretched as it is possible for human beings to be. In no respect has your vengeance failed. I—your old friend, playmate, brother, the son of your mother's dearest friend—have been made miserable for life. Your revenge was well chosen. You knew that, however I might worship Madaline, my wife, however much I might love her, she could never be mistress of Beechgrove, she could never be the mother of my children; you knew that, and therefore I say your revenge was admirably chosen. It were useless to comment on your wickedness, or to express the contempt I feel for the woman who could deliberately plan such evil and distress. I must say this, however. All friendship and acquaintance between us is at an end. You will be to me henceforward an entire stranger. I could retaliate. I could write and tell your husband, who is a man of honor, of the unworthy deed you have done; but I shall not do that—it would be unmanly. Before my dear wife and I parted, we agreed that the punishment of your sin should be left to Heaven. So I leave it. To a woman unworthy enough to plan such a piece of baseness, it will be satisfaction sufficient to know that her scheme has succeeded. Note the words 'my wife and I parted'—parted, never perhaps to meet again. She has all my love, all my heart, all my unutterable respect and deep devotion; but, as you know, she can never be mistress of my house. May Heaven forgive you.

Arleigh."

She could have borne with his letter if it had been filled with the wildest invictives—if he had reproached her, even cursed her; his dignified forbearance, his simple acceptance of the wrong she had done him, she could not tolerate.

She laid down the letter. It was all over now—the love for which she would have given her life, the friendship that had once been so true, the vengeance that had been so carefully planned. She had lost his love, his friendship, his esteem. She could see him no more. He despised her. There came to her a vision of what she might have been to him had things been different—his friend, adviser, counselor—the woman upon whom he would have looked as the friend of his chosen wife—the woman whom, after all, he loved best—his sister, his truest confidante. All this she might have been but for her revenge. She had forfeited it all now. Her life would be spent as though he did not exist; and there was no one but herself to blame.

Still she had had her revenge; she smiled bitterly to herself as she thought of that. She had punished him. The beautiful face grew pale, and the dark eyes shone through a mist of tears.

"I am not hardened enough," she said to herself, mockingly, "to be quite happy over an evil deed. I want something more of wickedness in my composition."

She parried skillfully all Lady Peters' questions; she professed entire ignorance of all that had happened. People appealed to her as Lord Arleigh's friend. They asked her:

"What does this mean? Lord Arleigh was married quietly, and separated from his wife the same day. What does it mean?"

"I cannot tell, but you may rely upon it that a reasonable explanation of the circumstances will be forthcoming," she would reply. "Lord Arleigh is, as we all know, an honorable man, and I knew his wife."

"But what can it mean?" the questioners would persist.

"I cannot tell," she would answer, laughingly. "I only know we must give the matter the best interpretation we can."

So she escaped; and no one associated the Duchess of Hazlewood with Lord Arleigh's strange marriage. She knew that when her husband returned she would have to give some kind of explanation; but she was quite indifferent about that. Her life, she said to herself, was ended.

When the duke did come home, after a few pleasant weeks on the sea, the first thing he heard was the story about Lord Arleigh. It astounded him. His friend Captain Austin related it to him as soon as he had landed.

"Whom did you say he married?" inquired the duke.

"Rumor said at first that it was a distant relative of yours," replied the captain, "afterward it proved to be some young lady whom he had met at a small watering-place."

"What was her name? Who was she? It was no relative of mine; I have very few; I have no young female relative at all."

"No—that was all a mistake; I cannot tell you how it arose. He married a lady of the name of Dornham."

"Dornham!" said the puzzled nobleman. "The name is not unfamiliar to me—Dornham—ah, I remember!"

He said no more, but the captain saw a grave expression come over his handsome face, and it occurred to him that some unpleasant thought occurred to his companion's mind.

Chapter XXX.

One of the first questions, after his return, that the Duke of Hazlewood put to his wife was about Lord Arleigh. She looked at him with an uneasy smile.

"Am I my brother's keeper?" she asked.

"Certainly not, Philippa; but, considering that Arleigh has been as a brother to you all these years, you must take some interest in him. Is this story of his marriage true?"

"True?" she repeated. "Why, of course it is—perfectly true! Do you not know whom he has married?"

"I am half afraid to ask—half afraid to find that my suspicions have been realized."

"He has married my companion," said the duchess. "I have no wish to blame him; I will say nothing."

"It is a great pity that he ever saw her," observed the duke, warmly. "From all I hear, the man's life is wrecked."

"I warned him," said Philippa, eagerly. "I refused at first to introduce her to him. I told him that prudence and caution were needful."

"How came it about then, Philippa?"

The duchess shrugged her shoulders.

"There is a fate, I suppose, in these things. He saw her one day when I was out of the way, and, according to his own account, fell in love with her on the spot. Be that as it may, he was determined to marry her."

"It seems very strange," said the Duke of Hazlewood, musingly. "I have never known him to do anything 'queer' before."

"He can never say that I did not warn him," she remarked, carelessly.

"But it was such a wretched marriage for him. Who was she, Philippa? I have never made many inquiries about her."

"I would really rather not discuss the question," said the duchess; "it has no interest for me now. Norman and I have quarreled. In all probability we shall never be friends again."

"All through this marriage?" interrogated the duke.

"All through this marriage," repeated his wife—"and I know no subject that irritates me so much. Please say no more about it, Vere."

"I should like to know who the girl is," he urged. "You have never told me."

"I shall be jealous of her in a few minutes!" exclaimed Philippa "Already she has sundered an old friendship that I thought would last forever; and now, directly you return, you can talk of no one else."

"I should like to see you jealous," said the duke, who was one of the most unsuspicious of men.

She smiled; yet there came to her a sharp, bitter memory of the night on the balcony when she had been jealous of the ideal woman, the unknown love whom Norman had sketched for her.

The duke, however, was pertinacious; he could not give up the subject.

"You told me," he resumed, "that she was the daughter of an old friend of yours named Dornham—and it seems to me, Philippa, that

I have some kind of remembrance of that name which is far from pleasant."

With an air of resignation the duchess rose from her seat.

"I am tired, Vere," she said, "quite tired of the subject. Yet I ought not to be selfish. Of course, the incident is all new to you—you have been away from all kinds of news; to us it is an old, worn-out story. Lord Arleigh and I quarreled and parted because of his marriage, so you may imagine it is not a very attractive subject to me."

"Well, I will say no more about it, but I am sincerely sorry, Philippa. Of all our friends, I like Lord Arleigh best; and I shall decidedly refuse to quarrel with him. His marriage is his own affair, not mine."

"Still, you cannot make a friend of the man whom I decline to know," she rejoined, hurriedly.

"Certainly not, if you place the matter in such a light," he said, gravely. "I shall always consider it my pleasure and duty to consult you on such points. I will call no man my friend whom you dislike."

So, for the time, all danger was tided over; the duke saw that the subject annoyed his wife, and did not voluntarily resume it. He was too true a gentleman to think of discussing with another lady what he did not discuss with his own wife, so that the subject was not mentioned between Lady Peters and himself.

Then for the fair young Duchess of Hazlewood began the new life which had in it no old friend. If she repented of her vengeance, she did not say so. If she would fain have undone her evil deed, she never owned it. But, as time wore on, people saw a great change in her. She gave herself more to the gayeties and follies of the world; there were few fashions which she did not lead, few gay pursuits in which she did not take an active part. The character of her beauty, too, seemed changed. She had always been brilliant, but somewhat of a strange unrest came into her face and manner; the dark eyes seemed to be always looking for something they could not find. Her mind, though charming and fascinating as ever, grew variable and unsteady. She had always been too proud for coquetry; she remained so now. But she no longer shunned and avoided all flattery and homage; it seemed rather to please her than not. And—greatest change of all—the name of Lord Arleigh never crossed her lips. He himself had retired from public life; the great hopes formed of him were all dying away. Men spoke of him with mystery, women with sad, gentle interest; those who had known him knew him no more.

He did not return to Beechgrove: it seemed to him that he could never again endure the sight of the place where he had separated from his wife—that his ancient home had been in some manner desecrated. The mansion was left in charge of Mrs. Chatterton, whose wonder at the new and strange state of things never ceased.

"Such a marriage!" She held up her hands in horror as she thought of it. Indeed, to her the event appeared like a wedding and a funeral on the same day. She had not seen Lady Arleigh since, yet she had never forgot the fair, lovely young face that had shone for so short a time in the grand old home.

Lord Arleigh saw that his wife had everything needful for her; he settled a large income on her; he sent from London horses, carriages, everything that her heart could desire; he saw that she had a proper household formed. Whatever else the world might say, it could not say that he showed her any want of respect or any want of attention. Lord Arleigh did not live with his wife, never visited her, never spoke of her; but it was quite clear that his motive for doing none of these things lay deeper than the world knew or could even guess.

The family solicitor went down to Winiston House occasionally, but Lord Arleigh never. The few who met him after his marriage found him strangely altered. Even his face had changed; the frank, honest, open look that had once seemed to defy and challenge and meet the whole world had died away; he looked now like a man with a secret to keep—a secret that had taken his youth from him, that had taken the light from his life, that hod shadowed his eyes, drawn hard lines of care round his lips, wrinkled his face, taken the music from his voice, and made of him a changed and altered, a sad, unhappy man.

There were one or two intimate friends—friends who had known him in his youth—who ventured to ask what this secret was, who appealed to him frankly to make his trouble known, telling him that sorrow shared was sorrow lightened; but with a sad smile he only raised his head and answered that his sorrow was one of which he could not speak. Sometimes a kindly woman who had known him as boy and man—one with daughters, and sons of her own—would ask him what was the nature of his sorrow. He would never tell.

"I cannot explain," he would reply.

Society tried hard to penetrate the mystery. Some said that Lady Arleigh was insane, and that he had not discovered it until the afternoon of his wedding-day. Others said that she had a fierce temper, and that he was unaware of it until they were traveling homeward. These were the most innocent rumors; others were more scandalous. It was said that he had discovered some great crime that she had committed. Few such stories; Lord Arleigh, they declared, was not the man to make so terrible a mistake.

Then, after a time, all the sensation and wonder died away, society accepted the fact that Lord Arleigh was unhappily married and had separated from his wife.

He went abroad, and then returned home, sojourning at quiet watering places where he thought his story and himself would be unknown. Afterward he went to Normandy, and tried to lose the remembrance of his troubles in his search after the picturesque. But, when he had done everything that he could do to relieve his distress of mind, he owned to himself that he was a most miserable man.

Chapter XXXI.

A year and a half bad passed, and Lord Arleigh was still, as it were, out of the world. It was the end of April, a spring fresh and beautiful. His heart had turned to Beechgrove, where the violets were springing and the young larches were budding; but he could not go thither—the picture-gallery was a haunted spot to him—and London he could endure. The fashionable intelligence told him that the Duke and Duchess of Hazlewood had arrived for the season, that they had had their magnificent mansion refurnished, and that the beautiful duchess intended to startle all London by the splendor and variety of her entertainments.

He said to himself that it would be impossible for him to remain in town without seeing them—and see them of his own free will he never would again.

Fate was, however, too strong for him. He had decided that he would leave London rather than run the risk of meeting the Duchess of Hazlewood. He went one morning to a favorite exhibition of pictures, and the first person he saw in the gallery was the duchess herself. As their eyes met her face grew deadly pale, so pale that he thought she would faint and fall to the ground; her lips opened as though she would fain utter his name. To him she looked taller, more beautiful, more stately than ever—her superb costume suited her to perfection—yet he looked coldly into the depths of her dark eyes, and without a word or sign of greeting passed on.

He never knew whether she was hurt or not, but he decided that he would leave London at once. He was a sensitive man more tender of heart than men as a rule, and their meeting had been a source of torture to him. He could not endure even the thought that Philippa should have lost all claim to his respect. He decided to go to Tintagel, in wild, romantic Cornwall; at least there would be boating, fishing, and the glorious scenery.

"I must go somewhere," he said to himself—"I must do something. My life hangs heavy on my hands—how will it end?"

So in sheer weariness and desperation he went to Tintagel, having, as he thought, kept his determination to himself, as he wished no one to know whither he had retreated. One of the newspapers, however, heard of it, and in a little paragraph told that Lord Arleigh of Beechgrove had gone to Tintagel for the summer. That paragraph had one unexpected result.

It was the first of May. The young nobleman was thinking of the May days when he was a boy—of how the common near his early home was yellow with gorse, and the hedges were white with hawthorn. He strolled sadly along the sea-shore, thinking of the sunniest May he had known since then, the May before his marriage. The sea was unusually calm, the sky above was blue, the air mild and balmy, the white sea-gulls circled in the air, the waves broke with gentle murmur on the yellow sand.

He sat down on the sloping beach. They had nothing to tell him, those rolling, restless waves—no sweet story of hope or of love, no vague pleasant harmony. With a deep moan he bent his head as he thought of the fair young wife from whom he had parted for evermore, the beautiful loving girl who had clung to him so earnestly.

"Madaline, Madaline!" he cried aloud: and the waves seemed to take up the cry—they seemed to repeat "Madaline" as they broke on the shore. "Madaline," the mild wind whispered. It was like the realization of a dream, when he heard his name murmured, and, turning, he saw his lost wife before him.

The next moment he had sprung to his feet, uncertain at first whether it was really herself or some fancied vision.

"Madaline," he cried, "is it really you?"

"Yes; you must not be angry with me, Norman. See, we are quite alone; there is no one to see me speak to you, no one to reveal that we have met."

She trembled as she spoke; her face—to him more beautiful than ever—was raised to his with a look of unutterable appeal.

"You are not angry, Norman?"

"No, I am not angry. Do not speak to me as though I were a tyrant. Angry—and with you, Madaline—always my best beloved—how could that be?"

"I knew that you were here," she said. "I saw in a newspaper that you were going to Tintagel for the summer. I had been longing to see you again—to see you, while unseen myself so I came hither."

"My dear Madaline, to what purpose?" he asked, sadly.

"I felt that if I did not look upon your face I should die—that I could live no longer without seeing you. Such a terrible fever seemed to be burning my very life away. My heart yearned for the touch of your hand. So I came. You are not angry that I came?"

"No, not angry; but, my darling, it will be harder for us to part."

"I have been here in Tintagel for two whole days," she continued. "I have seen you, but this is the first time you have gone where I could follow. Now speak to me, Norman. Say something to me that will cure my terrible pain—that will take the weary aching from my heart. Say something that will make me stronger to bear my desolate life—braver to live without you. You are wiser, better, stronger, braver than I. Teach me to bear my fate."

What could he say? Heaven help them both—what could he say? He looked with dumb, passionate sorrow into her fair loving face.

"You must not think it unwomanly in me to come," she said. "I am you wife—there is no harm in my coming. If I were not your wife, I would sooner have drowned myself than return after you had sent me away."

Her face was suffused with a crimson blush.

"Norman," she said gently, "sit down here by my side, and I will tell you why I have come."

They sat down side by side on the beach. There was only the wide blue sky above, only the wide waste of restless waters at their feet, only a circling sea-gull near—no human being to watch the tragedy of love and pride played out by the sea Waves.

"I have come," she said, "to make one more appeal to you, Norman—to ask you to change this stern determination which is ruining your life and mine—to ask you to take me back to your home and your heart. For I have been thinking, dear, and I do not see that the obstacle is such as you seem to imagine. It was a terrible wrong, a great disgrace—it was a cruel deception, a fatal mistake; but, after all, it might be overlooked. Moreover, Norman, when you made me your wife, did you not promise to love and to cherish, to protect me and make me happy until I died?"

"Yes," he replied, briefly.

"Then how are you keeping that promise—a promise made in the sight of Heaven?"

Lord Arleigh looked down at the fair, pure face, a strange light glowing in his own.

"My dear Madaline," he said, "you must not overlook what the honor of my race demands. I have my own ideas of what is due to my ancestors; and I cannot think that I have sinned by broken vows. I vowed to love you—so I do, my darling, ten thousand times better than anything else on earth. I vowed to be true and faithful to you—

so I am, for I would not ever look at another woman's face. I vowed to protect you and to shield you—so I do, my darling; I have surrounded you with luxury and ease."

What could she reply—what urge or plead?

"So, in the eyes of Heaven, my wife, I cannot think I am wronging you."

"Then," she said, humbly, "my coming here, my pleading, is in vain."

"Not in vain, my darling. Even the sight of you for a few minutes has been like a glimpse of Elysium."

"And I must return," she said, "as I came—with my love thrown back, my prayers unanswered, my sorrow redoubled."

She hid her face in her hands and wept aloud. Presently she bent forward.

"Norman," she said, in a low whisper, "my darling, I appeal to you for my own sake. I love you so dearly that I cannot live away from you—it is a living death. You cannot realize it. There are few moments, night or day, in which your face is not before me—few moments in which I do not hear your voice. Last night I dreamed that you stood before me with outstretched arms and called me. I went to you, and you clasped me in your arms. You said, 'My darling wife, it has all been a mistake—a terrible mistake—and I am come to ask your pardon and to take you home.' In my dream, Norman, you kissed my face, my lips, my hands, and called me by every loving name you could invent. You were so kind to me, and I was so happy. And the dream was so vivid, Norman, that even after I awoke I believed it to be reality. Then I heard the sobbing of the waves on the beach, and I cried out, 'Norman, Norman!' thinking you were still near me; but there was no reply. It was only the silence that roused me to a full sense that my happiness was a dream. There was no husband with kind words and tender kisses. I thought my heart would have broken. And then I said to myself that I could live no longer without making an effort once more to change your decision. Oh, Norman, for my sake, do not send me back to utter desolation and despair! Do not send me back to coldness and darkness, to sorrow and tears. Let me be near you! You have a thousand interests in life—I have but one. You can live without love, I cannot. Oh, Norman, for my sake, for my love's sake, for my happiness' sake, take me back, dear—take me back!"

The golden head dropped forward and fell on his breast, her hands clung to him with almost despairing pain.

"I will be so humble, darling. I can keep away from all observation. It is only to be with you that I wish—only to be near you. You cannot be hard—you cannot send me away; you will not, for I love you!"

Her hands clung more closely to him.

"Many men have forgiven their wives even great crimes, and have taken them back after the basest desertion. Overlook my father's crime and pardon me, for Heaven's dear sake!"

"My dearest Madaline, if you would but understand! I have nothing to pardon. You are sweetest, dearest, loveliest, best. You are one of the purest and noblest of women. I have nothing to pardon; it is only that I cannot take disgrace into my family. I cannot give to my children an inheritance of crime." "But, Norman," said the girl, gently, "because my father was a felon, that does not make me one— because he was led into wrong, it does not follow that I must do wrong. Insanity may be hereditary, but surely crime is not; besides, I have heard my father say that his father was an honest, simple, kindly northern farmer. My father had much to excuse him. He was a handsome man, who had been flattered and made much of."

"My darling I could not take your hands into mine and kiss them so, if I fancied that they were ever so slightly tainted with sin."

"Then why not take me home. Norman?"

"I cannot," he replied, in a tone of determination. "You must not torture me, Madaline, with further pleading. I cannot—that is sufficient."

He rose and walked with rapid steps down the shore. How bard it was, how terrible—bitter almost as the anguish of death!

She was by his side again, walking in silence. He would bare given the whole world if he could have taken her into his arms and have kissed back the color into her sad young face.

"Norman," said a low voice, full of bitterest pain, "I am come to say good-by. I am sorry I have done harm—not good. I am sorry—forgive me, and say good-by."

"It has made our lot a thousand times harder, Madaline," he returned, hoarsely.

"Never mind the hardship; you will soon recover from that," she said. "I am sorry that I have acted against your wishes, and broken the long silence. I will never do it again, Norman."

"Never, unless you are ill and need me," he supplemented. "Then you have promised to send for me."

"I will do so" she said. "You will remember, dear husband, that my last words to you were 'Good-by, and Heaven bless you.'"

The words died away on her lips. He turned aside lest she should see the trembling of his face; he never complained to her. He knew now that she thought him hard, cold, unfeeling, indifferent—that she thought his pride greater than his love; but even that was better than that she should know he suffered more than she did—she must never know that.

When he turned back from the tossing waves and the summer sun she was gone. He looked across the beach—there was no sign of her. She was gone; and he avowed to himself that it would be wonderful if ever in this world he saw her again. She did not remain at Tintagel; to do so would be useless, hopeless. She saw it now. She had hoped against hope: she had said to herself that in a year and a half he would surely have altered his mind—he would have found now how hard it was to live alone, to live without love—he would have found that there was something dearer in the world than family pride—he would have discovered that love outweighed everything else. Then she saw that her anticipations were all wrong—he preferred his dead ancestors to his living wife.

She went back to Winiston House and took up the dreary round of life again. She might have made her lot more endurable and happier, she might have traveled, have sought society and amusement; but she had no heart for any of these things. She had spent the year and a half of her lonely married life in profound study, thinking to herself that if he should claim her he would be pleased to find her yet more accomplished and educated. She was indefatigable, and it was all for him.

Now that she was going back, she was without this mainspring of hope—her old studies and pursuits wearied her. To what end and for what purpose had been all her study, all her hard work? He would never know of her proficiency; and she would not care to study for any other object than to please him.

"What am I to do with my life," she moaned. "Mariana in the moated grange was not more to be pitied than I."

How often the words occurred to her:

"The day is dreary,
'He cometh not,' she said:
She said, 'I am aweary, aweary,
would that I were dead.'"

It was one of the strangest, dullest, saddest lives that human being ever led. That she wearied of it was no wonder. She was tired of the sorrow, the suffering, the despair—so tired that after a time she fell ill; and then she lay longing for death.

Chapter XXXII.

It was a glorious September, and the Scottish moors looked as they had not looked for years; the heather grew in rich profusion, the grouse were plentiful. The prospects for sportsmen were excellent.

Not knowing what else to do, Lord Arleigh resolved to go to Scotland for the shooting; there was a sort of savage satisfaction in the idea of living so many weeks alone, without on-lookers, where he could be dull if he liked without comment—where he could lie for hours together on the heather looking up at the blue skies, and puzzling over the problem of his life—where, when the fit of despair seized him, he could indulge in it, and no one wonder at him. He hired a shooting-lodge called Glaburn. In his present state of mind it seemed to him to be a relief to live where he could not even see a woman's face. Glaburn was kept in order by two men, who mismanaged it after the fashion of men, but Lord Arleigh was happier there than he had been since his fatal marriage-day, simply because he was quite alone. If he spent more time in lying on the heather and thinking of Madaline than he did in shooting, that was his own concern—there was no one to interfere.

One day, when he was in one of his most despairing moods, he went out quite early in the morning, determined to wander the day through, to exhaust himself pitilessly with fatigue, and then see if he could not rest without dreaming of Madaline. But as he wandered east and west, knowing little and caring less, whither he went, a violent storm, such as breaks at times over the Scottish moors, overtook him. The sky grew dark as night, the rain fell in a torrent— blinding, thick, heavy—he could hardly see his hand before him. He wandered on for hours, wet through, weary, cold, yet rather rejoicing than otherwise in his fatigue. Presently hunger was added to fatigue; and then the matter became more serious—he had no hope of being able to find his way home, for he had no idea in what direction he had strayed.

At last he grew alarmed; life did not hold much for him, it was true, but he had no desire to die on those lonely wilds, without a human being near him. Then it became painful for him to walk; his fatigue was so great that his limbs ached at every step. He began to think his life was drawing near its close. Once or twice he had cried "Madaline" aloud and the name seemed to die away on the sobbing wind.

He grew exhausted at last; for some hours he had struggled on in the face of the tempest.

"I shall have to lie down like a dog by the road-side and die," he thought to himself.

No other fate seemed to be before him but that, and he told himself that after all he had sold his life cheaply. "Found dead on the Scotch moors," would be the verdict about him.

What would the world say? What would his golden-haired darling say when she heard that he was dead?

As the hot tears blinded his eyes—tears for Madaline, not for himself—a light suddenly flashed into them, and he found himself quite close to the window of a house. With a deep-drawn, bitter sob, he whispered to himself that he was saved. He had just strength enough to knock at the door; and when it was opened he fell across the threshold, too faint and exhausted to speak, a sudden darkness before his eyes.

When he had recovered a little, he found that several gentlemen were gathered around him, and that one of them was holding a flask of whisky to his lips.

"That was a narrow escape," said a cheery, musical voice. "How long have you been on foot?"

"Since eight this morning," he replied.

"And now it is nearly eight at night! Well, you may thank Heaven for preserving your life."

Lord Arleigh turned away with a sigh. How little could any one guess what life meant for him—life spent without love—love—without Madaline!

"I have known several lose their lives in this way," continued the same voice. "Only last year poor Charley Hartigan was caught in a similar storm, and he lay for four days dead before he was found. This gentleman has been fortunate."

Lord Arleigh roused himself and looked around. He found himself the center of observation. The room in which he was lying was large and well furnished, and from the odor of tobacco it was plainly used as a smoking-room.

Over him leaned a tall, handsome man, whose hair was slightly tinged with gray.

"I think," he said, "you are my neighbor, Lord Arleigh? I have often seen you on the moors."

"I do not remember you," Lord Arleigh returned; "nor do I know where I am."

"Then let me introduce myself as the Earl of Mountdean," said the gentleman. "You are at Rosorton, a shooting-lodge belonging to me, and I beg that you will make yourself at home."

Every attention was paid to him. He was placed in a warm bed, some warm, nourishing soup was brought to him, and he was left to rest.

"The Earl of Mountdean." Then this was the tall figure he had seen striding over the hills—this was the neighbor he had shunned and avoided, preferring solitude. How kind he was, and how his voice affected him! It was like long-forgotten melody. He asked himself whether he had seen the earl anywhere. He could not remember. He could not recall to his mind that they had ever met, yet he had most certainly heard his voice. He fell asleep thinking of this, and dreamed of Madaline all night long.

In the morning the earl came himself to his room to make inquiries; and then Lord Arleigh liked him better than ever. He would not allow his guest to rise.

"Remember," he said, "prevention is better than cure. After the terrible risk you have run, it will not do for you to be rash. You must rest."

So Lord Arleigh took the good advice given to him to lay still, but on the second day he rose, declaring that he could stand no further confinement. Even then Lord Mountdean would not hear of his going.

"I am compelled to be despotic with you," he said. "I know that at Glaburn you have no housekeeper, only men-servants—and they cannot make you comfortable, I am sure. Stay here for a few days until you are quite well."

So Lord Arleigh allowed himself to be persuaded, saying, with a smile, that he had come to Glaburn purposely for solitude.

"It was for the same thing that I came here," said the earl. "I have had a great sorrow in my life, and I like sometimes to be alone to think about it."

The two men looked at each other, but they liked each other all the better for such open confession.

When a few days had passed, it was Lord Arleigh who felt unwilling to leave his companion. He had never felt more at home than he did with Lord Mountdean. He had met no one so simple, so manly, so intelligent, and at the same time such a good fellow. There were little peculiarities in the earl, too, that struck him very forcibly; they seemed to recall some faint, vague memory, a something that he could never grasp, that was always eluding him, yet that was perfectly clear; and he was completely puzzled.

"Have I ever met you before?" he asked the earl one day.

"I do not think so. I have no remembrance of ever having sees you."

"Your voice and face are familiar to me," the younger man continued. "One or two of your gestures are as well known to me as though I had lived with you for years."

"Remembrances of that kind sometimes strike me," said the earl—"a mannerism, a something that one cannot explain. I should say that you have seen some one like me, perhaps."

It was probable enough, but Lord Arleigh was not quite satisfied. The earl and his guest parted in the most friendly manner.

"I shall never be quite so much in love with solitude again," said Lord Arleigh, as they were parting; "you have taught me that there is something better."

"I have learned the same lesson from you," responded the earl, with a sigh. "You talk about solitude. I had not been at Rosorton ten days before a party of four, all friends of mine, proposed to visit me. I could not refuse. They left the day after you came."

"I did not see them," said Lord Arleigh.

"No, I did not ask them to prolong their stay, fearing that after all those hours on the moors, you might have a serious illness; but now, Lord Arleigh, you will promise me that we shall be friends."

"Yes," he replied, "we will be friends."

So it was agreed that they should be strangers no longer—that they should visit and exchange neighborly courtesies and civilities.

Chapter XXXIII.

The Earl of Mountdean and Lord Arleigh were walking up a steep hill one day together, when the former feeling tired, they both sat down among the heather to rest. There was a warm sun shining, a pleasant wind blowing, and the purple heather seemed literally to dance around them. They remained for some time in silence; it was the earl who broke it by saying:

"How beautiful the heather is! And here indeed on this hill-top is solitude! We might fancy ourselves quite alone in the world. By the way, you have never told me, Arleigh, what it is that makes you so fond of solitude."

"I have had a great trouble," he replied, briefly.

"A trouble! But one suffers a great deal before losing all interest in life. You are so young, you cannot have suffered much."

"I know no other life so utterly helpless as my own."

The earl looked at him thoughtfully.

"I should like to know what your trouble is?" he said gently.

"I can tell you only one half of it," was the reply. "I fell in love with one of the sweetest, fairest, purest of girls. How I loved her is only known to myself. I suppose every man thinks his own love the greatest and the best. My whole heart went out to this girl—with my whole soul I loved her! She was below me in the one matter of worldly wealth and position—above me in all other. When I first asked her to marry me, she refused. She told me that the difference in our rank was too great. She was most noble, most self-sacrificing; she loved me, I know, most dearly, but she refused me. I was for some time unable to overcome her opposition; at last I succeeded. I tell you no details either of her name or where she lived, nor any other circumstances connected with her—I tell you only this, that, once having won her consent to our marriage, I seemed to have exchanged earth for Elysium. Then we were married, not publicly and with great pomp, but as my darling wished—privately and quietly. On the same day—my wedding-day—I took her home. I cannot tell how great was my happiness—no one could realize it. Believe me, Lord Mountdean, that she herself is as pure as a saint, that I know no other woman at once so meek and so lofty, so noble and so humble. Looking at her, one feels how true and sweet a woman's soul can be. Yet—oh, that I should live to say it!—on my wedding-day I discovered something—it was no fault of hers, I swear—that parted us. Loving her blindly, madly, with my whole heart and soul, I was still compelled to leave her. She is my wife in name only, and can never be more to me, yet, you understand, without any fault of hers."

"What a strange story!" said the earl, thoughtfully. "But this barrier, this obstacle—can it never be removed?"

"No," answered Lord Arleigh, "never!"

"I assure you of my deepest sympathy," said the earl. "It is a strange history."

"Yes, and a sad fate," sighed Lord Arleigh. "You cannot understand my story entirely. Wanting a full explanation, you might fairly ask me why I married with this drawback. I did not know of it, but my wife believed I did. We were both most cruelly deceived, it does not matter now. She is condemned to a loveless, joyless life; so am I. With a wife beautiful loving, young, I must lead a most solitary existence—I must see my name die out for want of heirs—I must see my race almost extinct, my life passed in repining and misery, my heart broken, my days without sunshine. I repeat that it is a sad fate."

"It is indeed," agreed the earl—"and such a strange one. Are you quite sure that nothing can be done to remedy it?"

"Quite sure," was the hopeless reply.

"I can hardly understand the need for separation, seeing that the wife herself is blameless."

"In this case it is unavoidable."

"May I, without seeming curious, ask you a question?" said the earl.

"Certainly—as many as you like."

"You can please yourself about answering it," observed the earl; and then he added: "Tell me, is it a case of insanity? Has your wife any hereditary tendency to anything of that kind?"

"No," replied Lord Arleigh; "it is nothing of that description. My wife is to me perfect in body and mind; I can add nothing to that."

"Then your story is a marvel; I do not—I cannot understand it. Still I must say that, unless there is something far deeper and more terrible than I can imagine, you have done wrong to part from your wife."

"I wish I could think so. But my doom is fixed, and no matter how long I live, or she lives, it can never be altered."

"My story is a sad one," observed Lord Mountdean, "but it is not so sad as yours. I married when I was quite young—married against my father's wish, and without his consent. The lady I loved was like your own; she was below me in position, but in nothing else. She was the daughter of a clergyman, a lady of striking beauty, good education and manners. I need not trouble you by telling you how it came about. I married her against my father's wish; he was in Italy at the time for his health—he had been there indeed for some years. I married her privately; our secret was well kept. Some time after our marriage I received a telegram stating that my father was dying and wished to see me. At that very time we were expecting the birth of what we hoped would be a son and heir. But I was anxious that my father should see and bless my wife before he died. She assured me that the journey would not hurt her, that no evil consequences would ensue; and, as I longed intensely for my father to see her, it

255

was arranged that we should go together. A few hours of the journey passed happily enough, and then my poor wife was taken ill. Heaven pardon me because of my youth, my ignorance, my inexperience! I think sometimes that I might have saved her—but it is impossible to tell. We stopped at a little town called Castledene, and I drove to the hotel. There were races, or something of the kind, going on in the neighborhood, and the proprietors could not accommodate us. I drove to the doctor, who was a good Samaritan; he took us into his house—my child was born, and my wife died there. It was not a son and heir, as we had hoped it might be, but a little daughter, as fair as her mother. Ah, Lord Arleigh, you have had your troubles, I have had mine. My wife was buried at Castledene— my beautiful young wife, whom I loved so dearly. I left my child, under the doctor's care, with a nurse, having arranged to pay so much per annum for her, and intending when I returned to England to take her home to Wood Lynton as my heiress. My father, contrary to the verdict of the physicians, lingered about three years. Then he died, and I became Earl of Mountdean. The first thing I did was to hurry to Castledene. Can you imagine my horror when I found that all trace of my child was lost? The poor doctor had met with some terrible death, and the woman who had charge of my little one had left the neighborhood. Can you imagine what this blow was to me? Since then my life has been spent in one unceasing effort to find my daughter."

"How strange!" said Lord Arleigh. "Did you not know the name of the nurse?"

"Yes, she lived at a little place called Ashwood. I advertised for her, I offered large rewards, but I have never gleaned the least news of her; no one could ever find her. Her husband, it appeared, had been guilty of crime. My opinion is that the poor woman fled in shame from the neighborhood where she was known, and that both she and my dear child are dead."

"It seems most probable," observed Lord Arleigh.

"If I could arrive at any certainty as to her fate," said the earl, "I should be a happier man. I have been engaged to my cousin Lady Lily Gordon for four years, but I cannot make up my mind to marry until I hear something certain about my daughter."

Chapter XXXIV.

Winiston House was prettily situated. The house stood in the midst of charming grounds. There was a magnificent garden, full of flowers, full of fragrance and bloom; there was an orchard filled with rich, ripe fruit, broad meadow-land where the cattle grazed, where daisies and oxlips grew. To the left of the house was a large shrubbery, which opened on to a wide carriage drive leading to the high road. The house was an old red-brick building, in no particular style of architecture, with large oval windows and a square porch. The rooms were large, lofty, and well lighted. Along the western side of the house ran a long terrace called the western terrace; there the sun appeared to shine brightest, there tender plants flourished, there tame white doves came to be fed and a peacock walked in majesty; from there one heard the distant rush of the river.

There Lady Arleigh spent the greater part of her time—there she wore her gentle life away. Three years had elapsed, and no change had come to her. She read of her husband's sojourn in Scotland. Then she read in the fashionable intelligence that he had gone to Wood Lynton, the seat of the Earl of Mountdean. He remained there three days, and then went abroad. Where he was now she did not know; doubtless he was traveling from one place to another, wretched, unhappy as she was herself.

The desolate, dreary life had begun to prey upon her at last. She had fought against it bravely for some time—she had tried to live down the sorrow; but it was growing too strong for her—the weight of it was wearing her life away. Slowly but surely she began to fade and droop. At first it was but a failure in strength—a little walk tired her, the least fatigue or exercise seemed too much for her. Then, still more slowly, the exquisite bloom faded from the lovely face, a weary languor shone in the dark-blue eyes, the crimson lips lost their color. Yet Lady Arleigh grew more beautiful as she grew more fragile. Then all appetite failed her. Mrs. Burton declared that she ate nothing.

She might have led a different life—she might have gone out into society—she might have visited and entertained guests. People knew that Lady Arleigh was separated from her husband; they knew also that, whatever might have been the cause of separation, it had arisen from no fault of hers. She would, in spite of her strange position, have been welcomed with open arms by the whole neighborhood, but she was sick with mortal sorrow—life had not a charm for her.

She had no words for visitors—she had no wish left for enjoyment. Just to dream her life away was all she cared for. The disappointment was so keen, so bitter, she could not overcome it. Death would free Norman from all burden—would free him from this tie that must be hateful to him. Death was no foe to be met and fought with inch by inch; he was rather a friend who was to save her from the embarrassment of living on—a friend who would free her husband from the effects of his terrible mistake.

Madaline had never sent for her mother, not knowing whether Lord Arleigh would like it; but she had constantly written to her, and had forwarded money to her. She had sent her more than Margaret Dornham was willing to accept. Another thing she had done—she had most carefully refrained from saying one word to her mother as to the cause of her separation from her husband. Indeed, Margaret Dornham had no notion of the life that her well-beloved Madaline was leading.

It had been a terrible struggle for Margaret to give her up.

"I might as well have let her go back years ago to those to whom she belonged," she said to herself, "as to let her go now."

Still, she stood in great awe of the Duchess of Hazlewood, who seemed to her one of the grandest ladies in all England; and, when the duchess told her it was selfish of her to stand in her daughter's light, Margaret gave way and let her go. Many times, after she had parted with her, she felt inclined to open the oaken box with brass clasps, and see what the papers in it contained, but a nameless fear came over her. She did not dare to do what she had not done earlier.

Madaline had constantly written to her, had told her of her lover, had described Lord Arleigh over and over again to her. On the eve of her wedding-day she had written again; but, after that fatal marriage-day, she had not told her secret. Of what use would it be to make her mother more unhappy than she was—of what avail to tell her that the dark and terrible shadow of her father's crime had fallen over her young life, blighting it also?

Of all her mother's troubles she knew this would be the greatest so she generously refrained from naming it. There was no need to tell her patient, long-suffering, unhappy mother that which must prove like a dagger in her gentle heart. So Margaret Dornham had one gleam of sunshine in her wretched life. She believed that the girl she had loved so dearly was unutterably happy. She had read the descriptions of Lord Arleigh with tears in her eyes.

"That is how girls write of the men they love," she said—"my Madaline loves him."

Madaline had written to her when the ceremony was over. She had no one to make happy with her news but her distant mother. Then some days passed before she heard again—that did not seem strange. There was, of course, the going home, the change of scene, the constant occupation. Madaline would write when she had time. At the end of a week she heard again; and then it struck her that the letter was dull, unlike one written by a happy bride—but of course she must be mistaken—why should not Madaline be happy?

After that the letters came regularly, and Madaline said that the greatest pleasure she had lay in helping her mother. She said that she intended to make her a certain allowance, which she felt quite sure would be continued to her after her death, should that event precede her mother's; so that at last, for the weary-hearted woman, came an interval of something like contentment. Through Madaline's bounty she was able to move from her close lodgings in town to a pretty cottage in the country Then she had a glimpse of content.

After a time her heart yearned to see the daughter of her adoption, the one sunbeam of her life, and she wrote to that effect.

"I will come to you," wrote Madaline, in reply, "if you will promise me faithfully to make no difference between me and the child Madaline who used to come home from school years ago."

Margaret promised, and Madaline, plainly dressed, went to see her mother. It was sweet, after those long, weary months of humiliation and despair, to lay her head on that faithful breast and hear whispered words of love and affection. When the warmth of their first greeting was over, Margaret was amazed at the change in her child. Madaline had grown taller, the girlish graceful figure had developed into a model of perfect womanhood. The dress that she wore became her so well that the change in the marvelous face amazed her the most, it was so wonderfully wonderful, so fair, so pure, so *spirituelle*, yet it had so strange a story written upon it—a story she could neither read nor understand. It was not a happy face. The eyes were shadowed, the lips firm, the radiance and brightness that had distinguished her were gone; there were patience and resignation Instead.

"How changed you are, my darling!" said Margaret, as she looked at her. "Who would have thought that my little girl would grow into a tall, stately, beautiful lady, dainty and exquisite? What did Lord Arleigh say to your coming, my darling?"

"He did not say anything," she replied, slowly.

"But was he not grieved to lose you?"

"Lord Arleigh is abroad," said Madaline, gently. "I do not expect that he will return to England just yet."

"Abroad!" repeated Margaret. "Then, my darling, how is it that you are not with him?"

"I could not go," she replied, evasively.

"And you love your husband very much, Madaline, do you not?" inquired Margaret.

"Yes, I love him with all my heart and soul!" was the earnest reply.

"Thank Heaven that my darling is happy!" said Margaret, "I shall find everything easier to bear now that I that."

Chapter XXXV.

Margaret Dornham was neither a clever nor a far-seeing woman; had she been either, she would never have acted as she did. She would have known that in taking little Madaline from Castledene she was destroying her last chance of ever being owned or claimed by her parents; she would have understood that, although she loved the child very dearly, she was committing a most cruel act. But she thought only of how she loved her. Yet, undiscerning as she was, she was puzzled about her daughter's happiness. If she was really so happy, why did she spend long hours in reverie—why sit with folded hands, looking with such sad eyes at the passing clouds? That did not look like happiness. Why those heavy sighs, and the color that went and came like light and shade? It was strange happiness. After a time she noticed that Madaline never spoke voluntarily of her husband. She would answer any questions put to her—she would tell her mother anything she desired to know; but of her own accord she never once named him. That did not look like happiness. She even once, in answer to her mother's questions, described Beechgrove to her—told her of the famous beeches, the grand picture gallery; she told her of the gorgeous Titian—the woman with rubies like blood shining on her white neck. But she did not add that she had been at Beechgrove only once, and had left the place in sorrow and shame.

She seemed to have every comfort, every luxury; but Margaret noticed also that she never spoke of her circle of society—that she never alluded to visitors.

"It seems to me, my darling, that you lead a very quiet life," she said, one day; and Madaline's only answer was that such was really the case.

Another time Margaret said to her:

"You do not write many letters to your husband, Madaline. I could imagine a young wife like you writing every day," and her daughter made no reply.

On another occasion Mrs. Dornham put the question to her:

"You are quite sure, Madaline, that you love your husband?"

"Love him!" echoed the girl, her face lighting up—"love him, mother? I think no one in the wide world has ever loved another better!"

"Such being the case, my darling," said Margaret, anxiously, "let me ask you if you are quite sure he loves you?"

No shadow came into the blue eyes as she raised them to her mother's face.

"I am as sure of it," she replied, "as I am of my own existence."

"Then," thought Margaret to herself, "I am mistaken; all is well between them."

Madaline did not intend to remain very long with her mother, but it was soothing to the wounded, aching heart to be loved so dearly. Margaret startled her one day, by saying:

"Madaline, now that you are a great lady, and have such influential friends, do you not think you could do something for your father?"

"Something for my father?" repeated the girl, with a shudder. "What can I do for him?"

A new idea suddenly occurred to Mrs. Dornham. She looked into Lady Arleigh's pale, beautiful face.

"Madaline," she said, earnestly, "tell me the whole truth—is your father's misfortune any drawback to you? Tell me the truth; I have a reason for asking you."

But Lady Arleigh would not pain her mother—her quiet, simple heart had ached bitterly enough. She would not add one pang.

"Tell me, dear," continued Margaret, earnestly; "you do not know how important it is for me to understand."

"My dear mother," said Lady Arleigh, gently clasping her arms round her mother's neck; "do not let that idea make you uneasy. All minor lights cease to shine, you know, in the presence of greater ones. The world bows down to Lord Arleigh; very few, I think, know what his wife's name was. Be quite happy about me, mother. I am sure that no one who has seen me since my marriage knows anything about my father."

"I shall be quite happy, now that I know that," she observed.

More than once during that visit Margaret debated within herself whether she would tell Lady Arleigh her story or not; but the same weak fear that had caused her to run away with the child, lest she should lose her now, made her refrain from speaking, lest Madaline, on knowing the truth, should be angry with her and forsake her.

If Mrs. Dornham had known the harm that her silence was doing she would quickly have broken it.

Lady Arleigh returned home, taking her silent sorrow with her. If possible, she was kinder then ever afterward to her mother, sending her constantly baskets of fruit and game—presents of every kind. If it had not been for the memory of her convict husband, Mrs. Dornham would for the first time in her life have been quite happy.

Then it was that Lady Arleigh began slowly to droop, then it was that her desolate life became utterly intolerable—that her sorrow became greater than she could bear. She must have some one near her, she felt—some one with whom she could speak—or she should go mad. She longed for her mother. It was true Margaret Dornham was not an educated woman, but in her way she was refined. She was gentle, tender-hearted, thoughtful, patient, above all, Madaline believed she was her mother—and she had never longed for her mother's love and care as she did now, when health, strength, and life seemed to be failing her.

By good fortune she happened to see in the daily papers that Lord Arleigh was staying at Meurice's Hotel, in Paris. She wrote to him there, and told him that she had a great longing to have her mother with her. She told him that she had desired this for a long time, but that she had refrained from expressing the wish lest it should be displeasing to him.

"Do not scruple to refuse me," she said, "if you do not approve. I hardly venture to hope that you will give your consent. If you do, I will thank you for it. If you should think it best to refuse it, I submit humbly as I submit now. Let me add that I would not ask the favor but that my health and strength are failing fast."

Lord Arleigh mused long and anxiously over this letter. He hardly cared that her mother should go to Dower House; it would perhaps be the means of his unhappy secret becoming known. Nor did he like to refuse Madaline, unhappy, lonely, and ill. Dear Heaven, if he could but go to her himself and comfort her.

Chapter XXXVI.

Long and anxiously did Lord Arleigh muse over his wife's letter. What was he to do? If her mother was like the generality of her class, then he was quite sure that the secret he had kept would be a secret no longer—there was no doubt of that. She would naturally talk, and the servants would prove the truth of the story, and there would be a terrible *exposé*. Yet, lonely and sorrowful as Madaline declared herself to be, how could he refuse her? It was an anxious question for him, and one that caused him much serious thought. Had he known how ill she was he would not have hesitated a moment.

He wrote to Madaline—how the letter was received and cherished no one but herself knew—and told her that he would be in England in a day or two, and would then give her a decided answer. The letter was kind and affectionate; it came to her hungry heart like dew to a thirsty flower.

A sudden idea occurred to Lord Arleigh. He would go to England and find out all about the unfortunate man Dornham. Justice had many victims; it was within the bounds of possibility that the man might have been innocent—might have been unjustly accused. If such—and oh, how he hoped it might be!—should prove to be the case, then Lord Arleigh felt that he could take his wife home. It was the real degradation of the crime that he dreaded so utterly—dreaded more than all that could ever be said about it. He thought to himself more than once that, if by any unexpected means he discovered that Henry Dornham was innocent of the crime attributed to him, he would in that same hour ask Madaline to forgive him, and to be the mistress of his house. That was the only real solution of the difficulty that ever occurred to him. If the man were but innocent he—Lord Arleigh—would never heed the poverty, the obscurity the humble name—all that was nothing. By comparison it seemed so little that he could have smiled at it. People might say it was a low marriage, but he had his own idea of what was low. If only the man could be proved innocent of crime, then he might go to his sweet, innocent wife, and clasping her in his arms, take her to his heart.

The idea seemed to haunt him—it seemed to have a fatal attraction for him. He resolved to go to London at once and see if anything could be done in the matter. How he prayed and longed and hoped! He passed through well-nigh every stage of feeling—from the bright rapture of hope to the lowest depths of despair. He went first to Scotland Yard, and had a long interview with the detective who had given evidence against Henry Dornham. The detective's idea was that he was emphatically "a bad lot."

He smiled benignly when Lord Arleigh suggested that possibly the man was innocent, remarking that it was very kind of the gentleman to think so; for his own part he did not see a shadow of a chance of it.

"He was caught, you see, with her grace's jewels in his pocket, and gold and silver plate ready packed by his side—that did not look much like innocence."

"No, certainly not," Lord Arleigh admitted; "but then there have been cases in which circumstances looked even worse against an innocent man."

"Yes"—the detective admitted it, seeing that for some reason or other his lordship had a great desire to make the man out innocent.

"He will have a task," the detective told himself, grimly.

To the inquiry as to whether the man had been sent out of England the answer was "No; he is at Chatham."

To Chatham Lord Arleigh resolved to go. For one in his position there would not be much difficulty in obtaining an interview with the convict. And before long Lord Arleigh, one of the proudest men in England, and Henry Dornham, poacher and thief, stood face to face.

Lord Arleigh's first feeling was one of great surprise—Henry Dornham was so different from what he had expected to find him; he had not thought that he would be fair like Madaline, but he was unprepared for the dark, swarthy, gypsy-like type of the man before him.

The two looked steadily at each other; the poacher did not seem in the least to stand in awe of his visitor. Lord Arleigh tried to read the secret of the man's guilt or innocence in his face. Henry Dornham returned the gaze fearlessly.

"What do you want with me?" he asked. "You are what we call a swell. I know by the look of you. What do you want with me?"

The voice, like the face, was peculiar, not unpleasant—deep, rich, with a clear tone, yet not in the least like Madaline's voice.

"I want," said Lord Arleigh, steadily, "to be your friend, if you will let me."

"My friend!" a cynical smile curled the handsome lips. "Well, that is indeed a novelty. I should like to ask, if it would not seem rude, what kind of a friend can a gentleman like you be to me?"

"You will soon find out," said Lord Arleigh.

"I have never known a friendship between a rich man and a ne'er-do-well like myself which did not end in harm for the poorer man. You seek us only when you want us—and then it is for no good."

"I should not be very likely to seek you from any motive but the desire to help you," observed Lord Arleigh. "It is not quite clear to me how I am to be helped," returned the convict with a cynical smile; "but if you can do anything to get me out of this wretched place, please do."

"I want you to answer me a few questions," said Lord Arleigh—"and very much depends on them. To begin, tell me, were you

269

innocent or guilty of the crime for which you are suffering? Is your punishment deserved or not?"

"Well," replied Henry Dornham, with a sullen frown, "I can just say this—it is well there are strong bars between us; if there were not you would not live to ask such another question."

"Will you answer me?" said Lord Arleigh, gently.

"No, I will not—why should I? You belong to a class I hate and detest—a class of tyrants and oppressors."

"Why should you? I will tell you in a few words. I am interested in the fate of your wife and daughter."

"My what?" cried the convict, with a look of wonder.

"Your wife and daughter," said Lord Arleigh.

"My daughter!" exclaimed the man. "Good Heaven! Oh, I see! Well, go on. You are interested in my wife and daughter—what else?"

"There is one thing I can do which would not only be of material benefit to them, but would make your daughter very happy. It cannot be done unless we can prove your innocence."

"Poor little Madaline," said the convict, quietly—"poor, pretty little girl!"

Lord Arleigh's whole soul revolted on hearing this man speak so of his fair, young wife. That this man, with heavy iron bars separating him, as though he were a wild animal, from the rest of the world, should call his wife "poor, pretty little Madaline."

"I would give," said Lord Arleigh, "a great deal to find that your conviction had been a mistake. I know circumstances of that kind will and do happen. Tell me honestly, is there any, even the least probability, of finding out anything to your advantage?"

"Well," replied Henry Dornham, "I am a ne'er-do-well by nature. I was an idle boy, an idle youth, and an idle man. I poached when I had a chance. I lived on my wife's earnings. I went to the bad as deliberately as any one in the world did, but I do not remember that I ever told a willful lie."

There passed through Lord Arleigh's mind a wish that the Duchess of Hazlewood might have heard this avowal.

"I do not remember," the man said again, "that I have ever told a willful lie in my life. I will not begin now. You asked me if I was really guilty. Yes, I was—guilty just as my judges pronounced me to be!"

For a few minutes Lord Arleigh was silent; the disappointment was almost greater than he could bear. He had anticipated so much from this interview; and now by these deliberately spoken words his hopes were ended—he would never be able to take his beautiful young wife to his heart and home. The bitterness of the disappointment seemed almost greater than he could bear. He tried to recover himself, while Henry Dornham went on:

"The rich never have anything to do with the poor without harm comes of it. Why did they send me to the duke's house? Why did be try to patronize me? Why did he parade his gold and silver plate before my eyes?"

The passion of his words seemed to inflame him.

"Why," he continued angrily, should he eat from silver while others were without bread? Why should his wife wear diamonds while mine cried with hunger and cold? I saw how unjust it was. Who placed his foot on my neck? Who made him my master and tyrant, patronizing me with his 'my good fellow' this and the other? What right had he to such abundance while I had nothing?"

"That which was his," said Lord Arleigh, bluntly, "at least was not yours to take."

"But I say it was! I helped myself before, and, if I were out of this place, having the chance, I would help myself again."

"That would be equally criminal," said Lord Arleigh, fearlessly and again Henry Dornham laughed his cynical laugh.

"It is too late in the day for me to talk over these matters," said the convict. "When I roamed in the woods as a free man, I had my own ideas; prison has not improved them. I shall never make a reformed convict—not even a decent ticket-of-leave man. So if you have any thought of reclaiming me, rid your mind of it at once."

"It will be best to do so, I perceive," observed Lord Arleigh. "I had some little hope when I came in—I have none now."

"You do not mean to say, though, that I am not to be any the better off for your visit?" cried the man. "I do not know your name, but I can see what you are. Surely you will try to do something for me?"

"What can I do?" asked Lord Arleigh. "If you had been innocent— even if there had been what they call extenuating circumstances—I would have spent a fortune in the endeavor to set you free; but your confession renders me powerless."

"The only extenuating circumstance in the whole affair," declared the man, after a pause, "was that I wanted money, and took what I thought would bring it. So you would give a small fortune to clear me, eh?" he interrogated.

"Yes," was the brief reply.

The man looked keenly at him.

"Then you must indeed have a strong motive. It is not for my own sake, I suppose?" A new idea occurred to him. A sudden smile curled his lip. "I have it!" he said. "You are in love with my—with pretty little Madaline, and you want to marry her! If you could make me out innocent, you would marry her; if you cannot—what then? Am I right?"

All the pride of his nature rose in rebellion against this coarse speech. He, an Arleigh of Beechgrove, to hear this reprobate sneering at his love! His first impulse was an angry one, but he controlled himself. After all, it was Madaline's father—for Madaline's sake he would be patient.

"Am I right?" the prisoner repeated, with the same mocking smile.

"No," replied Lord Arleigh, "you are not right. There is no need for me to offer any explanation, and, as I have failed in my object, I will go."

"You might just as well tell me if you are in love with my little Madaline. I might make it worth your while to let me know."

It was with great difficulty that Lord Arleigh controlled his indignation; but he replied, calmly:

"I have nothing to tell you."

A look of disappointment came over the dark, handsome face.

"You can keep your secrets," he said—"so can I. If you will tell me nothing, neither shall I; but I might make it worth your while to trust me."

"I have nothing to confide," returned Lord Arleigh; "all I can say to you on leaving is that I hope you will come to your senses and repent of your past wickedness."

"I shall begin to think that you are a missionary in disguise," said Henry Dornham. "So you will not offer me anything for my secret?" he interrogated.

"No secret of yours could interest me," rejoined Lord Arleigh abruptly, as he went away.

So, for the second time in his life, he was at the door of the mystery, yet it remained unopened. The first time was when he was listening to Lord Mountdean's story, when the mention of the name Dornham should lead to a denouement; the second was now, when, if he had listened to the convict, he would have heard that Madaline was not his child.

He left Chatham sick at heart. There was no help for him—his fate was sealed. Never, while he lived, could he make his beautiful wife his own truly—they were indeed parted for evermore. There remained to him to write that letter; should he consent to Madaline's mother living with her or should he not?

He reflected long and anxiously, and then having well weighed the matter he decided that he would not refuse his wife her request. He must run the risk, but he would not caution her.

He wrote to Madaline, and told her that he would be pleased if she were pleased, and that he hoped she would be happy with her mother, adding the caution that he trusted she would impress upon her mother the need of great reticence, and that she must not mention the unfortunate circumstances of the family to any creature living.

Madaline's answer touched him. She assured him that there was no fear—that her mother was to be implicitly trusted. She told him also how entirely she had kept the secret of his separation from her, lest it should add to her mother's trouble.

"She will know now that I do not live with you, that I never see you, that we are as strangers, but she will never know the reason."

He was deeply moved. What a noble girl she was, bearing her troubles so patiently, and confiding them to no human soul!

Then he was compelled to go to Beechgrove—it was long since he had been there, and so much required attention, he was obliged to go, sorely against his will, for he dreaded the sight of the place, haunted as it was by the remembrance of the love and sorrow of his young wife. He avoided going as long as possible, but the place needed the attention of a master.

It was June when he went—bright, smiling, perfumed, sunny June—and Beechgrove was at its best; the trees were in full foliage, the green woods resounded with the song of birds, the gardens were filled with flowers, the whole estate was blooming and fair. He took up his abode there. It was soon noticed in the house that he avoided the picture-gallery—nothing ever induced him to enter it. More than once, as he was walking through the woods, his heartbeat and his face flushed; there, beyond the trees lived his wife, his darling, from whom a fate more cruel than death had parted him. His wife! The longing to see her grew on him from day to day. She was so near him, yet so far away—she was so fair, yet her beauty must all fade and die; it was not for him.

In time he began to think it strange that he had never heard anything of her. He went about in the neighborhood, yet no one spoke of having seen her. He never heard of her being at church, nor did he ever meet her on the high-road. It was strange how completely a vail of silence and mystery had fallen over her.

When he had been some time at Beechgrove he received one morning a letter from the Earl of Mountdean, saying that he was in the neighborhood, and would like to call. Lord Arleigh was pleased at the prospect. There was deep and real cordiality between the two men—they thoroughly understood and liked each other; it was true that the earl was older by many years than Lord Arleigh, but that did not affect their friendship.

They enjoyed a few days together very much. One morning they rode through the woods—the sweet, fragrant, June woods—when, from between the trees, they saw the square turrets of the Dower House. Lord Mountdean stopped to admire the view.

"We are a long distance from Beechgrove," he said; "what is that pretty place?"

Lord Arleigh's face flushed hotly.

"That," he replied, "is the Dower House, where my wife lives."

The earl looked with great interest at Lady Arleigh's dwelling-place.

"It is very pretty," he said—"pretty and quiet; but it must be dull for a young girl. You said she was young, did you not?"

"Yes, she is years younger than I am," replied Lord Arleigh.

"Poor girl!" said the earl, pityingly; "it must be rather a sad fate—so young and beautiful, yet condemned all her life to live alone. Tell me, Arleigh, did you take advice before you separated yourself so abruptly from her?"

"No," replied Lord Arleigh, "I did not ever seek it; the matter appeared plain enough to me."

"I should not like you to think me curious," pursued the earl. "We are true friends now, and we can trust each other. You have every confidence in me, and I have complete faith in you. I would intrust to you the dearest secret of my heart. Arleigh, tell me what I know you have told to no human being—the reason of your separation from the wife you love."

Lord Arleigh hesitated for one half minute.

"What good can it possibly do?" he said.

"I am a great believer in the good old proverb that two heads are better than one," replied the earl. "I think it is just possible that I might have some idea that has not occurred to you; I might see some way out of the difficulty, that has not yet presented itself to you.

Please yourself about it; either trust me or not, as you will; but if you do trust me, rely upon it I shall find some way of helping you."

"It is a hopeless case," observed Lord Arleigh, sadly. "I am quite sure that even if you knew all about it, you would not see any comfort for me. For my wife's sake I hesitate to tell you, not for my own."

"Your wife's secret will be as safe with me as with yourself," said the earl.

"I never thought that it would pass my lips, but I do trust you," declared Lord Arleigh; "and if you can see any way to help me, I shall thank Heaven for the first day I met you. You must hold my wife blameless, Lord Mountdean," he went on. "She never spoke untruthfully, she never deceived me; but on our wedding-day I discovered that her father was a convict—a man of the lowest criminal type."

Lord Mountdean looked as he felt, shocked.

"But how," he asked, eagerly, "could you be so deceived?"

"That I can never tell you; it was an act of fiendish revenge—cruel, ruthless, treacherous. I cannot reveal the perpetrator. My wife did not deceive me, did not even know that I had been deceived; she thought, poor child, that I was acquainted with the whole of her father's story, but I was not. And now, Lord Mountdean, tell me, do you think I did wrong?"

He raised his care-worn, haggard face as he asked the question and the earl was disturbed at sight of the terrible pain in it.

Chapter XXXVII.

The reason of his separation from his wife revealed, Lord Arleigh again put the question:

"Do you think, Lord Mountdean, that I have done wrong?"

The earl looked at him.

"No," he replied, "I cannot say that you have."

"I loved her," continued Lord Arleigh, "but I could not make the daughter of a convict the mistress of my house, the mother of my children. I could not let my children point to a felon's cell as the cradle of their origin. I could not sully my name, outrage a long line of noble ancestors, by making my poor wife mistress of Beechgrove. Say, if the same thing had happened to you, would you not have acted in like manner?"

"I believe that I should," answered the earl, gravely.

"However dearly you might love a woman, you could not place your coronet on the brow of a convict's daughter," said Lord Arleigh. "I love my wife a thousand times better than my life, yet I could not make her mistress of Beechgrove."

"It was a cruel deception," observed the earl—"one that it is impossible to understand. She herself—the lady you have made your wife—must be quite as unhappy as yourself."

"If it be possible she is more so," returned Lord Arleigh; "but tell me, if I had appealed to you in the dilemma—if I had asked your advice—what would you have said to me?"

"I should have no resource but to tell you to act as you have done," replied the earl; "no matter what pain and sorrow it entailed you could not have done otherwise."

"I thought you would agree with me. And now, Mountdean, tell me, do you see any escape from my difficulty?"

"I do not, indeed," replied the earl.

"I had one hope," resumed Lord Arleigh; "and that was that the father had perhaps been unjustly sentenced, or that he might after all prove to be innocent. I went to see him—he is one of the convicts working at Chatham."

"You went to see him!" echoed the earl, in surprise.

"Yes; and I gave up all hope from the moment I saw him. He is simply a handsome reprobate. I asked him if it was true that he had committed the crime, and he answered me quite frank, 'Yes.' I asked him if there were any extenuating circumstances; he replied 'want of money.' When I had seen and spoken to him, I felt convinced that the step I had taken with regard to my wife was a wise one, however cruel it may have been. No man in his senses would voluntarily admit a criminal's daughter into his family."

"No; it is even a harder case than I thought it," said the earl. "The only thing I can recommend is resignation."

Lord Mountdean thought that he would like to see the hapless young wife, and learn if she suffered as her husband did. He wondered too what she could be like, this convict's daughter who had been gifted with a regal dower of grace and beauty—this lowly-born child of the people who had been fair enough to charm the fastidious Lord Arleigh.

Meanwhile Madaline was all unconscious of the strides that destiny was making in her favor. She had thought her husband's letter all that was most kind; and, though she felt that there was no real grounds for it, she impressed upon her mother the need of the utmost reticence. Margaret Dornham understood from the first.

"Never have a moment's uneasiness, Madaline," she said. "From the hour I cross your threshold until I leave, your father's name shall never pass my lips."

It was a little less dreary for Madaline when her mother was with her. Though they did not talk much, and had but few tastes alike, Margaret was all devotion, all attention to her child.

She was sadly at a loss to understand matters. She had quite expected to find Madaline living at Beechgrove—she could not imagine why she was alone in Winiston House. The arrangement had seemed reasonable enough while Lord Arleigh was abroad, but now that he had returned to England, why did he not come to his wife, or why did not she go to him? She could not understand it; and as Madaline volunteered no explanation, her mother asked for none.

But, when day after day she saw her daughter fading away—when she saw the fair face lose its color, the eyes their light—when she saw the girl shrink from the sunshine and the flowers, from all that was bright and beautiful, from all that was cheerful and exhilarating— she knew that her soul was sick unto death. She would look with longing eyes at the calm, resigned face, wishing with all her heart that she might speak, yet not daring to do so.

What seemed to her even more surprising was that no one appeared to think such a state of things strange; and when she had been at Winiston some few weeks, she discovered that, as far as the occupants of the house were concerned, the condition of matters was not viewed as extraordinary. She offered no remark to the servants, and they offered none to her, but from casual observations she gathered that her daughter had never been to Beechgrove, but had lived at Winiston all her married life, and that Lord Arleigh had never been to visit her.

How was this? What did the terrible pain in her daughter's face mean? Why was her bright young life so slowly but surely fading away? She noted it for some time in silence, and then she decided to speak.

One morning when Madaline had turned with a sigh from the old-fashioned garden with its wilderness of flowers, Margaret said, gently:

"Madaline, I never hear you speak of the Duchess of Hazlewood who was so very kind to you. Does she never come to see you?"

She saw the vivid crimson mount to the white brow, to be speedily replaced by a pallor terrible to behold.

"My darling," she cried, in distress, "I did not expect to grieve you!"

"Why should I be grieved?" said the girl, quietly. "The duchess does not come to see me because she acted to me very cruelly; and I never write to her now."

Then Margaret for awhile was silent. How was she to bring forward the subject nearest to her heart? She cast about for words in which to express her thoughts.

"Madaline," she said, at last, "no one has a greater respect than I have for the honor of husband and wife; I mean for the good faith and confidence there should be between them. In days gone by I never spoke of your poor father's faults—I never allowed any one to mention them to me. If any of the neighbors ever tried to talk about him, I would not allow it. So, my darling, do not consider that there is any idle curiosity in what I am about to say to you. I thought you were so happily married, my dear; and it is a bitter disappointment to me to find that such is not the case."

There came no reply from Lady Arleigh; her hands were held before her eyes.

"I am almost afraid, dearly as I love you, to ask you the question," Margaret continued; "but, Madaline, will you tell me why you do not live with your husband?"

"I cannot, mother," was the brief reply.

"Is it—oh, tell me, dear!—is it any fault of yours? Have you displeased him?"

"It is through no fault of mine, mother. He says so himself."

"Is it from any fault of his? Has he done anything to displease you?"

"No," she answered, with sudden warmth, "he has not—indeed, he could not, I love him so."

"Then, if you have not displeased each other, and really love each other, why are you parted in this strange fashion? It seems to me, Madaline, that you are his wife only in name."

"You are right, mother—and I shall never be any more; but do not ask me why—I can never tell you. The secret must live and die with me."

"Then I shall never know it, Madaline?"

"Never, mother," she answered.

"But do you know, my darling, that it is wearing your life away?"

"Yes, I know it, but I cannot alter matters. And, mother," she continued, "if we are to be good friends and live together, you must never mention this to me again."

"I will remember," said Margaret, kissing the thin white hands, but to herself she said matters should not so continue. Were Lord Arleigh twenty times a lord, he should not break his wife's heart in that cold, cruel fashion.

A sudden resolve came to Mrs. Dornham—she would go to Beechgrove and see him herself. It he were angry and sent her away from Winiston House, it would not matter—she would have told him the truth. And the truth that she had to tell him was that the separation was slowly but surely killing his wife.

Chapter XXXVIII.

Margaret Dornham knew no peace until she had carried out her intention. It was but right, she said to herself, that Lord Arleigh should know that his fair young wife was dying.

"What right had he to marry her?" she asked herself indignantly, "if he meant to break her heart?"

What could he have left her for? It could not have been because of her poverty or her father's crime—he knew of both beforehand. What was it? In vain did she recall all that Madaline had ever said about her husband—she could see no light in the darkness, find no solution to the mystery; therefore the only course open to her was to go to Lord Arleigh, and to tell him that his wife was dying.

"There may possibly have been some slight misunderstanding between them which one little interview might remove," she thought.

One day she invented some excuse for her absence from Winiston House, and started on her expedition, strong with the love that makes the weakest heart brave. She drove the greater part of the distance, and then dismissed the carriage, resolving to walk the remainder of the way—she did not wish the servants to know whither she was going. It was a delightful morning, warm, brilliant, sunny. The hedge-rows were full of wild roses, there was a faint odor of newly-mown hay, the westerly wind was soft and sweet.

As Margaret Dornham walked through the woods, she fell deeply into thought. Almost for the first time a great doubt had seized her, a doubt that made her tremble and fear. Through many long years she had clung to Madaline—she had thought her love and tender care of more consequence to the child than anything else. Knowing nothing of her father's rank or position, she had flattered herself into believing that she had been Madaline's best friend in childhood. Now there came to her a terrible doubt. What if she had stood in

Madaline's light, instead of being her friend? She had not been informed of the arrangements between the doctor and his patron, but people had said to her, when the doctor died, that the child had better be sent to the work-house—and that had frightened her. Now she wondered whether she had done right or wrong. What if she, who of all the world had been the one to love Madaline best, had been her greatest foe?

Thinking of this, she walked along the soft greensward. She thought of the old life in the pretty cottage at Ashwood, where for so short a time she had been happy with her handsome, ne'er-do-well husband, whom at first she had loved so blindly; she thought of the lovely, golden-haired child which she had loved so wildly, and of the kind, clever doctor, who had been so suddenly called to his account; and then her thoughts wandered to the stranger who had intrusted his child to her care. Had she done wrong in leaving him all these years in such utter ignorance of his child's welfare? Had she wronged him? Ought she to have waited patiently until he had returned or sent? If she were ever to meet him again, would he overwhelm her with reproaches? She thought of his tall, erect figure, of his handsome face, so sorrowful and sad, of his mournful eyes, which always looked as though his heart lay buried with his dead wife.

Suddenly her face grew deathly pale, her lips flew apart with a terrified cry, her whole frame trembled. She raised her hands as one who would fain ward off a blow, for, standing just before her, looking down on her with stern, indignant eyes, was the stranger who had intrusted his child to her.

For some minutes—how many she never knew—they stood looking at each other—he stern, indignant, haughty, she trembling, frightened, cowed.

"I recognize you again," he said, at length, in a harsh voice.

Cowed, subdued, she fell on her knees at his feet.

"Woman," he cried, "where is my child?"

She made him no answer, but covered her face with her hands.

"Where is my child?" he repeated. "I intrusted her to you—where is she?"

The white lips opened, and some feeble answer came which he could not hear.

"Where is my child?" he demanded. "What have you done with her? For Heaven's sake, answer me!" he implored.

Again she murmured something he could not catch, and he bent over her. If ever in his life Lord Mountdean lost his temper, he lost it then. He could almost, in his impatience, have forgotten that it was a woman who was kneeling at his feet, and could have shaken her until she spoke intelligibly. His anger was so great he could have struck her. But he controlled himself.

"I am not the most patient of men, Margaret Dornham," he said; "and you are trying me terribly. In the name of Heaven, I ask you, what have you done with my child?"

"I have not injured her," she sobbed.

"Is she living or dead?" asked the earl, with terrible calmness.

"She is living," replied the weeping woman.

Lord Mountdean raised his face reverently to the summer sky.

"Thank Heaven!" he said, devoutly; and then added, turning to the woman—"Living and well?"

"No, not well; but she will be in time. Oh, sir, forgive me! I did wrong, perhaps, but I thought I was acting for the best."

"It was a strange 'best,'" he said, "to place a child beyond its parent's reach."

"Oh, sir," cried Margaret Dornham, "I never thought of that! She came to me in my dead child's place—it was to me as though my own child had come back again. You could not tell how I loved her. Her little head lay on my breast, her little fingers caressed me, her little voice murmured sweet words to me. She was my own child—I loved her so, sir!" and the poor woman's voice was broken with sobs. "All the world was hard and cruel and cold to me—the child never was; all the world disappointed me—the child never did. My heart soul clung to her. And then, sir, when she was able to run about, a pretty, graceful, loving child, the very joy of my heart and sunshine of my life, the doctor died, and I was left alone with her."

She paused for some few minutes, her whole frame shaken with sobs. The earl, bending down, spoke kindly to her.

"I am quite sure," he said, "that if you erred it has been through love for my child. Tell me all—have no fear."

"I was in the house, sir," she continued, "when the poor doctor was carried home dead—in his sitting-room with my—with little Madaline—and when I saw the confusion that followed upon his death, I thought of the papers in the oaken box; and, without saying a word to any one, I took it and hid it under my shawl."

"But, tell me," said the earl, kindly, "why did you do that?"

"I can hardly remember now," she replied—"it is so long since. I think my chief motive was dread lest my darling should be taken from me. I thought that, if strangers opened the box and found out who she was, they would take her away from me, and I should never see her again. I knew that the box held all the papers relating to her, so I took it deliberately."

"Then, of course," said the earl, "you know her history?"

"No," she replied, quickly; "I have never opened the box."

"Never opened it!" he exclaimed, wonderingly.

"No, sir—I have never even touched it; it is wrapped in my old shawl just as I brought it away."

"But why have you never opened it?" he asked, still wondering.

"Because, sir, I did not wish to know who the little child really was, lest, in discovering that, I should discover something also which would compel me to give her up."

Lord Mountdean looked at her in astonishment. How woman-like she was! How full of contradictions! What strength and weakness, what honor and dishonor, what love and selfishness did not her conduct reveal!

"Then," continued Margaret Dornham, "when the doctor died, people frightened me. They said that the child must go to the work-house. My husband soon afterward got into dreadful trouble, and I determined to leave the village. I tell the truth, sir. I was afraid, too, that you would return and claim the child; so I took her away with me to London. My husband was quite indifferent—I could do as I liked, he said. I took her and left no trace behind. After we reached London, my husband got into trouble again; but I always did my best for the darling child. She was well dressed, well fed, well cared for, well educated—she has had the training of a lady."

"But," put in Lord Mountdean, "did you never read my advertisments?"

"No, sir," she replied; "I have not been in the habit of reading newspapers."

"It was strange that you should remain hidden in London while people were looking for you," he said. "What was your husband's trouble, Mrs. Dornham?"

"He committed a burglary, sir; and, as he had been convicted before, his sentence was a heavy one."

"And my daughter, you say, is living, but not well? Where is she?"

"I will take you to her, sir," was the reply—"at once, if you will go."

"I will not lose a minute," said the earl, hastily. "It is time, Mrs. Dornham, that you knew my name, and my daughter's also. I am the Earl of Mountdean, and she is Lady Madaline Charlewood."

On hearing this, Margaret Dornham was more frightened than ever. She rose from her knees and stood before him.

"If I have done wrong, my lord," she said, "I beg of you to pardon me—it was all, as I thought, for the best. So the child whom I have loved and cherished was a grand lady after all?"

"Do not let us lose a moment," he said. "Where is my daughter?"

"She lives not far from here; but we cannot walk—the distance is too great," replied Margaret.

"Well, we are near to the town of Lynton—it is not twenty minutes walk; we will go to an hotel, and get a carriage. I—I can hardly endure this suspense."

He never thought to ask her how she had come thither; it never occurred to him. His whole soul was wrapped in the one idea—that he was to see his child again—Madaline's child—the little babe he had held in his arms, whose little face he had bedewed with tears—his own child—the daughter he had lost for long years and had tried so hard to find. He never noticed the summer woods through which he was passing; he never heard the wild birds' song; of sunshine or shade he took no note. The heart within him was on fire, for he was going to see his only child—his lost child—the daughter whose voice he had never heard.

"Tell me," he said, stopping abruptly, and looking at Margaret "you saw my poor wife when she lay dead—is my child like her?"

Margaret answered quickly.

"She is like her; but, to my mind, she is a thousand times fairer."

They reached the principal hotel at Lynton, and Lord Mountdean called hastily for a carriage. Not a moment was to be lost—time pressed.

"You know the way," he said to Margaret, "will you direct the driver?"

He did not think to ask where his daughter lived, if she was married or single, what she was doing or anything else; his one thought was that he had found her—found her, never to lose her again.

He sat with his face shaded by his hand during the whole of the drive, thanking Heaven that he had found Madaline's child. He never noticed the woods, the high-road bordered with trees, the carriage-drive with its avenue of chestnuts; he did not even recognize the picturesque, quaint old Dower House that he had admired so greatly some little time before. He saw a large mansion, but it never occurred to him to ask whether his daughter was mistress or servant; he only knew that the carriage had stopped, and that very shortly he should see his child.

Presently he found himself in a large hall gay with flowers and covered with Indian matting, and Margaret Dornham was trembling before him.

"My lord," she said, "your daughter is ill, and I am afraid the agitation may prove too much for her. Tell me, what shall I do?"

He collected his scattered thoughts.

"Do you mean to tell me," he asked, "that she has been kept In complete ignorance of her history all these years?"

"She has been brought up in the belief that she is my daughter," said Margaret—"she knows nothing else."

A dark frown came over the earl's face.

"It was wickedly unjust," he said—"cruelly unjust. Let me go to her at once,"

Pale, trembling, and frightened, Margaret led the way. It seemed to the earl that his heart had stopped beating, and a thick mist was spread before his eyes, that the surging of a deep sea filled his ears. Oh, Heaven, could it be that after all these years he was really going to see Madaline's child, his own lost daughter? Very soon he found himself looking on a fair face framed in golden hair, with dark blue eyes, full of passion, poetry, and sorrow, sweet crimson lips, sensitive, and delicate, a face so lovely that its pure, saint-like expression almost frightened him. He looked at it in a passion of wonder and grief of love and longing; and then he saw a shadow of fear gradually darken the beautiful eyes.

"Madaline," he said gently; and she looked at him in wonder "Madaline," he repeated.

"I—I—do not know you," she replied, surprised.

She was lying, when he entered the room, on a little couch drawn close to the window, the sunlight, which fell full upon her, lighting up the golden hair and refined face with unearthly beauty. When he uttered her name, she stood up, and so like her mother did she appear that it was with difficulty he could refrain from clasping her in his arms. But he must not startle her, he reflected—he saw how fragile she was.

"You call me Madaline," she said again—"but I do not know you."

Before answering her, Lord Mountdean turned to Margaret.

"Will you leave us alone?" he requested, but Lady Arleigh stretched out her hand.

"That is my mother," she said—"she must not be sent away from me."

"I will not be long away, Madaline. You must listen to what this gentleman says—and, my dear, do not let it upset you."

Mrs. Dornham retired, closing the door carefully behind her, and Lady Arleigh and the earl stood looking at each Other.

"You call we Madaline," she said, "and you send my mother from me. What can you have to say?" A sudden thought occurred to her. "Has Lord Arleigh sent you to me?" she asked.

"Lord Arleigh!" he repeated, in wonder. "No, he has nothing to do with what I have to say. Sit down—you do not look strong—and I will tell you why I am here."

It never occurred to him to ask why she had named Lord Arleigh. He saw her sink, half exhausted, half frightened, upon the couch, and he sat down by her side.

"Madaline," he began, "will you look at me, and see if my face brings back no dream, no memory to you? Yet how foolish I am to think of such a thing! How can you remember me when your baby-eyes rested on me for only a few minutes?"

"I do not remember you," she said, gently—"I have never seen you before."

"My poor child," he returned, in a tone so full of tenderness and pain that she was startled by it, "this is hard!"

"You cannot be the gentleman I used to see sometimes in the early home that I only just remember, who used to amuse me by showing me his watch and take me out for drives?"

"No. I never saw you. Madeline as a child—I left you when you were three or four days old. I have never seen you since, although I have spent a fortune almost in searching for you."

"You have?" she said, wonderingly. "Who then are yon?"

"That is what I want to tell you without startling you, Madaline— dear Heaven, how strange it seems to utter that name again! You have always believed that good woman who has just quitted the room to be your mother?"

"Yes, always," she repeated, wonderingly.

"And that wretched man, the convict, you have always believed to be your father?"

"Always," she repeated.

"Will it pain or startle you very much to hear that they are not even distantly related to you—that the woman was simply chosen as your foster mother because she had just lost her own child?"

"I cannot believe it," she cried, trembling violently. "Who are you who tells me this?"

"I am Hubert, Earl of Mountdean," he replied, "and, if you will allow me, I will tell you what else I am."

"Tell me," she said, gently.

"I am your father, Madaline—and the best part of my life has been spent in looking for you."

"My father," she said, faintly. "Then I am not the daughter of a convict—my father is an earl?"

"I am your father," he repeated, "and you, child, have you, child, have your mother's face."

"And she—who has just left us—is nothing to me?"

"Nothing. Do not tremble, my dear child. Listen—try to be brave. Let me hold your hands in mine while I tell you a true story."

He held her trembling hands while he told her the story of his life, of his marriage, of the sudden and fatal journey, and her mother's death—told it in brief, clear words that left no shadow of doubt on her mind as to its perfect truth.

"Of your nurse's conduct," he said, "I forbear to speak—it was cruel, wicked; but, as love for you dictated it, I will say no more. My dear child, you must try to forget this unhappy past, and let me atone to you for it. I cannot endure to think that my daughter and heiress, Lady Madaline Charlewood, should have spent her youth under so terrible a cloud."

There came no answer, and, looking at her, he saw that the color had left her face, that the white eyelids had fallen over the blue eyes, that the white lips were parted and cold—she had fainted, fallen into a dead swoon.

He knelt by her side and called to her with passionate cries, he kissed the white face and tried to 'recall the wandering senses, and then he rang the bell with a heavy peal. Mrs. Dornham came hurrying in.

"Look!" said Lord Mountdean. "I have been as careful as I could, but that is your work."

Margaret Dornham knelt by the side of the senseless girl.

"I would give my life to undo my past folly," she said. "Oh, my lord, can you ever forgive me?"

He saw the passionate love that she had for her foster-child; he saw that it was a mother's love, tender, true, devoted and self-sacrificing, though mistaken. He could not be angry, for he saw that her sorrow even exceeded his own.

To his infinite joy, Madaline presently opened her dark eyes and looked up at him. She stretched out her hands to him.

"My father," she said—"you are really my father?"

He kissed her face.

"Madaline," he replied, "my heart is too full for words. I have spent seventeen years in looking for you, and have found you at last. My dear child, we have seventeen years of love and happiness to make up."

"It seems like an exquisite dream," she said. "Can it be true?"

He saw her lovely face grow crimson, and bending her fair, shapely head, she whispered:

"Papa, does Lord Arleigh know?"

"Lord Arleigh!" he repeated. "My dear child, this is the second time you have mentioned him. What has he to do with you?"

She looked up at him in wonder.

"Do you not know?" she asked. "Have they not told you I am Lord Arleigh's wife?"

Lord Arleigh felt very disconsolate that June morning. The world was so beautiful, so bright, so fair, it seemed hard that he should have no pleasure in it. If fate had but been kinder to him! To increase his dullness, Lord Mountdean, who had been staying with him some days, had suddenly disappeared. He had gone out early in the morning, saying that he would have a long ramble in the woods, and would probably not return until noon for luncheon. Noon had come and passed, luncheon was served, yet there was no sign of the earl, Lord Arleigh was not uneasy, but he longed for his friend's society.

At last he decided upon going in search of him. He had perhaps lost his way in the woods, or he had mistaken some road. It was high time that they looked after him—he had been so many hours absent without apparent cause. Lord Arleigh whistled for his two favorite dogs, Nero and Venus, and started out in search of his friend.

He went through the woods and down the high-road, but there was no sign of the earl. "He must have walked home by another route," thought Lord Arleigh; and he went back to Beechgrove. He did not find the earl there, but the groom, who had evidently been riding fast, was waiting for him in the hall.

"My lord," he said, "I was directed to give you this at once, and beg of you not to lose a moment's time."

Wondering what had happened, Lord Arleigh opened the note and read:

"My Dear Lord Arleigh: Something too wonderful for me to set down in words has happened. I am at the Dower House, Winiston. Come at once, and lose no time.

Mountdean."

"At the Dower House?" mused Lord Arleigh. "What can it mean?"

"Did the Earl of Mountdean send this himself?" he said to the man.

"Yes, my lord. He bade me ride as though for life, and ask your lordship to hurry in the same way."

"Is he hurt? Has there been any accident?"

"I have heard of no accident, my lord; but, when the earl came to give me the note, he looked wild and unsettled."

Lord Arleigh gave orders that his fleetest horse should be saddled at once, and then he rode away.

He was so absorbed in thought that more than once he had a narrow escape, almost striking his head against the overhanging boughs of the trees. What could it possibly mean? Lord Mountdean at the Dower House! He fancied some accident must have happened to him.

He had never been to the Dower House since the night when he took his young wife thither, and as he rode along his thoughts recurred to that terrible evening. Would he see her now, he wondered, and would she, in her shy, pretty way, advance to meet him? It could not surely be that she was ill, and that the earl, having heard of it, had sent for him. No, that could not be—for the note said that something wonderful had occurred.

Speculation was evidently useless—the only thing to be done was to hasten as quickly as he could, and learn for himself what it all meant. He rode perhaps faster than he had ever ridden in his life before. When he reached the Dower House the horse was bathed in foam. He thought to himself, as he rang the bell at the outer gate, how strange it was that he—the husband—should be standing there ringing for admittance.

A servant opened the gate, and Lord Arleigh asked if the Earl of Mountdean was within, and was told that he was.

"There is nothing the matter, I hope," said Lord Arleigh—"nothing wrong?"

The servant replied that something strange had happened, but he could not tell what it was. He did not think there was anything seriously wrong. And then Lord Arleigh entered the house where the years of his young wife's life had drifted away so sadly.

Chapter XXXIX.

Lord Arleigh was shown into the dining-room at Winiston House, and stood there impatiently awaiting the Earl of Mountdean. He came in at last, but the master of Beechgrove barely recognized him, he was so completely changed. Years seemed to have fallen from him. His face was radiant with a great glad light. He held out his hand to his friend.

"Congratulate me," he said; "I am one of the happiest men in the world."

"What has happened?" asked Lord Arleigh, in surprise.

"Follow me," said the earl; and in silence Lord Arleigh obeyed him.

They came to the pretty shaded room, and the earl, entering first, said:

"Now, my darling, the hour has come which will repay you for the sorrow of years."

Wondering at such words, Lord Arleigh followed his friend. There lay his beautiful wife, lovelier than ever, with the sunlight touching her hair with gold, her fair face transparent as the inner leaf of a rose—Madaline, his darling, who had been his wife in name only.

What did it mean? Why had the earl led him thither? Was it wanton cruelty or kindness? His first impulse was to fall on his knees by the little couch and kiss his wife's hands, his second to ask why he had been led thither to be tortured so. Madaline rose with a glad cry at his entrance, but Lord Mountdean laid a restraining hand on her shoulder.

"Lord Arleigh," said the earl, "tell me who this is."

"My wife, Lady Arleigh," he replied.

She bent forward with clasped hands.

"Oh, listen. Norman," she said, "listen."

"You looked upon her as the only woman you ever could love; you made her your wife; yet, believing her to be the daughter of a felon, you separated from her, preferring a life-time of misery to the dishonor of your name. Is it not so, Lord Arleigh?"

"Yes," he replied, "it is indeed so."

"Then now learn the truth. This lady, your wife, is not the daughter of a convict. In her—how happy the telling of it makes me—behold my daughter, the child whom for seventeen years I have sought incessantly—my heiress, Lady Madaline Charlewood, the descendant of a race as honored, as ancient, and as noble as your own!"

Lord Arleigh listened like one in a dream. It could not be possible, it could not be true, his senses must be playing him false—he must be going mad. His wife—his deserted wife—the earl's long-lost daughter! It was surely a cruel fable.

His dark, handsome face grew pale, his hands trembled, his lips quivered like a woman's. He was about to speak, when Madaline sprang forward and clasped her arms around his neck.

"Oh, my darling," she cried, "it is true—quite true! You need not be afraid to kiss me and to love me now—you need not be afraid to call me your wife—you need not be ashamed of me any longer. Oh, my darling, believe me, I am not a thief's daughter. My father is here— an honorable man, you see, not a convict. Norman, you may love me now; you need not be ashamed of me. Oh, my love, my love, I was dying, but this will make me well!"

Her golden head drooped on to his breast, the clinging arms tightened their hold of him. The earl advanced to them.

"It is all true, Arleigh," he said. "You look bewildered, but you need not hesitate to believe it. Later on I will tell you the story myself, and we will satisfy all doubts. Now be kind to her; she has suffered enough. Remember, I do not blame you, nor does she. Believing what you did, you acted for the best. We can only thank Heaven that the mystery is solved; and you can take a fair and noble maiden, who will bring honor to your race, to your home."

"My love," said Madaline, "it seems to me a happy dream." When Lord Arleigh looked around again the earl had vanished and he was alone with his fair young wife.

Half an hour afterward Lord Arleigh and his wife stood together under the great cedar on the lawn. They had left the pretty drawing-room, with its cool shade and rich fragrance, and Lord Arleigh stood holding his wife's hand in his.

"You can really forgive me, Madaline?" he said. "You owe me no ill-will for all that I have made you suffer?"

She smiled as she looked at him.

"No," she replied. "How could there be ill-will between you and me? You did right—in your place I should have acted as you did."

He caressed the fair, sweet face.

"Thank you, my darling," he said. "How thin you are!" he added. "How you have worn yourself away with fretting! What must I do to bring the roses back to this sweet face, and the light that I remember so well to the dear eyes?"

She looked up at him, her whole soul in her eyes.

"You have but one thing to do, and that is—love me," she said; "and then I shall be the happiest wife in all the world. If a choice were offered me of all the good gifts of this world, mine would be my husband's love."

Lord Arleigh looked thoughtfully at her. The sunshine glistened through the green boughs, and touched her graceful golden head as with an aureole of glory.

"I am beginning to think," he said, "that all that happens is for the best. We shall be wiser and better all our lives for having suffered."

"I think so too," observed Madaline.

"And my darling," he said, "I am quite sure of another thing. There are many good gifts in the world—wealth, fame, rank, glory—but the best gift of all is that which comes straight from Heaven—the love of a pure, good wife."

Looking up, they saw the earl crossing the lawn to meet them.

"Madaline," he said, gently, when he was close to them, "how rejoiced I am to see that look on your face. You have no thought of dying now?"

"Not if I can help it, papa," she replied.

"I think," continued the earl, "that this is the happiest day of my life. I must say this to you, Norman—that, if I had chosen from all the world, I could not have chosen a son whom I should care for more than for you, and that, if I had a son of my own, I should have wished him to be like you. And now we will talk about our future—I am so proud to have two children to arrange for instead of one—our future, that is to have no clouds. In the first place, what must we do with this good foster-mother of yours, Madaline, whose great love for you has led to all this complication?"

"I know what I should like to do," said Lady Arleigh, gently.

"Then consider it done," put in her husband.

"I should like her to live with me always," said Lady Arleigh any capacity—as housekeeper, or whatever she would like. She has had so little happiness in her life, and she would find her happiness now in mine. When her unfortunate husband is free again, she can do as she likes—either go abroad with him, or we can find them a cottage and keep them near us."

So it was arranged; and there were few happier women than Margaret Dornham when she heard the news.

"I thought," she sobbed, in a broken voice, "that I should never be forgiven; and now I find that I am to be always near to the child for whose love I would have sacrificed the world."

Lord Mountdean insisted on the fullest publicity being given to Madaline's abduction.

"There is one thing," he said, "I cannot understand—and that is how you came to misunderstand each other. Why did Madaline believe that you knew all about her story when you knew nothing of it? That secret, I suppose, you will keep to yourselves?"

"Yes," replied Lord Arleigh. "The truth is, we were both cruelly deceived—it matters little by whom and how.'"

"That part of the story, then, will never be understood," said Lord Mountdean. "The rest must be made public, no matter at what cost to our feelings—there must be no privacy, no shadow over my daughter's name. You give me your full consent, Norman?"

"Certainly; I think your proposal is very wise," Lord Arleigh replied.

"Another thing, Norman—I do not wish my daughter to go home to Beechgrove until her story has been made known. Then I will see that all honor is paid to her."

So it was agreed, and great was the sensation that ensued. "The Arleigh Romance," as it was called, was carried from one end of the kingdom to the other. Every newspaper was filled with it; all other intelligence sank into insignificance when compared with it. Even the leading journals of the day curtailed their political articles to give a full account of the Arleigh romance. But it was noticeable that in no way whatsoever was the name of the Duchess of Hazlewood introduced.

The story was fairly told. It recalled to the minds of the public that some time previously Lord Arleigh had made what appeared a strange marriage, and that he had separated from his wife on their wedding-day, yet paying her such honor and respect that no one could possibly think any the worse of her for it. It reminded the world how puzzled it had been at the time; and now it gave a solution of the mystery. Through no act of deception on the part of his wife, Lord Arleigh had believed that he knew her full history; but on their wedding-day he found that she was, to all appearance, the daughter of a man who was a convict. Therefore—continued the story—the young couple had agreed to separate. Lord Arleigh, although loving his wife most dearly, felt himself compelled to part from her. He preferred that his ancient and noble race should become extinct rather than that it should be tarnished by an alliance with the offspring of crime. Lady Arleigh agreed with her husband, and took up her abode at the Dower House, surrounded by every mark of esteem and honor. Then the story reverted to the Earl of Mountdean's lost child, and how, at length, to the intense delight of the husband and father, it was discovered that Lady Arleigh was no other than the long-lost daughter of Lord Mountdean.

As the earl had said, the only obscure point in the narrative was how Lord Arleigh had been deceived. Evidently it was not his wife who had deceived him—who, therefore, could it have been? That the world was never to know.

It was extraordinary how the story spread, and how great was the interest it excited. There was not a man or woman in all England who did not know it.

When the earl deemed that full reparation had been made to his daughter, he agreed that she should go to Beechgrove.

The country will never forget that home-coming. It was on a brilliant day toward the end of July. The whole country side was present to bid Lady Arleigh welcome—the tenants, servants, dependents, friends; children strewed flowers in her path, flags and banners waved in the sunlit air, there was a long procession with bands of music, there were evergreen arches with "Welcome Home" in monster letters.

It was difficult to tell who was cheered most heartily—the fair young wife whose beauty won all hearts, the noble husband, or the gallant earl whose pride and delight in his daughter were so great. Lord Arleigh said a few words in response to this splendid reception— and he was not ashamed of His own inability to finish what he had intended to say.

There had never been such a home-coming within one's memory The old house was filled with guests, all the *élite* of the county were there. There was a grand dinner, followed by a grand ball, and there was feasting for the tenantry—everything that could be thought of for the amusement of the vast crowd.

On that evening, while the festivities were at their height, Lord Arleigh and his lovely young wife stole away from their guests and went up to the picture-gallery. The broad, silvery moonbeams fell on the spot where they had once endured such cruel anguish. The fire seemed to have paled in the rubies round the white neck of Titian's gorgeous beauty. Lord Arleigh clasped his wife in his arms, and then he placed her at some little distance from himself, where the silvery moonlight fell on the fair, lovely profile, on the golden head, on the superb dress of rich white silk and on the gleaming diamonds.

"My darling," he said, "you are thousand times lovelier than even Titian's beauty here! Do you remember all we suffered in this spot?'

"I can never forget it," she replied.

"But you must forget it—it is for that I have brought you hither. This is the pleasantest nook in our house, and I want you to have pleasant associations with it. Where we suffered hear me say——" He paused.

"What is it?" she asked, quietly.

He threw his arms round her, and drew her to his breast.

"Hear me say this, my darling—that I love you with all my heart; that I will so love you, truthfully and faithfully, until death; and that I thank Heaven for the sweetest and best of all blessings, the gift of a good, pure, and loving wife."

Chapter XL.

Philippa, Duchess of Hazlewood, was sitting in the superb drawing-room at Vere Court. It was some time since she had left town, but she had brought some portion of the gay world back with her. The court was filled with visitors, and nothing was thought of but brilliant festivities and amusement. The duchess was queen of all gayety; the time that had passed had simply added to her beauty— she was now one of the handsomest women in society.

It was a warm day, the last day in June, and Vere Court had never seemed so brilliant. The lovely young duchess had withdrawn for a short time from her guests. Most of them had gone out riding or driving. There was to be a grand ball that evening and her Grace of Hazlewood did not wish to fatigue herself before it came off. As for driving or riding in the hot sun simply because the day was fine and the country fair, she did not believe in it. She had retired to her drawing-room; a soft couch, had been placed near one of the open windows, and the breeze that came in was heavy with perfume. On the stand by her side lay a richly-jeweled fan, a bottle of sweet scent, a bouquet of heliotrope—her favorite flower—and one or two books which she had selected to read. She lay, with her dark, queenly head on the soft cushion of crimson velvet in an attitude that would have charmed a painter. But the duchess was not wasting the light of her dark eyes over a book. She had closed them, as a flower closes its leaves in the heat of the sun. As she lay there, beautiful, languid, graceful, the picture she formed was a marvelous rich study of color. So thought the duke, who, unheard by her, had entered the room.

Everything had prospered with his grace. He had always been extremely wealthy, but his wealth had been increased in a sudden and unexpected fashion. On one of his estates in the north a vein of coal had been discovered, which was one of the richest in England. The proceeds of it added wonderfully to his income, and promised to add still more. No luxury was wanting; the duchess had all that her heart, even in its wildest caprices, could desire. The duke loved her with as keen and passionate a love as ever. He had refused to go out this morning, because she had not gone; and now he stood watching her with something like adoration in his face—the beautiful woman, in her flowing draperies of amber and white. He went up to her and touched her brow lightly with his lips.

"Are you asleep, my darling?" he asked.

"No," she replied, opening her eyes.

"I have something to read to you—something wonderful."

She roused herself.

"Your geese are generally swans, Vere. What is the wonder?"

"Listen, Philippa;" and, as the duke scanned the newspaper in his hands, he sang the first few lines of his favorite song:

"'Queen Philippa sat in her bower alone.'

"Ah, here it is!" he broke off. "I am sure you will say that this is wonderful. It explains all that I could not understand—and, for Arleigh's sake, I am glad, though what you will say to it, I cannot think."

And, sitting down by her side, he read to her the newspaper account of the Arleigh romance.

He read it without interruption, and the queenly woman listening to him knew that her revenge had failed, and that, instead of punishing the man who had slighted her love, she had given him one of the sweetest, noblest and wealthiest girls in England. She knew that her vengeance had failed—that she had simply crowned Lord Arleigh's life with the love of a devoted wife.

When the duke looked up from his paper to see what was the effect of his news, he saw that the duchess had quietly fainted away, and lay with the pallor of death on her face. He believed that the heat was the cause, and never suspected his wife's share in the story.

She recovered after a few minutes. She did not know whether she was more glad or sorry at what she had heard. She had said once before of herself that she was not strong enough to be thoroughly wicked—and she was right.

A year had elapsed, and Lord Arleigh and his wife were in town for the season, and were, as a matter of course, the objects of much curiosity. He was sitting one evening in the drawing-room of his town-house, when one of the servants told him that a lady wished to see him. He inquired her name and was told that she declined to give it. He ordered her to be shown into the room where he was, and presently there entered a tall stately lady, whose face was closely vailed; but the imperial figure, the stately grace were quite familiar to him.

"Philippa!" he cried, in astonishment.

Then she raised her vail, and once again he saw the grandly-beautiful face of the woman who had loved him with such passionate love.

"Philippa!" he repeated.

"Yes," said the duchess, calmly. "And do you know why I am here?"

"I cannot even guess," he replied.

"I am here to implore your pardon," she announced, with deep humility—"to tell you that neither by night nor by day, since I planned and carried out my revenge, have I known peace. I shall neither live nor die in peace unless you forgive me, Norman."

She bent her beautiful, haughty head before him—her eyes were full of tears.

"You will forgive me, Norman?" she said in her low, rich voice. "Remember that it was love for you which bereft me of my reason and drove me mad—love for you. You should pardon me."

Leaving her standing there, Lord Arleigh drew aside the velvet hangings and disappeared. In a few moments he returned leading his wife by the hand.

"Philippa," he said, gravely, "tell my wits your errand; hear what she says. We will abide by her decision."

At first the duchess drew back with a haughty gesture.

"It was you I came to see," she said to Lord Arleigh; and then the sweet face touched her and her better self prevailed.

"Madaline," she said, quietly, "you have suffered much through me—will you pardon me?"

The next moment Lady Arleigh's arms were clasped round her neck, and the pure sweet lips touched her own.

"It was because you loved him," she whispered, "and I forgive you."

The Duke of Hazlewood did not understand the quarrel between his wife and Lord Arleigh, nor did he quite understand the reconciliation; still he is very pleased that they are reconciled, for he likes Lord Arleigh better than any friend he has ever had. He fancies, too, that his beautiful wife always seems kinder to him when she has been spending some little time with Lady Arleigh.

In the gallery at Verdun Royal there is a charming picture called "The Little Lovers." The figures in it are those of a dark-haired, handsome boy of three whose hand is filled with cherries, and a lovely little girl, with hair like sunshine and a face like a rosebud, who is accepting the rich ripe fruit. Those who understand smile as they look at this painting, for the dark-haired boy is the son and heir of the Duke of Hazlewood, and the fair-faced girl is Lord Arleigh's daughter.

The Earl of Mountdean and his wife, *neé* Lady Lily Gordon, once went to see that picture, and, as they stood smiling before it, he said:

"It may indicate what lies in the future. Let us hope it does for the greatest gift of Heaven is the love of a good and pure-minded wife."